ROYAL INSTITUTE OF MAGIC

Elizabeth's Legacy

VICTOR KLOSS

An Original Publication From Victor Kloss

Royal Institute of Magic Elizabeth's Legacy
Written and published by Victor Kloss
Cover by Andrew Gaia
Formatted by Frostbite Publishing
Copyright © 2015 by Victor Kloss
All rights reserved.

***

***

www.RoyalInstituteofMagic.com

— CHAPTER ONE —

Unwanted Rescue

Date: *18th December 1589*

The guard removed the blindfold and Michael squinted as his eyes adjusted to the torchlight.

"Ask no questions. Be seated," the guard said.

Michael James Greenwood found himself in a lavish hallway with a group of nobles sitting opposite each other. Most ignored him and those who glanced his way did so with a disdainful air, as if his very presence were an insult. To be fair, Michael didn't exactly blend in. He was half their age and had scruffy blond hair tinted white from flour, having been dragged from his father's bakery less than an hour ago.

Michael turned to the huge guard standing behind him and raised his eyebrows. Until now, protesting had accomplished nothing except a cuff on the head, but looking at the present company, he felt compelled to give it one more try.

"Sir, this is absurd," he said. "You have the wrong Greenwood. There must be a lord or nobleman with the same surname. I have no association with whoever organised this meeting."

The guard's face darkened. "This meeting has been organised by Her Majesty, the Queen. Unfortunately, there has been no mistake. Now, be seated and be silent."

Michael bit back a reply, not because he was scared but because he was now genuinely curious. The Queen was responsible for this strange congregation? He had only seen the Queen once and that had been from a distance. He was positive she didn't know he existed.

He sat down between two well-to-do gentlemen, giving them both a nod and a smile. He wasn't surprised when neither returned the compliment. They inched away from him, trying to avoid flour ruining their expensive garments.

Michael noticed many were fidgeting. Did they know something he didn't? The guards had told him nothing when they had appeared at his father's bakery and whisked him to the castle. They would only say he wasn't in trouble and he would be returned unharmed before the end of the day. Michael had been escorted to the main entrance and then blindfolded before entering.

"Lord Frederick Arnold," the guard said, breaking the nervous silence and interrupting his thoughts.

A heavyset man rose and walked to the guard, who was standing next to a door halfway down the corridor. The guard spoke quietly to the Lord. Michael couldn't hear what was said, but the Lord pulled out a handkerchief and wiped his gleaming forehead. He took a deep breath, opened the door and disappeared inside. There were a few restrained gasps. Michael saw fear in some faces but respect in others.

Michael tapped his fingers on his knees. He was tempted to ask someone if they knew what was happening, but was fairly certain it would earn him another cuff from the guard. Could there have been some instruction he had missed? More likely these lords and ladies, with their wealth and contacts, knew something. Whatever they had learnt, it wasn't inspiring them with confidence.

After the Lord disappeared through the door, Michael had expected the excitement to build, but silence resumed. Five minutes passed before the guard opened the same door and poked his head through. Evidently he was satisfied with what he saw, for he called another name. A "Lady Janet Harris" stood up and walked to the guard, showing marginally more composure than the Lord. Hushed whispers were again exchanged and the woman stepped through the same door.

Twenty more times this happened, until it was just Michael Greenwood sitting among all the empty chairs, feeling just as clueless as when he had arrived.

"Master Michael Greenwood."

He felt a flutter of nerves as he stood up. He knew he should have been scared or at least concerned like the others, but he wasn't. He was curious. What lay behind the door? He had seen the guard whisper instructions countless times in the last hour and he was itching to know what the man said.

"You will not be held accountable for whatever decision you make beyond this door," the guard said.

Michael felt both short-changed by the brevity of the instructions and excited by the mystery of them.

"Can you tell me what this is all about?" Michael asked.

"No, but I can tell you why you found yourself surrounded by nobility. You are part of a small group of citizens they are experimenting with to see how certain commoners perform on the test."

"What sort of commoners?"

"Young, able to read and write, physically and mentally adept. There aren't many of you, thankfully."

"So I'm an experiment?"

"Yes." The guard's face showed less empathy than the surrounding stone walls. "If you want my advice, you should walk away. The Institute is an elite organisation and should not be sullied by the common man."

"Thank you for your kind words of support, sir," Michael said. He turned the handle before the guard could reply and entered the room.

His body was tense and on edge, ready to react to any potential danger that might emerge. Michael was half expecting a fully suited knight to come flying at him and he was almost disappointed when his eyes adjusted to the dim light inside the room.

It was empty, except for a single chair and an ornate desk in the centre of a small square room. At the back were double doors, so large they spanned most of the wall. On the left was a much smaller door. The only thing that caught Michael's interest was a golden sword hanging on the right-hand wall. It was encased in an elaborate frame, behind a sheet of glass. Inlaid in the handle were jewels that made him stare in wonder.

Dragging his eyes away from the sword, he walked to the desk; perhaps there was something in the many drawers that would enlighten him.

He stopped sharply before he had taken his first step.

There was something *floating* inches above the desk.

It was parchment standing upright as if it were attached to a piece of string that hung from the ceiling. Though there was no wind in the room, the parchment was rippling gently.

Had it been there a moment ago? Surely he would have noticed it? But then, he wasn't accustomed to checking for items floating above desks.

Even from a distance he could see the flowing script of ink on the parchment. He moved closer and ran his hand above it, searching for the fine piece of string that held it afloat. He felt nothing. Intrigued, Michael walked around the desk, inspecting the parchment from all angles, but he couldn't see anything holding it in place. Michael gave the parchment an experimental poke. It rippled and smoothly returned to its original position.

Michael rubbed his chin. Whatever trickery was being employed, it was nothing he had ever seen before. He turned his attention to the writing on the parchment with growing curiosity.

"To: All Royal Institute of Magic applicants

"From: Queen Elizabeth, Commander of the Royal Institute of Magic

"Welcome,

"I imagine you are full of questions and, I hope, curiosity rather than fear. Let me assure you that you are in no kind of difficulty; quite the opposite.

"You have been carefully selected to apply for a position in the Royal Institute of Magic. Due to the secretive nature of our organisation, you will be unaware of its value to our country. Allow me to enlighten you.

8

"*Last year we fought and achieved a great victory against the Spanish Armada. That victory was made possible through the Royal Institute of Magic. I cannot reveal the part the Institute played except to stress its importance.*"

Michael stopped reading and sat down before he fell down. If he weren't in the castle right now, he would have disregarded the whole document as some sort of joke. His eyes flicked to the bottom of the document and he saw the Queen's signature. This Royal Institute of Magic was responsible for the victory against the Spanish? His curiosity well and truly piqued, Michael continued reading.

"*Your application to the Institute is subject to your willingness and an entrance examination.*

"*I will not lie to you. This examination will frighten you. It will shake your beliefs to the core. I would not have passed what you are about to attempt. Four weeks it took me to learn and accept the truth. You will have one hour.*

"*I can give you some advice. Forget what you think you know about witchcraft and its association with the devil. Look and listen to what you encounter; true observation is more important than hearsay.*

"*Should you fail the examination or wish to stop, you may leave at any time. You shall not be punished. The success rate is less than one per hundred, so do not be disheartened.*

"*If you succeed, you shall work for our country's most prestigious institute and you will serve directly under me. The government has no knowledge of our existence.*

"*Choose wisely. Though you will be remunerated well, you shall also face great evil. We have enemies far more dangerous than the Spanish or the French and only the Royal Institute of Magic can stand against them.*

"*Should you wish to apply, proceed through the double doors that lie ahead of you – if not, take the door to the left and you will never hear from us again.*

"*Whatever your choice, I wish you good fortune.*

"*Elizabeth.*"

Michael leant back on the chair and took a deep breath in an attempt to calm his thumping heart.

This was crazy! The Queen – *the Queen* – was talking about witchcraft and the devil. No wonder this document could only be read in this enclosed room. If this got to the wrong people, civil war could break out.

The letter answered some questions, but it posed many more. What exactly was this Royal Institute of Magic? The document was very careful not to reveal anything about it. Michael re-read the section about the test and his stomach gave a little lurch.

How long did he have to make a decision? Surely the guard would come in soon to check on him. Would he be disqualified if he were still in here?

It didn't matter. Michael had made his mind up even before he'd finished reading. He was not yet twenty, but already he knew the baker's life was not for him. His father had told him many times if he worked hard, he would one day inherit the bakery. But working sixty hours a week for the next twenty years in a profession he had no affection for was a very dispiriting thought.

Besides, Michael wasn't sure he could stand walking away from something as crazy as this. The test scared him a little, but Michael was a fool for mysteries and had always been too curious for his own good. How could he *not* go in?

He eyed the double doors. What dangers lay beyond them? Whatever they were, Michael had nothing to defend himself with. That could be a problem.

Michael remembered the golden sword. He went up to it, feeling the glass, tapping it with his knuckles. Emblazoned on its hilt was Queen Elizabeth's royal coat of arms. Was the sword there for a reason? He briefly weighed the dangers of getting in trouble with the guard versus the potential advantage of passing the test armed with a shining sword. It wasn't a hard decision to make.

He grabbed the chair and with a giant heave swung it into the glass frame. There was an almighty crash and the sword fell to the floor, along with shards of glass.

He picked up the weapon. Before the guard had time to investigate the noise, Michael ran to the double doors, grabbed the iron handle and disappeared through them.

— CHAPTER TWO —

A Single Clue

Present Day

Ben Greenwood sees the two police cars from the top of the hill, parked on either side of his dad's Mini Cooper. He stops and squints, searching for anything that might explain their presence. He's not concerned they might be there because of his parents; they're the last people who would ever get in trouble with the law. Nevertheless, he starts jogging down the hill, eager to get home and find out if they know what's going on.

He is almost at the driveway when he sees the shattered front window.

Their shattered front window.

Ben stops, as if his jogging is somehow impairing his vision. It can't be his house. But next to the broken window is the yellow front door, painted with the number 68. He leaps down the driveway, practically crashing through the entrance.

13

Ben's run comes to a shuddering halt in the hallway, as he stares in horror at the scene before him. It looks like a bomb has exploded. The coat rack, ordinarily piled with clothes, is empty. Jackets and hats flung across the floor, along with enough shoes to cover the carpet. Ben picks his way through the mess and enters a lounge from hell.

The furniture is upended, including a glass table lying shattered on the floor. Broken photo frames lie strewn across the room, shards of glass sprinkling the carpet.

Ben's attention to the devastation lasts only a moment; there are people in the room – lots of people, making lots of noise.

He feels dizzy watching everyone. Is this real or just a dream? Is this even his house? There are police officers and people in suits tearing around the place as if someone has hidden the crown jewels. The cacophony of stampeding feet and shouting voices creates an energy in the air that sets Ben's hair on end. He stands there, lost in the maelstrom until one of the police officers spots him.

"You okay, son?" the officer asks, tapping him on the shoulder.

The touch snaps Ben out of his stupor.

"Are my parents here?"

The officer curses under his breath and turns to the others in the room.

"Jamie! The son's arrived. Get over here!"

Something soft and fluffy connected with Ben's head and his dream came to an abrupt end.

"Charles, you'd better be up – it's 8:20am!"

There was the sound of shuffling feet and then another voice, this one far closer. The pillow hit him again.

"Wake up, Ben," Charlie said. "My worthless alarm didn't go off again. You need to get out of here before my mum comes in!"

Ben sat up, still half asleep, and rubbed his back. There was something about Charlie's bedroom floor that always made it ache.

"Don't make me come upstairs, Charles Hornberger!"

Charlie's mum sounded like she was holding a megaphone, her voice penetrating through doors as if they didn't exist.

"I'm coming!" Charlie shouted back with nearly as much gusto.

Charlie was trying to put on his trousers, hopping on alternate feet, like a waddling penguin. His large cheeks rippled with every jump and his tongue was thrust out – a reminder that coordination was not Charlie's strong suit.

"Please get a move on, Ben. You know my mum will go mental if she finds you here on a school night," Charlie said, panting a little from the constant hopping.

"I thought she was already mental."

Charlie was too freaked out to appreciate the joke.

"Relax, Charlie," Ben said. "I'm practically ready."

He threw on his school clothes and walked into Charlie's en-suite bathroom. He took a moment to make sure his mop of blond hair was ruffled enough to look good without being messy and then washed his face, inspecting it hopefully for a sign of facial hair in the mirror – nothing doing. Ben wiped the sleep from his dark blue eyes. He could never understand how they looked so bright despite his lack of sleep, though he didn't complain. His eyes had got him into, and out of, more trouble than he could remember.

A sudden thumping noise made Ben freeze. Someone was coming up the stairs.

"Right, that's it. I'm throwing you out of bed!"

Ben left the bathroom and saw Charlie with his mouth agape and eyes wide with horror.

"Stall her, would you, Charlie?" Ben asked, giving his friend a pat on the shoulder as he moved toward the bedroom window. He grabbed his backpack, slung it over his shoulder and pushed the window open. He stuck one leg out and turned back to Charlie, who was looking increasingly terrified.

"I can't stall her," Charlie replied in a fierce whisper, his face swiftly resembling a ripe tomato. "A loaded machine gun wouldn't stall her."

The footsteps got louder as she marched up the stairs. Ben thought he could hear Charlie's mum breathing behind the door, like a raging bull about to charge. He hung both legs out the window. There was an apple tree outside and he focused on the exact spot his feet would have to hit to make a safe landing.

He gave one last look to Charlie who was waving frantically at him to go.

"Remember my breakfast," Ben said with a smile and a little salute. "I like my eggs over easy."

Ben jumped just as he heard the door being thrown open. He landed with a soft thud on the trunk and quickly climbed down until he was safely in Charlie's back garden. He sneaked a look through the kitchen windows and saw Charlie's dad eating breakfast, his back turned. Ben sprinted to a hedge that ran along the side of the garden, keeping as low as possible. He got onto his hands and knees and squeezed through a tiny gap in the bushes, ignoring the scratchy branches, and re-appeared in the adjacent garden. The Lamberts, Charlie's neighbours, were early risers and their place was always empty. He dusted himself off and walked round the side of their house. Jumping over the gate, he walked up their driveway and on to the pavement. There he merged with the other kids making their way to school.

At the corner of the road Ben stopped and leant against a large tree to wait for Charlie. Several of the boys, some a year or two older, stopped and asked if he were playing any football over the summer. The girls in his class smiled and waved as they passed.

All of them would have woken up in their comfy beds, probably eaten cooked breakfasts and then would have been nagged out the door by their mums. Ben never thought he'd miss the nagging.

Charlie turned up moments later, holding a sandwich in his hands.

"I didn't have time to do eggs, so you'll have to settle for peanut butter and jam. Unfortunately, it's not up to my usual standard, as my mum kicked me out before I could finish. She thinks I have an eating problem."

"It's perfect, Charlie, thanks," Ben said, taking the sandwich and attacking it with relish.

They started their journey to school, walking through well-kept but uninspiring neighbourhoods filled with neat flower beds and silver hatchbacks.

Ben's dream came drifting back despite his best efforts to forget it.

"Seventeen days," he said, his voice tinged with frustration.

Charlie groaned. "I was sure you'd got rid of it this time."

"So was I," Ben said, kicking a pebble.

Ben mentally put the counter back at zero. Seventeen days without having the dream had been a record and he'd begun to believe it had finally gone. Two years was a long time to have a recurring dream, but maybe that was normal when it was based on such a traumatic experience. Was it really two years since his parents disappeared? He was almost fifteen now, so it must be. Ben still remembered the weeks after they vanished as if it were yesterday. Every time someone came in the house, every time the phone rang, every letter they received, Ben thought it would be his parents explaining where they had gone and why. But after a few months he had stopped rushing downstairs to collect the mail and he had stopped asking his grandma "Who called?" every time she hung up the phone. Then the nightmares had begun and he had to relive the incident every night.

"Speaking of which," Charlie said, "I have some news. Guess who emailed me this morning?"

There was something about Charlie's voice – it was too casual. Charlie was never casual.

"Someone important, judging by the way you're trying to stay relaxed but look as if you're about to burst."

Charlie slapped his thigh in frustration. "How do you do that calm look? You need to teach me."

"Impossible, Charlie, with your hamster-like face. So who emailed?"

"The textile expert!" Charlie raised his arms as if he'd just scored. "We even agreed a price that doesn't involve selling one of my kidneys. Best of all, he's based up in London so we don't have to ship it – we can travel there ourselves. I know you were concerned about that. He's really good. If he can't answer our question, nobody can."

Ben suppressed his excitement in a manner Charlie had failed to do moments earlier. There had been too many false leads already to get his hopes up. Charlie, though, seemed oblivious to the dozen experts they'd already gone through.

In Ben's left pocket was a small piece of fabric that he ran between his fingers. Ben knew the feel of the fabric down to the last stitch. He pulled it out and admired it as he had done a thousand times before. As always, he was struck by its beauty. It was no bigger than a handkerchief, but it was the colour and texture that stood out, not the size. It constantly shifted colours to match its surroundings. Right now it was light brown and blended in perfectly with Ben's hand. As soon as he moved it against his trousers, it turned black.

He still remembered finding the fabric hidden amongst the wreckage of their house after the police had gone. It was his one link to the crime scene and he'd never told anyone in case they took the swatch away. Ben felt certain it was a unique piece of material and a valuable clue. The only problem: it was too unique – nobody had ever seen it before and, though he had lots of offers to buy it, nobody could tell him anything about it.

"Sounds good, Charlie. Let's see him this weekend."

"Already booked," Charlie said, rubbing his hands together and grinning.

Ben had a sudden thought. "How much is he going to cost?"

Charlie's grin vanished. "It doesn't matter. I'm paying."

Ben shook his head and wagged his finger. "I'm paying at least half. How much is he charging? And don't even think about lying to me."

Charlie stared at him and sighed. "It's £100 for a fifteen-minute consultation."

Ben cringed. "Wow – does that include breakfast?"

"Very funny, Ben. This guy is a professional; he's worth it."

"I hope so," Ben said, "because I'll need to take an extra paper round for this." There was a little pause and he grabbed a handful of his blond hair. "Can we pay him at a later date? Because I'm a little short right now. Otherwise, we might have to postpone it."

Charlie rolled his eyes and threw his arms up in the air in a fit of theatrics.

"Come on, Ben," he said. "I'm sorry, but you can't even afford a place to live while you're down here for school. You are *not*" – Charlie stamped his foot – "paying for this."

Ben was torn between stubborn refusal and amusement at Charlie's little drama show. Down here was Dukinfield, a little town in West Sussex and home until his parents had disappeared. A wealthy family had agreed to take him in afterwards and he had spent his weekdays in Sussex at school and his weekends up in Croydon with his grandma. It was the perfect arrangement, until last year when the family moved abroad. He had asked around, but none of his other friends' parents could afford to let him stay. Ben, however, wasn't deterred. Rather than tell his grandma, he took living arrangements into his own hands. He had enough close friends, so why not sleep over on a rotating schedule? It was perfect – none of the parents would suspect a thing as he'd only ever stay at the same house once per week. Unfortunately, Ben hadn't accounted for the secret pact between mums – no weekday sleepovers. This made things trickier, but Ben still managed two or three nights a week at someone's with their parents' permission. The other nights, like the last, were slightly more adventurous.

"I'm going to pay you back," Ben said. "I'm getting some extra work this holiday."

Summer holidays were right round the corner and Ben was grateful that this was the last Monday at school for several weeks.

With the trip to the textile expert and end of term on the horizon, the final week of school dragged on forever. When Friday eventually arrived, Ben slept over at Charlie's again and the following morning they were on the bus heading up to London.

"Do we really have to detour to your grandma's?" Charlie asked.

"It's hardly a detour, we pass right through Croydon. I just need to drop my stuff off."

"Will the devil be home?"

"My grandma is not the devil," Ben said, smiling despite the insult. "Besides, isn't the devil a male?"

"I thought so until I met your grandma. Could you tell her to stop calling me Fatty?"

"You could stand to lose a little weight."

"My mum says it's just baby fat," Charlie said a little defensively.

In truth, Ben felt no great urge to defend his grandma. Charlie's accusations weren't far off the mark, which was why Ben put up with such peculiar living arrangements down in Sussex. But she was the only family he had left.

Ben felt the fabric in his pocket and stopped thinking about his grandma. Would this textile expert finally be the one to shed some light on it? What if he knew nothing? Their one and only lead to his missing parents would be gone. Ben refused to think about that possibility. He knew his parents were out there somewhere; the only mystery in his mind was why they were unable to come back.

Half an hour passed before the bus turned down Galaxy Lane and pulled over at his local stop. They got out and walked through a council estate and into a tiny neighbourhood of houses. Ben and Charlie followed a winding road that led to a cul-de-sac, where they eventually arrived at a small, characterless brick house that for the last two years Ben had called home. It didn't have the quirky yellow door of his parents' place, nor the crazy front garden, but it was better than no home at all.

Ben delved into his pocket for the key, but to his surprise the door was already open. A police officer stood just outside. Ben stopped, his heart lurching.

He recognised the man instantly – he was in Ben's dream nearly every night.

— CHAPTER THREE —
The Jewellery Box

The police officer was just leaving, but he stopped when he saw the two boys running towards him.

"Ben Greenwood?"

Ben nodded, trying to read the officer's face to determine the reason for his visit. His breath quickened and hope swelled despite his efforts to stop it. The officer looked smaller, but that must have been because Ben had grown.

"You probably don't remember me. I was one of the officers who answered the police call when your parents disappeared."

"Inspector Wilkins," Ben said. "What's happened? Have you found something?"

Wilkins' eyebrows flickered in surprise and he hesitated; Ben knew then the news wasn't good.

"I'm sorry, Ben." Wilkins rubbed his forehead, looking uncomfortable. "We haven't made any progress for some time. I came by to return some evidence we took from your parents' house."

"Why are you returning it?" Ben asked, his voice soft. "You're not giving up, are you?"

"No," Wilkins said, because he didn't have the heart to say otherwise. "We won't close the investigation until we find your parents. But we have several new cases and there isn't enough space to keep all the evidence at the station."

Ben wanted to believe him. "They're still alive." His throat suddenly felt constricted, but he pressed on. "I don't know how, but I'm sure of it."

"I believe you," the inspector said with a solemn face.

Ben watched Wilkins take his leave and drive away; with him went Ben's last hope in the police.

"He's lying," Charlie said, watching the car. "If he's returning evidence, it means they are closing the investigation."

Ben wanted to disagree, but he didn't doubt Charlie's hunch.

"Let's dump my bag and get out of here," Ben said.

Charlie nodded. "I wonder what evidence they returned."

Ben was wondering the same thing. Whatever it was hadn't helped the police, but that didn't dampen his curiosity.

"Jesus, what's that smell?" Charlie asked as they entered the house.

The answer came from the kitchen. Even from the hallway Ben could see dishes piled high in the sink, dirty plates covering every inch of the table tops. Ben held his breath and rushed over to close the fridge; it was almost empty except for some revolting cheese that looked as though it had evolved into an entirely new organism.

They shut the kitchen door to block off the smell and entered the dining room. On a small table were two big boxes; in one of them a frail lady's head was so immersed only her bushy white hair could be seen. She was throwing books and other bits out carelessly, scattering objects on the floor.

"Rubbish – junk!" the lady said.

"Grandma, what are you doing?" Ben asked, rushing forward and picking up the items off the floor. "That's not yours."

Grandma Anne looked up and scowled at Ben and then Charlie as a way of greeting.

"They should have taken this all straight to the tip," she said, pushing a box away in disgust. "It's hard enough keeping the house clean with you here."

"It's not junk, Grandma." Ben's eyes widened when he spotted a large binder. "Look at this. It's a family photo album."

Anne ignored the album entirely and pointed a bony finger at him. "What did I tell you about calling me Grandma? I've got enough real grandchildren as it is."

"I forgot," Ben said.

He felt strangely reluctant to break such an old habit. It was only after his parents disappeared that he learnt Anne was his step-grandmother.

Ben started sifting through the boxes. Immediately Anne dipped her head back into the box, her long, pointed nose almost touching its contents. "I'm entitled to fifty percent of anything you sell, so don't think about cheating me."

There was a subtle cough from the corner of the room. Anne turned to the source. "What is it, Fatty?"

"Nothing – just that, as next of kin, Ben is legally entitled to all his parents' possessions."

Anne's eyes, already set in a permanent squint, narrowed to slits. Her scowl made Charlie flinch. "If Fatty is right, then I don't want these boxes making a mess in here. Get them up to your bedroom."

Without waiting for a reply, she picked up her cane and walked back into the lounge. The TV went on and she forgot all about them.

Ben and Charlie grabbed the boxes and lugged them up the stairs into his bedroom. Upon entering, he did a quick inspection to make sure nothing was out of place. Anne liked to poke around and "borrow" things. Last week the batteries from his alarm clock had gone missing; Ben had found them later in the TV remote. Thankfully, the bed was unruffled, his family photos were still on the windowsill and the mini football was still on his desk.

They dumped everything on Ben's bed. But instead of heading out, their eyes lingered on the boxes.

"I wonder if there is anything useful in there," Ben said.

Charlie rubbed his chin thoughtfully. "The police would have been through it all, of course."

"Of course."

They both kept staring at the boxes.

"We've got time before the meeting with the textile guy," Ben said. "Why don't we take a look?"

Charlie nodded vigorously, his cheeks wobbling.

They sat down on the bed and each of them put a box on their lap.

Ben found himself subconsciously holding his breath when he picked up the first item – a phone book. He looked through each page, enjoying the look of his mum's handwriting. There were lots of other books, a couple of photo albums, which Ben marvelled over, and even an old iPod with a dead battery. A couple of times he glanced over and saw Charlie examining his own box carefully. His friend was a one-man Scotland Yard and Ben had faint hopes that Charlie might somehow spot something the police had missed. But though Charlie was clearly fascinated, he remained quiet.

Ben couldn't help feeling a little disappointed when he neared the end of his box. He peered in to survey the last few items.

Something shiny stared back at him, partially hidden underneath a binder.

It was a small, wooden jewellery box. Ben picked it up. The wood was beautifully crafted and inlaid with fine gold carvings.

Charlie put down a photograph he had been examining and looked over with interest.

Ben opened the box and stared at the contents. There was a handful of small jewellery pieces inside, but none of them looked particularly valuable. Ben wasn't surprised; his parents weren't exactly dripping money.

"Can I have a look?" Charlie asked, and Ben handed him the box. Charlie held it to the light, examining it from every angle with an intense expression.

"I bet this jewellery box is worth more than its contents," Charlie said. "The craftsmanship is amazing. Look at this engraving! Edward Clavell, 1548. This box is hundreds of years old."

Ben's fascination did not quite match Charlie's. "I'm guessing you still watch *Antiques Roadshow* every Sunday?"

"My dad always has it on and I've become hooked. I bet we could get this valued if we went on there." Charlie started tapping the base of the box and his excitement grew. "Do you hear that? It sounds like it could be hollow."

Ben listened carefully, but it was difficult to tell and he had a feeling Charlie was getting a little carried away.

Charlie began probing the delicate engravings. "Sometimes these things have a false bottom – I saw it on the *Roadshow* once."

After several minutes of prodding and probing, Charlie's excitement dimmed and he finally handed it back.

Ben gave the jewellery box a final inspection. There was something about the gold carvings that caught his eye; they seemed to glow the more he stared at them. It was almost hypnotic. He felt his eyes watering, unable to take them away from the gold flecks of light. They appeared to dance and shine, getting brighter by the second. Just as he thought he would be blinded by the display, Ben imagined the lights spelling out a word.

Greenwood.

The jewellery box gave a soft click and a tiny drawer just above the base slid open.

The shock made Ben blink and the trance was broken.

"How did you do that?" Charlie asked with a gasp. "What did you touch?"

Ben rubbed his eyes. "I'm not sure."

Inside the little drawer were a couple of cards on top of a piece of paper. Ben went for the cards, but the piece of paper below caught his attention.

It was a letter. Ben picked it up.

It wasn't your typical A4; it was thick, yellow parchment with elegant handwriting that he could barely decipher. At the top of the letter was a logo with the letters R.I.M. embossed over an elaborate coat of arms. The logo looked familiar somehow, but Ben couldn't place it.

"Dear Jane,

"It has been a week since you and Greg have been in. If you don't arrive tomorrow morning, I shall be forced to come knocking on your door.

"I do not believe the rumours, but there is no doubt they could put you and your son in considerable danger. I know your views on keeping Ben unaware of us, but the Institute is still the one place the enemy cannot reach. I implore you and Greg to come see me.

"Regards,

"Wren Walker"

The letter was dated the day before his parents disappeared.

Ben re-read it three times and stared at it long after he was finished. His head was spinning and his stomach was doing somersaults.

"I think we have something," Charlie said softly, breaking Ben's trance. He had read the letter over Ben's shoulder.

There were so many questions, Ben hardly knew where to start. Charlie, however, had no such problem. He was already moving back and forth on the carpet like a mad scientist brainstorming.

"Your parents must have known they were in danger. Apparently you were also in danger."

"I've never felt in danger," Ben said, his head going side to side to track Charlie's pacing.

Charlie nodded. "And since it's been two years, I think we can assume you're safe."

"What sort of danger could my parents have been in?" Ben asked. "They worked at Greenpeace, not MI5."

"The logo on the letter has nothing to do with Greenpeace."

"What else could it be?"

"I have no idea, but I know how we can find out."

Ben looked down at the letter. "By finding this Wren Walker lady?"

"Exactly. Who is she? More importantly, what is this R.I.M. logo? I bet it belongs to the institute she refers to. If we can identify the logo, we might be able to track her down."

Charlie's face was red and he was breathing a little quickly from talking so fast.

Ben stared at the logo on the parchment again. There was definitely something familiar about it. The coat of arms was shaped like a shield and cut into four quarters. Each quarter alternated between a red background with golden lions and a blue background with peculiar flowers, also golden. Where had he seen it before? Ben shut his eyes trying to visualise the moment he'd seen it. In a museum perhaps? No. On TV? No. On a building somewhere? Yes! In town...

Ben's eyes shot open.

"I don't believe it," he said.

Charlie looked confused.

"I used to pass this logo every weekend." It was Ben's turn to stand up and pace the room.

"There is a Sainsbury's near the town centre. I used to walk there every Saturday morning. On the other side of the main street was an old, narrow building. I remember because there was always a security guard standing outside a revolving door. Above it, where shop signage normally sits, was *this*."

Ben pointed to the R.I.M. logo.

Charlie, normally so vocal, was struck dumb. He kept opening and closing his mouth, but no words came out.

Ben felt like dancing, but settled for an ear-splitting grin. He headed for the door, giving Charlie a pat on the shoulder as he passed.

"No time to lose, Charlie – let's go."

"Where?"

"To get some answers."

"If they have a security guard stationed there, I don't think we'll be able to just walk in, do you?"

"Of course not," Ben said. He stopped and turned to face Charlie who was biting his lip.

"We're not going to do anything against the law again, are we? I always feel uncomfortable with that."

"Charlie, please – I have two, possibly three, solid plans brewing before we even have to *think* about breaking the law."

"How wonderfully reassuring."

— Chapter Four —
The Impossible Lift

Ben walked quickly, weaving his way through the morning shoppers. He wanted to jog, but Charlie was already huffing and puffing to keep up.

"So what's your plan?" Charlie asked. He had produced a white handkerchief from his pocket and was using it to dab his forehead.

Ben side-stepped an oncoming pram. "I need to see the building again."

Charlie groaned. "You don't have a plan, do you? You're just going to make something up when we get there."

"Nonsense," Ben said, flashing Charlie a look of mock outrage.

He did have a plan, of sorts, but he was hoping he'd have a better one when he got there.

"What about the textile expert?" Charlie asked.

"We're still going, but the appointment isn't until 3pm. We've got plenty of time."

It had been a while since Ben had been down this road, but it hadn't changed much. There were several department stores, as well as the usual array of mobile phone and coffee shops. Ben didn't slow his pace until he saw the orange signage of Sainsbury's in the distance. He scanned the row of shops carefully, his stomach tightening with the thought that the strange building might now be gone.

There it was! Squashed between Starbucks and an O2 Mobile shop. The front had a revolving door and frosted windows. Above the door, inlaid into the brickwork, was the logo they'd seen in the letter. The letters R.I.M. were cast in bronze over a coat of arms. With the glow from the surrounding shop signs it was easy to see why the building received nothing more than the odd curious glance.

"Incredible," Charlie said, staring up at the logo with his mouth open.

Ben gave him a little shove. "Keep walking."

They crossed the road and stopped next to Waterstones. Ben made a show of inspecting the books in the window.

"What are we doing?" Charlie asked. He was still staring at the strange building when Ben grabbed a cheek and turned his head away.

"Trying not to be suspicious," Ben answered, "though your gawking is ruining it."

"Sorry. What could a place like that be doing here?"

"It's not selling anything, that's for sure," Ben said, sneaking a glance at it. It was impossible to see anything beyond the frosted windows. "Do you see the guard?"

"It's hard not to."

The guard stood in front of the revolving door. His black suit stood out amongst the crowd of multi-coloured shoppers, as did his huge bulk, which would struggle making it through the door.

"I think now is a good time to reveal your plan," Charlie said.

"It's simple really. We go through the front."

"I'm sorry?"

"It's a revolving door," Ben said. "It's built to help people come in and out freely. If we act like we belong, we'll be fine."

Charlie looked at him as if he were mad. "What's the point of the troll-like guard then? To wish you good morning?"

Ben knew his logic was dubious. The frosted windows were a clear sign that they didn't want to attract attention, but it was the best he could do. He had hoped he could enter from the back or through one of the adjacent buildings, but that seemed impossible.

"He's just to deter shoppers," Ben said.

"You don't believe that and neither do I."

Ben gave him a lopsided smile, his blue eyes lighting up. "We'll soon find out. Are you ready?"

"Are you serious? Of course not."

"Do you have a better idea?" Ben asked, feeling a stab of frustration. They were so close to unravelling the mystery behind the letter, yet it was tantalisingly out of reach because of one stupid guard.

Charlie took his hanky out and dabbed his forehead.

"I think we should wait," he said. Ben was about to protest, but Charlie raised a pudgy finger. "Fifteen minutes, to see if anyone else goes in so we can see what security procedure they go through."

"And if nobody does?"

Charlie gave a theatrical sigh. "Then we do it your way."

They lounged by Waterstones, chatting idly and taking turns to keep an eye on passers-by, hoping someone would walk into the building. After less than ten minutes, Ben spotted a well-dressed man in a purple shirt walking twice as fast as the surrounding shoppers. The purpose and intensity of his stride reminded Ben of someone late for work.

"I see him," Charlie said when Ben picked him out.

The purple-shirted man stopped in front of the building. For a moment Ben thought it was just to answer his phone, but then he turned to the security guard and showed him something in his hand. The guard nodded and the man walked through the revolving door.

"Did you see that?" Ben asked. It was over in a heartbeat. "He must have showed the guard some sort of ID or pass."

Ben turned to Charlie and was surprised to see his face flushed with excitement. His hand was rummaging around in his pocket.

"I had a feeling these were important," Charlie said. He took out two cards and handed one to Ben. "They were lying on the letter. We left the house in such a rush that we didn't have time to inspect them."

Each was the size of a credit card, but the similarities ended there. They were made of silver and heavy enough to feel valuable. Embossed on them was the now familiar logo. The name "Greg Greenwood" was etched into the silver with four tiny green diamonds next to it. Ben's heart gave a great leap at the sight of his dad's name.

"Charlie, you genius, this is it!"

But Charlie's own elation was fleeting and soon replaced with worry.

"These are your parents' ID cards. I'm not sure they will work for us. How am I supposed to pass as your mum?"

Ben refused to be downcast. "There's no photo on them so I doubt they check if you're the card holder."

"What if they do?"

"Then he'll tell us to get lost. He's not going to chop our heads off in the middle of a busy shopping street."

Charlie tucked his hanky away and took a deep breath, his little pot belly expanding until he resembled a teddy bear.

"I'll approach him first," Ben said. "Just follow my lead and act casual. We won't have any problems."

Ben crossed the road, whistling softly to himself, one hand holding the ID card in his pocket. On the outside, he was calm; inside his heart was thumping like a drum. If this didn't work, they would have to come back at night and break in. But that was messy, illegal and, worst of all, a whole twelve hours from now.

As Ben approached he made eye contact with the guard and gave him a polite smile. The guard was big enough to wrestle a polar bear and had a face that could give you nightmares. When he was close enough to smell the guard's unpleasant breath, he stopped and produced his ID as if the guard were a train conductor. The guard's eyes flicked to the card and Ben felt his stomach lurch, though he kept a cool exterior. The guard's eyes narrowed for a split second and then he nodded. Ben wanted to punch the air in celebration; instead he pushed the revolving door gently until he was inside. He glanced back in time to see the guard waving Charlie through.

The moment he entered Ben felt a million miles from the bustling shops outside. The building was narrow but longer than

ROYAL INSTITUTE OF MAGIC

he had expected. It looked like a hotel reception yet to be furnished, with high ceilings and a pristine white marble floor. The room was empty except for one large reception desk to the side, manned by a woman tapping away on a computer. Charlie was right, this place had nothing to do with Greenpeace.

"Incredible," Charlie said. He had passed through the revolving door and was staring at the long, spacious room.

Their gawking was interrupted by a couple of women entering the building. They quickly stepped aside and watched the women walk to the end of the room, where they stopped and waited. After a moment the wall slid open. It was a concealed lift, Ben realised, and the two women stepped inside and disappeared.

Ben exchanged a curious glance with Charlie.

"Now what?" Charlie whispered.

"Follow me."

He strode towards the expensive-looking reception desk. It came up to Ben's chest, but he still attempted to look at home, folding his hands and resting them on the top surface.

"May I help you, sir?"

The woman's voice was polite and efficient, a perfect match for her crisp suit and pulled-back hair.

"I'm looking for Wren Walker. I have an appointment," Ben said with a smile.

Ben wanted to kick Charlie to stop his fidgeting. Thankfully, the receptionist didn't seem to notice, nor did she seem surprised by Ben's request.

"May I have your name, please?"

"Ben Greenwood."

The receptionist's reaction was subtle, but Ben caught it – a widening of the eyes, a look of recognition and a quick intake of breath.

"Ben Greenwood?" she repeated, recovering quickly, but he noticed the way she emphasised his surname. "If you'll wait here, I'll see if I can find Ms. Walker for you."

She disappeared through a discreet door behind the desk.

As soon as she left, Ben's plastered smile vanished.

"What do you make of that?"

"Intriguing," Charlie said. "Did you see the way she reacted to your surname? She recognised it instantly."

Ben ruffled his mop of blond hair. There was something he didn't like about the receptionist's reaction. He was beginning to doubt she had gone to get Wren. He glanced at the revolving door, then at the concealed lift at the end of the room. They could either wait for the receptionist to return or — he slapped the desk.

"Let's go."

To his surprise, Charlie didn't protest.

Ben walked quickly, but resisted the urge to run. Their steps echoed so loudly on the marble floor that Charlie kept glancing anxiously back to the reception desk. The lift doors blended into the back wall and Ben would have missed them had they not opened before. He pressed a small button and the doors slid open. He was expecting to see a small empty cubicle. He was wrong.

"What on earth is this?" Charlie asked.

Facing them were rows of black leather seats, complete with arm and headrests, inside a space far larger than your average lift. Each seat had a padded bar that you could pull down over your chest, reminding Ben of a roller-coaster ride.

"I have no idea, but I suggest we buckle up," Ben said, and sat down in one of the middle seats. Charlie ogled the chairs a moment longer before sitting next to Ben.

The doors remained open, leaving them staring at the reception desk and the exit in the distance.

"How do we shut this thing?" Ben asked.

He was still searching for a button when he heard the tapping noise. Shoes against marble floor. The receptionist was back and with her were two guards.

"Mr. Greenwood!"

Ben searched frantically for something to shut the doors, but there was simply nothing there.

"Mr. Greenwood! *Do not use that lift!*"

"Oh god, we're in trouble," Charlie said. He wiggled his legs, which were dangling off the chair. "Go, you stupid lift – go!"

Both guards were now running, the soles of their shiny shoes making a terrible clacking noise that echoed right into the lift.

Ben squeezed the armrests, willing the doors shut. The guards were less than twenty paces away. He could see the shine of sweat on their foreheads.

The doors closed, locking with a satisfying click.

Ben heard a thud as the two guards reached the lift and started hammering the button. The lift was still stationary and Ben thought for a moment that the doors would slide open again.

The lift gave a jerk and started descending.

"Yes!" Ben said, thumping the armrest.

"My heart," Charlie gasped, clutching his chest. "I think I just had a minor heart attack."

The lift descended slowly and Ben wondered why there were seatbelts, though he didn't take his off. Now that they were safe, Ben looked round the strange lift in more detail. He counted thirty chairs in rows of five. Above the lift doors he spotted the R.I.M. logo. Below it was some writing.

Ben read the words. His mouth opened slowly and he blinked. He read them again, not believing his eyes.

"Ben, can you stop that?"

He was tapping Charlie repeatedly, unaware where or how hard. He pointed a shaky finger at the lettering.

Royal Institute of Magic.

R.I.M.

"No," Charlie whispered. "That can't be right."

They both started talking at once, but their incoherent blabber was cut off by a violent lurch. Ben gripped the armrests instinctively.

The lift plummeted.

Their shoulder straps saved them from smashing into the ceiling, but they did nothing to stop Ben's stomach, which stayed behind as they went into a free fall. He screamed in horror and then delight when his brain had time to process what was happening.

Ben tensed himself for the stop, but it didn't come. Down they went, until it felt like they were going to hit the Earth's core. Just as Ben was starting to relax, the lift slowed dramatically and gravity squashed him against his seat.

The lift came to a gentle halt.

There was a soft ding and the doors opened.

— CHAPTER FIVE —
No Electronics Beyond This Point

A stone corridor greeted them, lit by torches hanging from the walls. It seemed to go on forever, the light and dancing shadows slowly fading in the distance, ending in ominous blackness.

Ben and Charlie lifted their shoulder straps and stumbled out of the lift. The doors closed behind them and an instant later, they heard the lift depart.

Everything was silent except the soft burning of the torches and each other's breathing, which sounded like two Darth Vaders – such was the echo.

Ben stood there, motionless, seemingly hypnotised by the torches. Charlie did the exact opposite. He started pacing back and forth, huffing and puffing like he'd run a marathon.

"Deep breaths, Charlie, *deep* breaths," he kept repeating.

Ben watched him for a moment, torn between amusement and impatience.

"Whenever you're ready, I need your help to work out where we are and what's going on."

Charlie kept his manic pacing. "Where we are? That's easy. We're so far below the Earth's surface we should be dead – crushed by the pressure or boiled to a crisp."

Ben raised a hand. "It is rather warm here, isn't it?"

"Let's try to ignore the unexplained miracle of our continued existence," Charlie said, ploughing on at a million miles an hour. "What is this place? How does it even exist? I have so many questions circling my head I can't think!"

Ben grabbed Charlie by the shoulders and pinned him against the wall.

"Would a slap help?"

Charlie took a deep breath. "You're right, I'm sorry. I need to calm down."

Ben released him and gave him a pat on the shoulder.

"Let's start at the top with the most important issue:

why did the guards try to stop us coming down here? Is this because the receptionist recognised my surname?"

"Is that really the most important issue? What about the fact that we're trapped a mile underneath the earth?" Charlie asked, already struggling to stay calm.

"One thing at a time."

Charlie took a deep breath. "The receptionist must know your parents."

Ben wished he could have asked her, but it was too late now.

"What do you make of this 'Royal Institute of Magic'?" Ben asked.

"Normally an institute is an organisation founded for particular work, such as education or research," Charlie said. "But an institute for magic?"

Ben nodded. "Magic tricks, illusions achieved through the sleight of hand."

Charlie gave him a quizzical look. "Why would an institution like that build something like this?"

"We'll soon find out."

Their conversation was interrupted by a noise from behind, making them both jump.

It was the soft ding of the lift.

They exchanged alarmed looks and Ben cursed. Why had they dallied? They could flee down the corridor, but they had no idea where they were going and almost anyone could outrun Charlie. Ben grit his teeth. Whatever happened, they weren't going back, not when they'd got this far.

The lift opened, but it wasn't the guards.

A dozen men and women strode out, chatting amongst themselves. Ben and Charlie flattened themselves against the passageway as they walked by, giving the boys no more than a passing glance.

"What happened to the guards?" Charlie asked, once everyone had passed.

Ben was wondering the same thing.

"Let's follow these people before they get away."

Charlie gave a longing look at the open lift. With a puff of his cheeks he turned his back on the quick way out and set off with Ben down the tunnel.

The stone passage had a vaulted ceiling, creating a rounded tunnel like a miniature version of the Underground. Occasionally the corridor turned and they would momentarily lose sight of the people in front, but their echoing voices were always present. Ben was so intent on following their target that he was only dimly aware of Charlie's frequent remarks about the length and scope of the tunnel.

Eventually the group ahead stopped and formed a queue down the tunnel. They had no choice but to catch up and join the line.

"Try and act casual," said Ben.

Ben peered ahead and saw the tunnel open up to a small room, which people were entering one at a time. Just before the entrance was a slab of stone jutting from the ceiling. On it the word "SECURITY" was engraved in Gothic font. They were glowing, as if LEDs had been embedded into the letters.

"If this leads to another heart-attack-inducing, free-falling lift, I'm turning around," Charlie said.

The queue moved forward quickly and before Ben knew it, he was next in line, standing at the entrance.

The room was small and bare except for a large woman who stood in the middle. Ben's blue eyes strayed past her to a peculiar stone archway that stood just in front of the exit. It was black and engraved with silver hieroglyphs. At the top was a large, green eye that looked so real Ben could have sworn it blinked. He was so captivated by the eye it took a moment to notice the sign next to him.

Warning:

Electronics at serious risk of spontaneous combustion beyond this point. Please dispense with all such items before proceeding through the arch.

Maximum penalty for smuggling science: £10,000 and three years in prison."

"We don't have all day, luv. Remove all electronics and step through," the large woman said, beckoning him impatiently with her hand.

Her order went in one ear and out the other the moment he saw what she was wearing. Strapped to her ample waist was a holster carrying the strangest-looking gun Ben had ever seen. It was made of wood and the barrel was a gnarled, tapered stick with no visible exit for bullets. On top of the handle sat a glass orb, partially encased by delicately carved tendrils of wood. Inside the orb were dozens of small, coloured pellets that floated around like they were in water.

"Just because there's no queue behind you doesn't mean you can stand there like a lemon," she said.

"Sorry," Ben replied, pulling himself together and giving her a sheepish smile. He slapped his jeans, pulled out a mobile phone and looked at her quizzically.

"In the safe," she said, pointing a long, pink-nailed finger at the wall to Ben's left.

Ben saw nothing but stone. There was clearly no safe anywhere. He walked to the wall anyway, examining every crevice. When he got there he was forced to give the lady another enquiring look.

She rolled her eyes and muttered something under her breath. Walking over to him, she thrust her hand out.

What did she want? Ben thought fast. He delved into his pocket, past the peculiar piece of fabric, and pulled out the ID card. She snatched it from him and inserted it into a tiny gap in the wall. Ben could have spent an hour looking and not seen it. It was the size of a card slot in an ATM machine.

There was a soft humming noise and the stone in front of him faded away, revealing a small empty cubicle within the wall.

He stared at the cubicle in astonishment, thrusting an experimental hand inside.

"It's for your phone, not your hand, luv," the lady said. "Phone in, card out, today if possible."

Ben did as she asked and the stone faded back into existence.

"Step on through," the woman ordered.

Ben wanted to examine the disappearing stone, but he could feel her growing irritation. He walked to the exit, approaching the black arch slowly. To his amazement, the green eye followed his progress. Underneath the arch, the air appeared to be shimmering and beyond it everything looked out of focus.

He could feel the large woman's eyes on him. His incompetence was arousing suspicion and he knew he couldn't afford to attract any more attention. If she stopped to question him, they would be in trouble. Trying to ignore the eye, he passed under the arch. His skin tingled and there was a moment of resistance, then he was through and into the passage beyond.

A few moments later a bug-eyed Charlie appeared.

"Ingenious," Charlie said, his voice brimming with excitement as they resumed their journey. "That illusion with the stone was as good as I've seen. I wonder where they hid the projector."

For some reason Ben felt disappointed at Charlie's logical explanation.

"That archway was odd, wasn't it?"

Charlie shrugged, as if the shimmering archway with the green eye was nothing compared to the disappearing stone.

Ben wasn't so easily convinced. "What did you make of that warning about electronics blowing up?"

"A silly joke," Charlie said, waving his hand. "You were right, by the way. The magic refers to illusion and trickery. I've heard of other such organisations, like the Magic Circle."

Ben didn't want to burst Charlie's bubble, but the idea of his parents spending endless hours mastering crazy card tricks was unthinkable. And how much trouble could one get into being in the magic business? It didn't add up.

Before he could argue the matter, the sound of voices echoed down the tunnel. Lots of voices, too many for a narrow tunnel, unless there was an almighty queue ahead. But they could see nothing for the passage curved out of sight.

A rush of air threw Ben's tousled hair back and he exchanged a surprised look with Charlie. There shouldn't be any wind underground.

Ben hurried forward, ignoring Charlie's pleas of caution. With every step the noise grew – voices, footsteps, even laughter. As he approached what must be the final bend, Ben saw a sign hanging from the tunnel ceiling. He recognised it instantly and stopped.

It was the London Underground symbol: a red circle with a blue horizontal bar and the word "Croydon" written on it.

He stared at it until Charlie caught up. Neither of them said anything. They both knew Croydon had no Underground station and if it did, it certainly wouldn't be this far below the Earth's surface.

With overwhelming curiosity, Ben rounded the final bend.

— CHAPTER SIX —

Trains and Dragons

Despite the sign, Ben didn't believe they were about to enter Croydon Underground Station. He assumed somebody had put up the symbol as a joke, a memento or maybe even a tribute to the real Underground.

He assumed wrong.

It wasn't the same as the more familiar London Underground, but there was no denying this was a station. The platform was half the usual length and the track only a foot below the ground. A gentle glow came from the great vaulted ceiling, casting ample light on the scene below.

The platform was buzzing with people. Some were waiting at the edge of the platform, others sat around circular wooden tables chatting. Several had drinks and food, perhaps sourced from the small shops that hugged the back of the platform. Ben spotted people wearing holsters with the strange toy guns, but nobody was giving them a second glance.

Ben and Charlie stood together, staring openly at everyone and everything. After a moment, Ben realised something wasn't right.

"Ben," whispered Charlie. He was watching the nearest table, looking slightly bemused. "Look closely at the two on the left," Charlie said softly, pointing.

They were wearing elaborate masks, giving them pointed ears, unnaturally high cheek bones and big, slanted eyes. Their casual jeans and long-sleeve shirts were a bizarre contrast to the facial get-up.

It wasn't just them, Ben realised. There were three on the next table with painted green faces and several others walking round with similar costumes.

"They must be going to a fancy dress party."

"Why would they walk around like that here though?" Charlie asked. "Check out that guy on that table. If he ever came to our school, the bullies would forget I ever existed."

Ben's reply died in his throat. Standing near the platform's edge was the most peculiar man Ben had ever seen. He was less than three feet high and painted green from head to toe. He had huge ears, a pointed nose and a comically long chin. His pot belly was poorly concealed by a faded green t-shirt. He was holding a tall sign that said "INFORMATION".

"Do you see that?" Ben asked.

Charlie's dramatic gasp was a "yes".

Ben turned his attention to the big sign. "Information – that's just what we need."

"Can we ask someone who doesn't look clinically insane?"

But Ben was already moving, picking his way through the crowd along the platform edge.

The mask the little man wore was extremely good, right down to the sharp, yellow teeth, but the effect was ruined slightly by the chewing gum.

"Alright, lads," the little man said in a high-pitched voice. "What can I do for ya?"

Obvious questions would arouse too much suspicion, but Ben had to ask something.

"Where does this line go?"

"Northbound takes you into London Victoria. Southbound takes you to Taecia. From there you can pretty much get to any kingdom you choose."

Ben attempted a casual nod of understanding, trying to disguise the fact that he had no clue what the man was talking about. He decided to take a calculated risk and ask a more direct question.

"Can you tell me how to get to the Institute?"

"You want the next train, which arrives any minute now. Anything else?"

Ben thanked him, unable to think of anything further to ask.

"Something wrong with your gawking friend? He looks like he's never seen a goblin before."

Before Ben could reply, the ground shuddered. It felt like a mini earthquake.

"Your ride," the goblin said. "You should step back, unless you want to be eaten."

The goblin had already taken his own advice, stepping away from the platform. Everyone else near the edge was doing the same. Several people were now peering into the inky blackness of the tunnel to their right.

Ben heard a soft rumbling noise, which quickly got louder until it sounded like a jumbo jet was careering down the tunnel right at them. The wind picked up, sweeping his hair back. Two green dots appeared in the depths of the tunnel; their oval shape and colour were an unusual choice for headlights.

The headlights blinked.

A dragon came flying down the tunnel and entered the platform with a deep-throated roar. It had teeth the size of daggers, flaring nostrils and red, scaly skin. Its leathery wings were short and stubby, suited to the deep tunnels rather than the open air. Ben flung himself backwards at the last minute, taking Charlie with him and landed hard on his backside. The sight before him made the pain insignificant. The dragon was pulling a dozen bright red carriages. They were far smaller than their London Underground counterparts. Elbows rested on half-doors and the windows had no glass, leaving the passengers open to the elements. It reminded Ben of the trams at theme parks, which took you from the car park to the entrance. On the dragon's neck sat three men on a huge saddle, each holding a harness.

The dragon came to a halt, steam hissing from its nostrils. The small half-doors swung open and people started filing out as if it were nothing more than the 9:07 from London Victoria.

Impossible. *Impossible!* But there it was, living and breathing. The shades of red on its scaly armour, rising and falling with every breath, were so real that Ben had the insane urge to touch them.

"I'm dreaming," Charlie whispered. "It's the only possible explanation."

They picked themselves off the floor, eyes still glued to the dragon.

"You'd better get in. Next one's not for an hour."

It was the little green man, or goblin, as he called himself. Was he a real goblin? A minute ago Ben would have scoffed at the prospect, but then came the dragon.

Charlie was lost in his own world, incapable of thought or reason. Ben gave the goblin a nod of thanks and shoved Charlie into one of the carriages, shutting the door behind him. It was crowded and Ben squeezed into a seat on the end, his elbow resting on the top of the small half-door.

"All aboard – she's about to depart!" the goblin shouted.

After a final flurry of doors closing, the goblin stuck two fingers in his mouth and whistled. The carriage gave a gentle jerk and starting moving slowly along the platform. Ahead, Ben could see the mighty black tunnel. The dragon broke into a gentle canter, flapping its stubby wings to help it along. The black tunnel engulfed them. For a moment Ben couldn't see his hand in front of his face, then the roof lit up, casting a soft, warm glow on the passengers. The wind rushed in, gently buffeting their faces.

Ben sat in silence until his heart rate returned to something approaching normal.

"Well, we're on our way," he said with a smile.

Thankfully, Charlie seemed to have returned to the world of the living. He still looked pale, but his crazed eyes had disappeared.

"Where to?"

"The Royal Institute of Magic, of course."

"But where *is* that?"

Ben shrugged. "We'll soon find out."

As the train trundled along, Ben thought of his parents. Had they known about all of this? If so, why keep it secret? Ben was starting to feel he had been missing out on something huge.

An announcement interrupted his thoughts. It came from the ceiling, though Ben saw no speakers, and had the same poorly masked boredom associated with most train conductors.

"Welcome, those joining us from Croydon," the voice droned. "We have a clear tunnel all the way to Taecia this morning, which means our journey time will be approximately forty-eight minutes. Thank you."

Ben frowned. "Taecia? I thought we were heading to the Institute?"

"Maybe the little green man lied to us," Charlie said.

Ben glanced cautiously at the nearby passengers, but thankfully nobody seemed to have heard Charlie's comment. With the noise from the carriage, plus the general murmur of conversation, Ben was fairly certain no one was listening to them. Nevertheless, he tried to keep his voice down.

"The goblin, you mean."

"You can't be serious," Charlie said.

"Why – because goblins don't exist?"

"I can't believe I'm saying this, but no, goblins don't exist."

Ben didn't know whether to laugh or to slap Charlie round his ample chops.

"Have you seen what's pulling us along?"

Charlie gave a furtive glance towards the back of the dragon's mighty neck. He shook his head, looking troubled.

"I can't," he said.

"Try harder."

Charlie took his hanky out and wiped his forehead. "How do you do it? How do you simply accept all this?"

"Because it's happening."

"I could be dreaming," Charlie mused. "Or maybe someone spiked our drinks. Maybe I'm hallucinating. Or maybe—"

"Do you want me to slap you?" Ben asked.

"Yes, please."

But Ben didn't. "It's not easy for me either. Every time I look outside I want to pinch myself."

This seemed to help Charlie relax and he put his hanky away. "If the *goblin*" – Charlie faltered, but only a little – "isn't lying, then perhaps Taecia is where the Royal Institute of Magic is."

"That makes sense."

"A more pressing question," Charlie said, "is the location of Taecia."

"Have you worked out where we're going?"

Charlie ticked off the facts on his stubby fingers. "I'd say we are doing no more than 40mph and we are heading south-west. The conductor says we will be travelling for forty-eight minutes, which means we will end up somewhere short of Portsmouth."

Ben didn't doubt Charlie's calculations or his in-built compass, which had saved them many times before.

"Seems like a lot of work for a simple network between towns. We already have trains and buses," Ben said.

The conductor's voice intervened before Charlie could reply.

"Ladies and gentlemen, we are about to take off. Please brace yourselves."

Ben exchanged an alarmed look with Charlie, whose face went pale, having only just regained colour.

"Take off?" Charlie said, a little too loudly for Ben's liking. "We're in a *tunnel.*"

Ben's initial anxiety was tempered by the calm exuding from the other passengers. They didn't even seem to be doing anything to brace themselves. A moment later, a metallic bar fastened to the back of the seat in front started sliding forward until it pressed down gently on their laps.

"Is that it?" Charlie asked, staring at the bar. "How about some seat belts, air bags or at least something that has a slim chance of preventing our untimely deaths?"

Charlie had a point. The bar reminded him of a cheap theme park ride, one that he could climb out of if he desired.

Ben wanted to reassure Charlie by pointing out that nobody else was panicking. He didn't get the chance.

The carriage accelerated like a modern-day roller-coaster. Ben's head yanked back and he grabbed hold of the metal bar for dear life. The wind buffeted him, screaming in his ears, watering his eyes. The carriage gave a little hop and its wheels left the ground. The roof screeched as they grazed the top of the tunnel. Ben braced himself for impact, but the carriages levelled out. There was a bang, like a gun being fired, and immediately the wind stopped, as did the rocking. The train cruised along smoothly through the tunnel, making a gentle purring noise.

Ben stuck a tentative hand against the side of the carriage, where a window would have been, and felt an unseen barrier. He poked it, softly, then harder – the barrier bent his finger painfully.

"Some sort of invisible shield," Ben said.

Charlie had his hand half-extended, perhaps wanting to touch it, but not quite daring.

"The technology doesn't exist for that yet," Charlie said.

"Maybe it's not technology," Ben said after a moment.

"What do you mean?"

"Maybe it's something else. Something other than science."

"Please, don't go there," Charlie said, massaging his temples.

"Is the prospect of magic any more outrageous than a dragon train?"

Charlie had no reply and Ben decided not to press the matter. Instead he turned his attention to the tunnel, which was now just a blur.

"If we were going 40mph before, what are we doing now?"

"It's hard to be accurate, but I would say at least 300mph." Charlie tapped his fingers together. "Which means, if we maintain this speed, we will end up somewhere in the Celtic Sea, south-west of England and west of France."

"What's out there?"

"Water, Ben – just water."

"No islands or anything?"

"Nothing that far out. The Isles of Scilly are the closest, but at this rate we will go way past them."

"Well then, I'm sure we'll slow down," Ben said.

But for the next forty-five minutes, the dragon train didn't slow down. Several times Ben was tempted to ask one of the other passengers, but the danger of arousing suspicion always stopped him. Nobody else seemed concerned, which reassured him, but did nothing to ease his curiosity.

Ben never thought he would get bored being pulled by a flying dragon in a carriage at 300mph, but he was grateful when the conductor's voice finally echoed throughout the cabin.

"Ladies and gentlemen, we are approaching Taecia. We will be coming out of Dragon Flight momentarily. For those of you travelling onwards, please note that all transport to Aven is currently suspended while the Empire determines whether they are now hostile. Have a pleasant day."

"What was that?" Charlie asked.

"God knows. File it for later. We're about to stop."

Ben had barely finished his sentence when the carriage suddenly broke hard. His stomach squashed against the metal bar and the train's wheels screeched as they touched the ground. There was another bang and the invisible barrier vanished, letting the rushing air in. Soon the dragon was cantering along no faster than a horse.

The tunnel started heading upwards and they began ascending.

"This isn't possible," Charlie said. His fingers were white, holding the metal bar in a death grip. "We're going to pop up in the middle of the sea."

Ben saw bright sunlight rapidly approaching as they neared the surface.

"Let's see, shall we?" Ben said, grinning at Charlie's horrified face. "You might be wrong."

"I'm not wrong," Charlie said, breathing so quickly that he was almost hyperventilating. "Did you know I can't swim?"

— CHAPTER SEVEN —
Tea and Treason

They weren't in the middle of the sea. They had emerged
into what loosely resembled an overground train station, with
platforms left and right, some of them occupied by other squat
dragons pulling carriages. Above the platforms was a walkway
that crossed over the tracks. Their train came to a gentle stop,
signalled by a jet of smoke from the dragon's nostrils. Ben pulled
the handle, the door swung open and he stumbled out.

There was so much to see Ben didn't know where to look
first. His attention was drawn to the people; they ranged from
the ordinary to off-the-wall. Some had pointed ears so subtle he
barely noticed until they passed by. Others were over seven feet
tall and looked carved from rock. Then there were those no
higher than his waist, with beards that swept the ground. In the
middle of the platform was a large map illustrating a complex
network of rail lines. Most of the station names he didn't

recognise, but he did spot Croydon, as well as other familiar places, like New York, Johannesburg and even Sydney. On top of the sign was a heading that read "Her Majesty's Dragonway Transport".

"Excuse me," a nearby voice said.

Charlie was standing by the door of the carriage, stopping people from exiting. Ben hauled him to the middle of the platform, right next to a sign that read, *"Welcome to Taecia: Founding Kingdom of the Elizabethan Empire and Home to the Royal Institute of Magic."*

They could have stood there for hours – Charlie certainly would have – but Ben shook himself out of his stupor and they wandered down the platform. There were stairs at the end that led to the overhead walkway and, Ben assumed, the way out of the station. He constantly fought the impulse to stop and stare and followed the exit signs that led up to and along the gangway. Eventually they spilled out into a town that belonged in another era. The buildings were white, with timber frames and narrow doors and windows. They looked like Tudor houses, if Ben remembered his history correctly. The road was cobbled and filled with horses and other animals Ben was sure only existed in fairytales and video games.

They collapsed on a nearby bench and, like tourists, stared at everything that moved.

"Looks like our sun," Ben said, glancing up at the clear blue sky.

It was a ridiculous comment, but instead of scoffing, Charlie just nodded.

"How do you hide an entire island? It's not possible."

Ben didn't have an answer. The more he looked around, the more incredible the place became. He felt like he was dreaming.

Ben leapt off the bench and rubbed his hands together.

"Are you ready?" he asked Charlie with a grin.

Charlie took a deep breath and nodded. "Where can we get directions for the Institute?"

Ben spotted a road sign that stood at a four-way junction. When they got close enough, one of the directions read "Royal Institute of Magic: 500 yards".

"Uphill – my favourite," Charlie said, patting his little pot belly.

The town was built on a steep hill and at the top was a castle wall, which they could not see beyond. Ben guessed it protected the Institute.

They made their way through a hodgepodge of winding lanes and crooked intersections. Horses and antique cars shared the roads, reminding Ben of early 20th century photos he had seen in libraries. Occasionally they took a wrong turn because they were too busy looking at everything and had to double back to continue up the hill. Many of the shops looked as though they had been around for centuries. There was an ironmonger, a dress maker and all sorts of food stores, including some divine-smelling bakeries. Among them were modern establishments – Ben spotted a Tesco's, a Greggs and even a Starbucks. How on earth did they get here? Apart from the logo and branding, they managed to nestle in among the older shops without looking too out of place.

Ben's stomach rumbled as he passed a Starbucks, but it was Charlie who stopped, staring at the familiar logo that hung out the front, his nose twitching at the smell of coffee.

"Do you think it's the same as home?" he asked, rubbing his stomach absently.

"They're always the same, Charlie."

Ben peered through the window. It certainly didn't appear too different, though he noticed the lack of electrical equipment and wondered how they made the hot drinks.

"Let's find out," Ben said, pulling open the small wooden door.

The moment he entered, Ben felt the hairs on his neck rise. A flash of light caught his eye and he turned sharply, stopping right under the doorway. Charlie ran into him and the momentum took them both into the café.

"Ow – what was that for?" Charlie asked, rubbing his nose.

Ben peered out of the window. "For a moment I thought someone was watching me."

Charlie's eyes widened. "Did you see anyone?"

"I'm not sure. I may have just imagined it."

Charlie was shaking his head before Ben finished speaking. "You're forgetting your incredible sixth sense – not that I believe in that sort of thing. Someone must have been watching you."

Ben knew Charlie was right. "Let's eat and see if they're still out there when we leave."

He forced the problem aside and went up to the counter. The sandwiches and drinks were similar to home, but there were also some strange additions. The "Elf Espresso" (roasted especially for the coffee connoisseur) and the "Pixie Latte" (sweet and spicy) caught Ben's eye.

"This Dodo salad sandwich sounds good," Ben said, taking one from the display.

"I'd say they became extinct in the 17th century, but what would be the point?" Charlie said, taking the same sandwich himself.

The lady serving them had perfect pale skin, huge almond eyes and ears that, at home, would be common at a Star Trek convention.

Ben had a sudden thought as he went to pay.

"Do you accept English currency?" Ben asked. He was trying not to stare, knowing Charlie was doing enough gawking for both of them.

"Of course," she said, giving him a quizzical look.

Ben slapped his pockets and realised he was broke. The sickening thought barely had time to register before Charlie slapped a ten-pound note on the counter.

"You are new here," the lady said as they made their way to a table.

"Is it that obvious?" Ben asked.

The lady smiled. "I see it in your faces." She gave them both a searching look. "You know the Institute is watching you?"

Ben almost dropped his sandwich. "How do you know that?"

The lady turned to the window. "I can see with more than just my eyes. There is a Warden standing outside the bar across the street. He watched you come in."

"A Warden?"

"They are responsible for border control and immigration. You don't fool around with them."

More customers entered and the lady turned away to serve them. Ben and Charlie sat themselves down on a small wooden table, next to a group of elves drinking coffee.

"The receptionist," Ben said, leaning forward so he could speak softly, "she must have sent warning."

Charlie was still looking at the lady who had served them, a peculiar glint in his eye. "Security cameras," he said, after a moment. "Do you think that's what she meant when she said she sees with more than just her eyes?"

Ben slammed his hand on the table with such vigour that Charlie nearly fell off his seat.

"Stop trying to explain everything scientifically," Ben said loudly enough to disturb the nearby table.

"I can't help it," Charlie said, his voice rising an octave in desperation. "I know it's ridiculous, but I keep trying to rationalise everything and it's driving me crazy. Did you spot that flying horse earlier? I found myself trying to explain it with Darwin's Theory of Evolution."

Ben would have laughed if it weren't for Charlie's genuine look of concern.

"Look, I know this is crazy, but I'm sure when we get to the Institute they will explain everything."

Charlie brightened considerably at the prospect and the dazed stupor that had gripped him finally dissipated. "You're right. I will feel better once we get some answers."

He stared at his sandwich with the sort of look Ben was more accustomed to and tucked in. The dodo, as it turned out, was delicious.

Ben kept thinking about the Warden, wondering why they were being watched. He was tempted to go outside and ask.

"We could ask if there is another way out," Charlie said, licking the last bits of sauce from his fingers.

"What's the point? We have nothing to hide. I say we continue to the Institute. If he wants to stop us, he's welcome to. One way or the other we'll get answers."

They left Starbucks with a full stomach and resumed their journey. As they climbed the hill, the buildings got bigger and the roads, such as they were, became wider. Trees and torch-lit lamp posts started lining the cobbled path and they soon had a clearer view of the stone wall at the top of the hill. It was at least ten feet high and spanned as far as the eye could see. Ben imagined it forming a ring round the entire top of the hill, fortifying the Institute. Other roads joined the main one, which led to a large open gate. It appeared to be the only way in.

Ben felt his body start to tingle with anticipation. He felt sure they were on the verge of unravelling something huge. Would this "Wren" person know what happened to his parents? Were they really still alive? Ben had never doubted it, but what if the news were bad? The thought made him shiver and he cast it from his mind. He felt the peculiar fabric in his pocket; surely he would get answers here.

"Can we take a breather?" Charlie asked from behind. He was bent over, hands on knees, panting heavily.

Ben realised he had been practically running up the hill. They were a mere twenty yards from the gate, but he waited for Charlie to get his breath back. There were two guards either side of the open gate, doing a good impression of the ones at

Buckingham Palace. Both wore the strange toy guns by their sides. Hanging on the stone wall was a black marble plaque with the words "Royal Institute of Magic" etched in silver. Above it was the same coat of arms Ben had seen outside their building in Croydon; a shield with four distinct quarters, alternating between a red background with golden lions and a blue background with three golden flowers.

Neither guard moved a muscle as they passed through the gate and into the grounds of the Institute.

Ben never thought he'd have the patience to stop now that he was this close, but one look at the Institute and they both came to a standstill.

To call it a house would have been an injustice, but it did look like a mighty version of the Tudor homes that populated the town. It was pristine white, dotted with dozens of leaded windows with black-timbered frames. Ben counted a dozen gables, creating a mini mountain range, and half a dozen outside balconies. There was a pair of mighty wooden double doors at the front. Above them the words "Royal Institute of Magic" were etched and seemed to pulse with a warm, silver glow.

An open courtyard surrounded the building, consisting of manicured gardens, trimmed hedges and even a water fountain. A generous cobbled path led to the entrance and there was a welcoming light coming from within.

Ben was concentrating so hard on peering through the windows that he didn't hear Charlie's cry of alarm as they approached the entrance. Ben felt something grab him from behind and yank him to a standstill.

Charlie was staring in horror at a large noticeboard. Ben hadn't even seen it, so intent had he been on reaching the front doors. It was big enough to warrant its own gable and on it were several A4-sized notices. But Ben saw only one. It was a head shot of his mum and dad. Underneath it read:

"Wanted on suspicion of high treason:

Greg and Jane Greenwood.

Rewards given for any information leading to their capture."

— CHAPTER EIGHT —
An Unpleasant Welcome

Ben stared at the poster, numb with shock. Seeing a photo of his parents, here of all places, was just as staggering as the declaration of treason. They looked just as he remembered. His mum was smiling, a sparkle in her blue eyes. His dad was also smiling, his ridiculous moustache and raised eyebrow giving the impression he knew something you didn't.

A wave of emotions swept through him as he examined every inch of their faces. The surprise and astonishment were interspersed with anxiety every time he glanced at the word "treason". But bubbling beneath it all was a peculiar sense of joy that, given the poster's message, took him a second to understand.

"They're alive," he whispered. The relief was such that he found it difficult to speak. A weight had been lifted, one he had borne so long he'd forgotten how heavy it was. He had always believed they were alive, but nagging in the back of his mind had been the lack of evidence.

"They're alive," he said, louder this time, turning to Charlie with a lopsided grin – his blue eyes shining.

"You always said they were," Charlie said, returning the smile, "and I never doubted you. What about the high treason?"

"I don't know."

Ben felt a growing concern now that the initial shock had subsided. "There must be some great misunderstanding." His voice trailed off. What misunderstanding could lead to a declaration of high treason?

They entered the Royal Institute of Magic cautiously. Ben had planned to be on alert, but that went out the window the moment he stepped inside. They found themselves in a huge sky-lit atrium, staring up at a dozen open galleries accessed via an old- fashioned staircase. There were wooden beams everywhere making the place seem cosy despite its size. The vast lobby was bare except for the staircase and a huge statue in the middle, which sat on a pedestal, towering over everyone.

Ben was so lost in the building that he didn't realise people were looking at him.

Lots of people.

"Ben Greenwood?"

A stout-looking man was watching him. He was shorter than those surrounding him, but Ben could tell by the room he was given that he was important. He had a scruffy beard, a scar that ran along his chin and an expression of such menace he looked ready to bite someone's head off.

"Yes," Ben said, just as Charlie whispered, "*Don't answer.*"

The effect was immediate. There was a flurry of soft chatter and a few people crossing the threshold stopped. Ben felt like he was suddenly in a Western duel.

"Look at their right shoulders," Charlie whispered.

Ben had already seen them. Each of them had tiny three-dimensional red diamonds hovering an inch above their shoulders. Most of them had just one or two, but the man addressing Ben had five.

"About bloody time," the man said gruffly. "Detain them."

Two men standing either side of the leader pulled out their strange guns and took aim. Ben could see the coloured pellets floating within the glass orb. But the barrel was a knotted wooden stick; surely it didn't function?

They pressed the triggers.

The barrels lit up and out shot a red pellet that swiftly expanded to the size of a tennis ball. From the corner of his eye Ben could just make out Charlie raising his hands in surrender as a pellet hit him full on the chest. Ben reacted instinctively, diving to his right, and the pellet flew by. He rolled and leapt to his feet. Another two pellets whipped by his face and a third struck him square on the back. It stung, but only a little and he even managed a few more steps before something yanked him back. A rope materialised around him like a perfectly thrown lasso, wrapping his arms against his chest. He struggled violently, but the rope held fast and yanked him around. It extended into the gun barrel of a slender woman who held it effortlessly.

"Slippery, like a weasel," the man said. He turned and glared at the congregation around him. "What are you lot looking at?"

The crowd thinned, leaving just the grizzled man and half a dozen others who were clearly his entourage. Ben noticed they had the same red diamonds as the man's, though not as many.

"This is wrong, Draven."

Not everyone had been scared away by the man's glare. Facing the group was a tiny woman with four white diamonds floating above her shoulder.

"Rubbish, Lana. I'm trying to find the Greenwoods. We're desperate, not that you'd know, living in the library."

Lana didn't flinch. "I'm going to stop this."

"Oh, put a cork in it," Draven said, waving a hand at her.

Lana turned to Ben and he met her level-headed stare. He saw a flicker of curiosity before she finally turned and left.

"Let's go," Draven said.

The woman holding his leash gave a little tug and Ben was yanked forward up the grand staircase. He tried to resist, but it was futile and he soon realised it would be better to save his energy.

"What's going on?" Ben asked.

"Silence," the woman said. "You will find out soon enough. You are not in any danger here."

"Really? Are all newcomers treated like dogs then?"

"I said, be quiet," she said and flicked the rope. Ben felt a painful shock run through his body. "You will find out soon enough."

They climbed to the fourth floor where they left the stairs and stopped in front of double doors. On them was a sign in red lettering that read "Department of Wardens" and below it was a symbol of a miniature world map. They went through the doors into a grand hallway that spanned left and right. In front of them, facing the doors, was a mighty statue of a large, rather pompous-looking fellow. Before Ben could read the description at the statue's base, he was jerked right. The hallway was lavishly decorated, with deep red walls and wood panelling. There were doors at regular intervals with signs like "Goblin Search – South East", "Illegal Elf Immigrants", "Tracking Centre" and many more, each more bizarre than the last.

"I want the team ready in five," Draven said. Two of the group instantly peeled off and doubled back the way they had come. Ben turned to see which door they might enter, but his head was forced forward.

Despite the woman's earlier claim that they weren't in danger, Ben's heart was beating hard. He thought about shouting for help, but who would come? Besides, it would only result in getting hurt again.

Ben forced his own anxiety aside. Draven seemed to think this would help the search for Ben's parents. Did he think Ben knew something?

Draven cursed loudly the moment they turned the next corner.

The lady waiting by the nearest door caught Ben by surprise. She wore a flowery red dress and had long, silvery hair elegantly piled up on her head. She wasn't young, but her wrinkles were so fine and delicate Ben couldn't decide whether she was old enough to be his mother or his grandmother. Her eyes were a sparkling grey and her ears were slightly pointed. Floating above her right shoulder were five small green diamonds.

"Good afternoon, Mr. Bogvid," she said in a rich voice.

"What do you want, Wren?" Draven asked roughly.

They had stopped by the door, which, Ben noticed, said "Warden Director".

"I have come for these two charming young boys," Wren said.

Draven stepped forward, thrusting his chin out. "They're not yours to take."

Wren raised a slender finger. "Quite true, Draven. However, they arc not yours cithcr and thcy arc certainly not under arrest." She turned to Ben, and Charlie. "If you'll come with me, I can provide you with some long overdue answers."

Draven glared, daring Ben or Charlie to defy him.

"Yes, please," Ben said and Charlie nodded vigorously. The leashes around their torsos immediately disappeared.

"You idiot," Draven said, shaking a hairy fist at Wren. "You realise what you're doing? You're jeopardising my rescue operation. The entire Institute and England could fall because of you."

"Oh, don't be so melodramatic, Draven."

Draven turned to Ben, a look of desperation in his eyes. "There could be spells on the boy. I'd stake my life on Greg and Jane putting some sort of tracking spell or even a shield. If we could trace that, we might be able to locate them."

For the first time, Ben started listening.

"You might be right. Why don't you convene the Executive Council and arrange something properly?"

"We don't have time for that," Draven said, raising his voice. "Our position weakens every minute we waste in bringing the Greenwoods to justice." His eyes narrowed to slits and he pointed a finger at Wren's face. "When the Council asks why we delayed, you're going to be in deep trouble, and I'm going to *love* watching you squirm and plead your innocence."

He opened the door and stormed through, his entourage following behind. It slammed shut.

Wren smiled serenely at them. "Who fancies a cup of tea?"

— CHAPTER NINE —

Answers at Last

They followed Wren back to the grand staircase.

"A few more flights, I'm afraid," she said in her rich voice. "Allow me to apologise on behalf of Draven. I know he might come across as the devil incarnate, but deep down he's not a bad person."

"Could he really track my parents if they had cast spells on me?"

"In theory, yes."

Ben couldn't believe he was throwing the word "spell" around with such nonchalance. Spells meant magic. The evidence was everywhere, but hearing adults say it gave it credence.

Charlie was puffing by the time they left the staircase and entered another set of double doors. This time the sign said "Department of Spellswords" with a sword shown below it.

Beyond the doors was another statue, this one of a cheerful man holding a sword in one hand and one of those strange guns in the other.

"Michael James," Wren said, noticing their interest. "He was the first Spellsword Director; quite a man by all accounts."

Without the pre-occupation of being captured, lassoed and marched by a raving madman, Ben was able to admire the hallway. This floor wasn't as lavish, but it felt spacious, with white walls and wooden beams. As they followed the hallway round the corners, Ben started to get a feel for the place. On every floor there seemed to be a corridor that looped round, with rooms branching off. Ben was sure that if they kept walking they would be back at the double doors.

The hallway was busy and several people passed by, nodding respectfully at Wren and giving Ben and Charlie curious looks. Wren seemed to know everyone's name and graced all who passed with a smile.

"Here we are," she said.

They stopped by a door that said "Spellsword Director" and Wren pushed it open.

Ben wasn't sure if he'd stepped into a luxurious office or a hotel suite. At the back of the long room, by the window, was a sturdy wooden desk and an ornate antique chair. Against one of the walls was a suite of high-backed, deep brown furniture surrounding a small, exquisitely carved oak table. There were paintings of incredible landscapes on the walls and behind the sofa was a mural of a world map. Light spilled in from the window as if the sun had parked itself just outside the Institute, giving the room a bright, airy feel.

"Natalie, could you make tea for three please – plus yourself if you want a cup?" Wren said. She had popped her head in an adjacent room Ben hadn't noticed.

Charlie walked over to the sofa and was staring at the map on the wall. "Oh my," he said.

Ben couldn't see what the fuss was about. It was a map – albeit a big one at least ten feet wide.

"Look, Ben," Charlie said. He leant on the sofa and pointed up at different countries. "These countries don't exist on our maps."

He pointed to a dozen countries – some small, some as big as France – scattered across the map.

"You know your geography, Charlie," Wren said. She sat down on the sofa. Charlie took a step back and half fell into a luxurious, brown chair. Ben sat down on the remaining chair.

"I can only imagine the questions you must have," Wren said, giving them both a lengthy look. "So, you tell me, where would you like to start?"

"My parents," Ben replied instantly. Questions buzzed round his head, but he chose his first one carefully. There was one thing he needed to be absolutely certain of. "Are they okay?"

It was clear Wren saw Ben's concern. "They are alive. We'd know if they weren't. As to their well-being, that is harder to say as we don't know where they are."

Ben's elation at their safety was tempered by their unknown whereabouts.

"Why are they being accused of treason?"

Her grey eyes held his and Ben had a feeling she was considering withholding the truth. He was about to demand it when she broke the little stand-off.

"There is a dark elf king by the name of Suktar. It would take hours to recount the long and bloody history of his empire. Suffice it to say that over the centuries it is not the French or the Spanish who have been England's greatest threat, but Erellia, King Suktar's kingdom."

"What does he have to do with my parents?"

"Suktar is accusing your parents of murdering his son, Prince Ictid. He is threatening to break a truce we have worked hard to establish unless they are brought to justice."

Ben was grateful he was sitting down. Head spinning, he grabbed the armrests.

"Murder?"

Wren's kind eyes found his and their warmth soothed his rising panic. "I am convinced it's nonsense," she said, "as is the majority of the Institute. Your dad can be unruly at times and a terrible influence on your mother, but they are two of the most honest people I know."

Ben was struck by how well Wren seemed to know his mum and dad. "Did my parents work here?"

"They do work here," Wren replied. "In fact, they are two of my best Spellswords."

"What is a Spellsword?"

"Sorry, how would you know that?" Wren said, admonishing herself. "Spellswords are the Institute's armed forces. As the name suggests, they are trained in both spell and sword to combat everything the Unseen Kingdoms can offer."

Ben turned away, staring into light coming from the window, trying to take everything in.

"I thought my parents worked for Greenpeace. I thought they had a normal life – you know, drive to work, do normal work stuff, pick me up, bug me about homework." He smiled sadly. "Turns out I didn't know them as well as I thought."

"That's not true," Wren said softly. "Yes, they didn't reveal their true occupation, but you knew them in every other sense."

Ben knew he should be delighted to discover their exciting profession, but he felt slightly empty. Why had they never told him about it? Why conceal something as incredible as this?

"Not everyone seems as convinced as you that my parents are innocent," Ben said, thinking of Draven's remarks. *Our position weakens every minute we waste in bringing the Greenwoods to justice.*

"There is little evidence of their guilt and certainly not enough to convict them, but Suktar is very persuasive and very powerful. Even so, had Greg and Jane fought their case, they would have had every chance of proving their innocence. Unfortunately, they have disappeared without a trace, which is a big mark against them."

Disappeared without a trace. The words lingered in his head. All this time he had assumed they had been forced to flee and were unable to return. But what if they left voluntarily? What if they could come back, but wouldn't? The thought rocked him and made him go cold.

"They must have a reason," Ben said softly, trying to keep the doubt from his voice.

"I am sure they did," Wren agreed, "but they have yet to share it with anyone. And if Suktar decides to break the truce, there could be a full-scale war. To buy ourselves time, it was decided we should side with Suktar. Once we find the Greenwoods, we will decide what to do."

"We found a letter you wrote to my mum. You mentioned rumours that put them in danger?"

"Yes, I remember writing that," Wren said, nodding. "The rumours were in relation to the murder. I urged your parents to come in and prove their innocence, but they didn't."

"Why would Suktar want Ben's parents if they didn't kill his son?" Charlie asked, finally plucking up the courage to ask a question.

"We don't know," Wren said, "but I can tell you, Ben, your parents are the most wanted people in the Unseen Kingdoms. Between the Institute and Suktar's empire, ninety percent of the population are looking for them."

Ben smiled, feeling a peculiar sense of pride. In five minutes they had gone from being Greenpeace employees to the most wanted couple in the... in the what?

"What are the Unseen Kingdoms?" Charlie asked, getting there a fraction before Ben.

Before Wren could answer a girl came in carrying a pot of tea and a plate of biscuits. She couldn't have been much older than Ben with dark brown hair that fell in curls over her shoulders. There was something exotic about her green eyes, which were intent on balancing the tray. Her ears were pointed, but less than Wren's. There was a single colourless diamond hovering over her shoulder.

"Sorry it took so long," she said, in a down-to-earth way that was at odds with her movie star looks. "We were out of biscuits, so I had to run out and get more. I hope you two like ginger snaps."

After an awkward pause Ben realised she was talking to him and Charlie.

"I love them, thanks," he said, giving her a lopsided smile. He knew from school that girls liked his smiles, but this time it did nothing. Charlie mumbled a response, but most of it was lost because he had said it to his lap.

"Excellent call, Natalie," Wren said. Natalie smiled again and left the room.

"She looks young," Charlie blurted out, before he could stop himself. "Compared to everyone else I've seen, I mean."

"She's fourteen," Wren said, as if Charlie's statement was perfectly acceptable. She started pouring them tea. "Fourteen is the minimum age to start the apprenticeship. Biscuits?"

Ben took a sip of his tea, tried forgetting about Natalie's green eyes and focused on the map.

"So where do you start explaining all this?" Ben asked.

"Simple," Wren said. "We start at the beginning. What do you know of Queen Elizabeth I?"

Ben immediately thought of the current queen and was glad he kept his mouth shut.

"She was queen during the war against the Spanish Armada, back in the 16th century," Charlie said.

"Very good. Our history lesson starts with her because she was the first to discover one of the Unseen Kingdoms – Taecia to be precise, which is where you find yourselves."

"Unseen Kingdoms?" both Charlie and Ben said at the same time.

"Twenty-four special islands shielded by magic innate to the land. Their laws of physics and energy resemble something you would call magic rather than science. These islands are as real as England or France, but the shield means they remain unseen and untouched by the outside world."

"How?" Charlie asked. His eyes flashed to the map. "Some of those lands are massive. Surely a ship must have passed through them at some point?"

"Most of the lands are not in the path of ships."

"And those that are?"

Wren smiled. "They detour."

Charlie puffed his cheeks – Ben could tell he was trying hard to stay calm.

"That's it?" he said. "They detour? Why would they voluntarily choose to steer round an invisible patch of land? Wouldn't somebody notice? I mean, they have all sorts of navigational technology now."

Wren's laugh sounded strangely melodic. "I can understand your frustration, Charlie. Consider magic as another source of energy, one that is senior to science. You know the laws of science but not the laws of magic and therefore you cannot possibly know what can and can't be done."

"That makes some sense, I guess," Charlie conceded.

Ben, however, had spotted a flaw in the explanation. "If we cannot see these islands, how did Queen Elizabeth discover them in the first place?"

"That is not fully known. It is thought that somebody from the Unseen Kingdoms introduced them to her. However, it was never documented. I have a feeling Queen Elizabeth wanted it that way."

"Who inhabits these Unseen Kingdoms?" Ben asked. "If these lands are magical, does everyone have a wand and fly broomsticks?"

"Not quite," Wren said with a smile. "The magic comes from the Unseens."

Ben frowned. "What are they?"

"The Unseens are magic inhabitants. It is another word for a non-human entity. They are the elves, dragons and innumerable other creatures once considered fantasy. The Unseens have co-existed with humans native to the Kingdoms for hundreds of years."

"Are these people – these humans – just like us?" Charlie asked.

"Yes, but they have become accustomed to using magic. The Unseens trade it with them in a packaged form that anyone can use. You may have seen the Spellshooters already."

"Those peculiar guns?"

Wren nodded. "That's right. They fire spells made by the Unseens."

Charlie stood up and started pacing the large office, with his hands behind his back, staring hard at the floor. Wren watched him with a small smile, continuing to sip her tea. Ben could almost feel the cogs in Charlie's head dusting themselves off.

"I'm beginning to understand," Charlie said, his voice infused with excitement Ben hadn't heard since this morning's detective work at his grandma's house. "But how much does our government know?"

"Nothing," Wren said. "Elizabeth kept this discovery to herself. She formed the Royal Institute of Magic to explore these new lands. They conquered and colonised many of them, forming an Elizabethan Empire within the Unseen Kingdoms. The two worlds gradually meshed, creating a peculiar mix of old world magic with modern culture. Today the Institute no longer conquers and rules, but our political influence is equal to the native monarchs throughout the kingdoms. We continue to trade and we are always learning. Most importantly, we are the buffer between the Unseen Kingdoms and the rest of the world."

Charlie's pacing continued unabated. "What about that King Suktar bloke, he must be powerful if you're concerned by his threat?"

Wren's expression was momentarily serious. "Suktar is an elf king of immense power. During the years after Queen

Elizabeth's death he took his mighty army and conquered many of the Unseen Kingdoms. It's only in the last century that we have established an uneasy truce."

Ben felt worn out listening to the stream of revelations. He stood up and walked past Charlie to the window. Hills and trees lined the horizon, but it was the town Ben noticed most. It was such a bizarre mix of old and new. He spotted several antique cars buzzing along the narrow roads. Were they running on magic? Ben would have loved to peer into one of the engines to find out. Flying over the timber-framed houses were enough mounted creatures to create an aerial traffic jam. Not far off was the bustling dragon train station.

His parents were out there somewhere.

"So what now?" Ben asked, turning back round to face Wren.

"Draven will be working to convene the Executive Council, to which you will be summoned and questioned."

"Is that where they can figure out if my parents have any spells on me?"

"Among other things, yes," Wren said.

Ben glanced briefly at Charlie. "Let's do it."

Wren put down her cup of tea and stood up. Her tall hairdo sparkled against the sunlight streaming from the window.

"Draven will also push to cast a Memory Search."

"What's that?"

97

"It's a powerful spell that enables us to see your memories like watching TV. It will replay in your mind as if it's happening again. We can use it to search for any hidden memories."

Ben frowned. "What do you mean?"

"Your parents worked hard to keep the Institute a secret. What if you accidentally overheard something? They may have cast a spell to make you forget."

"My parents would never do that," Ben said with more conviction than he felt.

"I believe you, but Draven will argue we might be able to learn something."

"Does it hurt?" Charlie asked, looking at Wren anxiously, as if it were his memory being searched.

"Not physically – but it can be emotionally unpleasant. I can move to block this procedure if you don't want it, Ben."

The idea of a bunch of strange adults watching his memories like a TV show was not appealing. But if it had the slightest chance of helping find his parents, he didn't have much of a choice.

"I'm okay with the Memory Search," he said after a moment.

Wren gave a small smile. "In that case, I should get going. They will be meeting about you as we speak and will want to know what you said."

"How long until I'm needed?"

"I would imagine this evening."

Ben guessed it to be about four in the afternoon though he hadn't seen a clock. That left at least three hours to occupy themselves.

"I thought you two might like a tour of the place," Wren suggested, smiling at their lost expressions.

They nodded enthusiastically and Wren called Natalie back in. Ben's stomach tightened as she re-entered, but he met her dazzling smile without showing it. Charlie suddenly became very interested in his feet.

"I must warn you," Wren said, looking at Ben. "Your surname might attract attention because of your parents. Your arrival was mentioned in an executive meeting."

"I was announced in a meeting?" Ben asked, feeling slightly light-headed.

"Only because we were looking out for you. We had people in the town searching to make sure you got here okay."

So someone *had been* spying on them when they entered Starbucks. All this because of his parents? It was crazy.

— CHAPTER TEN —
A Tour of the Institute

It wasn't as awkward as Ben envisioned. Charlie did go bright red whenever he imagined Natalie's eyes on him, but thankfully she didn't seem to notice or perhaps pretended not to.

"You must have a thousand questions," she said in a cheerful voice. As she talked she curled one of her dark brown locks around her finger. "Is it true you only found about the Institute today?"

"That's right."

"Wow," Natalie said. "You're both taking it really well. Most people would still be flipping out."

Ben warmed to Natalie's easy-going manner and he even saw Charlie relax a fraction, which in the presence of a girl as pretty as Natalie bordered on a miracle.

He tried not to stare at her bright eyes or her pointed ears, but his curiosity soon got the better of him. He plucked up the courage to ask a question he would have laughed at yesterday.

"Are you an elf?" Ben asked, trying to keep a straight face.

Natalie grinned. "I was wondering when you would ask that. Technically I'm a half-elf. My grandmother on my mum's side was an elf."

"Wouldn't that make you a quarter-elf?"

Ben didn't see anything wrong with the question, but Charlie shut his eyes and pinched the bridge of his nose.

"It should do, shouldn't it?" Natalie said, proving Charlie's embarrassment unfounded. "However, we call any elf with non-elf blood a half-elf."

"I pictured elves a little differently," Ben admitted.

"You thought we'd have the whole serene, angelic thing going on?"

"Yeah. I've been horribly misled by the *Lord of the Rings* movies."

"There are some elves still like that, but they live secluded from the modern world."

"Can you do magic at least?"

"Very little unfortunately," Natalie said with a little sigh. "I'm too human to classify as an Unseen."

"So I guess you live in one of the Unseen Kingdoms?"

"That's right. I live in Osium, a small country off the coast of Italy."

Ben thought he detected a slight accent and she definitely looked Italian with her tanned skin and dark hair.

"What's it like there?"

"It's a bit like Italy was a couple hundred years ago and a lot of people, even the Unseens, speak both Italian and English."

The idea of a goblin speaking Italian was almost too weird.

"So if you use magic instead of science, does that mean you've never used a mobile phone before?"

Natalie laughed. "Not quite. My parents travel a lot and I have spent half my life in Milan and London."

They arrived back at the grand staircase and Charlie stared at them like Mt. Everest. "Please tell me we're not going up again," he said.

"I'm sorry," Natalie said. "You'll hate me now, but once we're at the top it's all downhill, which makes the tour easier."

"Are there no lifts?" Ben asked as they started their ascent.

"Unfortunately not. There are alternatives, but not for apprentices."

Ben counted three open galleries before they would reach the top. Sunshine poured in from the glass roof, warming his shoulders.

"Wren mentioned an apprenticeship?" Ben said.

"That's right. Everyone here starts with the apprenticeship."

"How do you enrol? I can't imagine you advertise much."

"Generally it stays in the family, but when there aren't enough apprentices we look outside. We have a division that specialises in recruiting members who know nothing of the Unseen Kingdoms."

"Is the apprenticeship long?" Charlie asked.

"Four years. For the first two you work everywhere in the Institute. After that there is a test. If you pass, you are selected to specialise in one of the departments for another two years before taking a final examination to become a full Institute member."

"Sounds like a lot of work," Ben said. The exams and tests reminded him of school.

Natalie frowned and Ben caught a flicker of surprise. "Oh, no, it's not work. There is a lot to do, but it's so much fun. I couldn't imagine doing anything else."

Ben was slightly taken aback by her dedication. "Wren seems like a good person to work for."

This was apparently the right thing to say, for Natalie gave him a dazzling smile.

"She is the most wonderful person I know," Natalie said. "She is kind, generous, wise and, of course, extremely gifted."

She spoke with such reverence Ben half expected her to get down and pray.

"Ah, here we are. That wasn't too bad, was it?" Natalie said.

They had made it up the stairs and found themselves on the top open gallery. Looking over the railing, Ben could just make out the statue in the lobby far below. The glass roof was actually a huge gable and near its base was a door that led outside.

"Prepare yourself – it smells out here," she said, as she turned the door handle.

The wind hit them and, with it, the unmistakable smell of hay and manure, making Ben wrinkle his nose. But the smell was instantly forgotten by the sight that greeted them. It looked like a farm with paddocks spanning the vast expanse of the rooftop all around the glass gable. These paddocks were not filled with cows or sheep like an ordinary farm. There were huge eagles, horses with wings, animals that looked like a cross between a bird and a lion and even small dragons, each with its own paddock. Most were content to eat or bathe, but others were more interested in talking, creating a cacophony of roars, squawks and growls. Ben spotted a dozen boys and girls dealing manfully with the mayhem. He watched in fascination as a couple of them tried dragging a pint-sized dragon out of a paddock.

"Steeds," Natalie said, having to shout to be heard.

"People fly these things?" Charlie asked, his bashfulness in front of Natalie momentarily forgotten.

"Sure, if you're a qualified rider and you can afford it," Natalie said. She led them between the paddocks pointing at each of the strange animals. "The cheapest option is the Great Eagle. Most people start off with one of them. Above that is a winged horse, called a pegasus. Then there is the middle-class steed – the griffin. They have the wings and head of an eagle with the body of a lion."

"What about those bad boys?" Ben said. He was pointing at the little dragon with a long, skinny neck that two girls were currently scrubbing.

"Wyverns. They are very expensive and high maintenance."

Ben admired the power that oozed from every part of its body – from its jaws to its mighty wings.

"Please tell me you're not dreaming about riding that thing," Charlie said, noticing Ben's smile.

Ben slapped Charlie on the shoulder. "It's on my to-do list."

"What a coincidence – it's on my never-to-do list, underlined with one of those black permanent markers."

Ben felt a tap on his back. Natalie was behind him, pointing to another section of the roof. It was empty except for a man who stood there alone.

"That's the take-off zone," Natalie said. "He's waiting for his animal – watch."

Sure enough, a young girl soon walked over with one of the winged horses – a pegasus – in tow. She handed the man the reins and he mounted it. The girl stepped back and the pegasus started a gallop towards the end of the building. It unfolded its huge, white wings and leapt off the edge. Ben saw it plummet to the earth and then it vanished from view. A moment later it re-appeared, soaring upwards towards the blue sky.

"Who looks after all these animals?" Charlie asked, watching the departing pegasus.

"We do, the apprentices," Natalie said. "It's hard work, but really fun, except when you're shovelling poop or trying to avoid being eaten, pecked or crushed."

"That doesn't sound fun at all," Charlie said.

"I'm not selling it very well, am I?" Natalie said. "But it's a unique experience and really good exercise."

"You're still not selling it."

Natalie smiled at Charlie and he blushed, as if he suddenly realised whom he was talking to.

"I guess not. I'll stop before I make it any less inviting. Would you both like to head down? There's a lot to see."

They went back through the glass door and down the stairs. The noise receded and Ben inhaled the clean air trying to ignore the horrible smell that clung to his clothes. Instead of stopping by the double doors at the first landing they kept descending.

"That floor holds all the executive offices," Natalie said. "We aren't allowed in there. There isn't much to see anyway, just meeting rooms and offices."

Ben's stomach gave an unpleasant lurch and his eyes lingered on the doors. Was this where the Executive Council was meeting? If so, he would be back shortly.

The next floor was the Department of Spellswords and they were soon walking through the familiar hallway again.

"Spellswords are the Institute's elite combat unit. They must be expert Spellshooters with the ability to cast the most powerful spells. They must also be fit to fight."

"That sounds pretty cool," Ben said.

"A typical guy response," Natalie said, rolling her green eyes. "It's actually a lot of work."

She stopped by a door that said "Spell Training".

"You'll like this room," she said as they entered.

Ben and Charlie exchanged curious looks and followed her in.

The first thing Ben noticed were the high ceilings, which made the large room feel even bigger. It was busy and there was a buzz of activity. In the middle of the room was a large table, chest high. Surrounding it were stools, most of them occupied by people talking with great animation to one another. But it was to Ben's right where the real interest lay. It looked like a bowling alley except for the glass windows partitioning each lane. Instead of bowling pins at the end, there was a circular target like a big dartboard. Most of the lanes were occupied by one or two people. They had their Spellshooters out and were using them.

It was like a great fireworks display, except these "fireworks" shot towards the dartboard with varying degrees of accuracy. Some were fireballs and engulfed the dartboard completely; others were beams of light, with every colour on display; some zigzagged, others made the whole lane flash with light or go pitch black.

They stared in mute astonishment until Ben felt tapping on his shoulder. He turned and found himself staring up at a large, friendly man with his hand extended. He looked like a Viking, with shoulder-length, blond hair, deep blue eyes and a frame you could build a house on.

"Ben Greenwood?"

The name attracted a few curious looks, not helped by the man's deep, penetrating voice. Ben shook his hand and resisted the urge to grimace when it was half squeezed to death.

"James McFadden," he said effusively and then introduced himself to Charlie.

"I know your father well," he said. Ben wasn't sure if he shouted because of all the noise or if he just had a loud voice. "Fantastic Spellsword, one of the best. Is this your first time here?"

Ben nodded. He wanted to ask how well James knew his dad, but the big man was already moving.

"Follow me," he boomed. "I'll show you the ropes."

They followed James into a glass corridor that ran behind the lanes and provided the only way in and out of them. Each time they passed an occupied lane James would shout out his commentary.

"Frank, a fly could withstand the heat from your fireball – Amy and Jo, stop chatting and get back to work – Luke, stop watching Amy and Jo – Graham, clear your mind and concentrate or you won't cast a damn thing."

They each gave him an evil eye, which James completely ignored. Eventually they came to an empty lane. James opened the glass door and Ben, Charlie and Natalie followed him through.

The room was partially soundproof and shut out the cacophony from the spells in the adjacent lanes. The target at the end of the room was a good fifty yards away. Next to them, by the door, was a bookcase with four shelves. On each shelf there were three trays with coloured pellets Ben had seen in the orbs of the Spellshooters. Close up they looked even more remarkable, each one was a different size and shape. Some vibrated, others glowed and a few were transparent.

"Spells," James said, grabbing the shelf so firmly it jolted. "I won't go into detail about how they're made and packaged – the boffins downstairs can do that."

He took his Spellshooter out and pointed to each shelf.

"The red spells are fire-based. Blue is water, green is earth and white is air. Combine them and you can cast every spell known to man." He touched the top three trays. "Each tray represents the strength of spell. We classify them from a One to a Five. The Fours and Fives are too expensive for common practice so we don't supply them freely."

James grabbed a red pellet from the top left tray. He pressed it into the surface of the glass orb. There was a moment's resistance, then the pellet penetrated the orb and joined its friends, floating as if in water.

"The spell doesn't want to leave the orb. You have to command it to." James tapped his temple. "The spell will resist, but if you concentrate it will obey."

James lifted the Spellshooter and pointed at the target. Ben expected a look of concentration, but James seemed almost bored as he pulled the trigger. Everything happened in a flash. The little pellet shot down the orb and disappeared. The barrel glowed red and from its tip a small red pellet exploded leaving a trail of vapour as it sped towards the dartboard, hitting the middle with a soft thud.

"Concentration and will power," James said again, holstering his Spellshooter. "The rest is a piece of cake."

Before they could say anything, James turned and shouted "CONCENTRATION!" to the adjacent lane. There was an explosion of spells going horribly wrong.

"As you can see, they're mainly beginners in here right now," he said, grinning broadly. "Natalie is showing promise though. You should be ready for the Grade 1 exam soon."

"Thank you," Natalie said. "I want to run through the Distraction List one more time before I take it. I don't think I'm ready to face you yet."

"Nonsense," James said, giving Natalie a clap on the back that Ben feared might dislocate something. "You can deal with me. I'm like a fluffy pussy cat for the Grade 1 exam. It's a piece of cake."

"Of course it is," Natalie said, giving James a smile and then rolling her eyes as soon as he turned away.

To Ben's disappointment, the demonstration appeared to be over. James led them back out, slamming his hand on each glass door they passed and screaming "WILL POWER", all the while grinning broadly.

They left, with Natalie promising James she would return soon to take her exam.

"That was cool, right?" Natalie said. "But I think I can top it."

Ben, who couldn't possibly see how anything could top that, followed Natalie with Charlie along the hallway and round the corner until they came to another door that said "Spell Training – Combat".

"You'll like this," Natalie said and she opened the door.

At first glance the room looked similar to the last one. There was a high table surrounded by stools. To the right were the glass practice ranges, except there were just two and they were much wider. Only one was occupied and most of the people were watching the scene unfold.

"Oh my god," Charlie whispered.

There was a fight going on inside the glass room. On one side was a big green thing that Ben, with his knowledge of fantasy limited to the *Lord of the Rings* movies, assumed was an orc. It was all muscle, with nasty, yellow teeth. In its hand was a spiky wooden club. On the other side were two Spellswords armed with Spellshooters, circling the orc warily. The orc was clearly confused, unsure who to strike. He bellowed in frustration and swung his club. The first Spellsword ducked and rolled, the club missing by inches. The second one fired some sort of blue spray, but it did nothing except annoy the orc who swung back round in anger and charged at his attacker. The Spellsword fired and a crescent moon-shaped shield blocked the club, but the sheer strength of the blow knocked the Spellsword backwards. He got up quickly, back-peddled and then fled in a mad panic. In the confines of the glass room, he was reduced to ducking, rolling and dodging. It was as if he were playing "It" with the orc, but instead of tagging the Spellsword, the orc was trying to club him to death. While this was happening, the other

Spellsword was firing off a series of feeble spells that either spluttered into nothing or missed the orc completely.

The crowd watching the display was laughing hysterically, except for one rotund woman. She was shaking her head, her thumb and finger pinching the bridge of her nose.

"Help!" cried the Spellsword doing the running. "A little help!"

The woman sighed and stepped into the glass room through the glass passage at the back. She raised her Spellshooter and fired. Something green hit the orc and it vanished with a pop.

"Don't worry, it wasn't real," Natalie said, seeing their reaction. "It's just a spell that is able to replicate certain semi-intelligent creatures – useful for combat practice."

Ben watched as the woman berated the two Spellswords, though he couldn't make out her voice behind the glass.

"We should probably go," Natalie said. "Kate is a nice lady, but seeing her pupils crash and burn can put her in a bad mood."

With great reluctance they followed Natalie out and back to the grand staircase, which they descended to the next floor. Ben was still buzzing, scenes of the orc fighting, spells flying, Spellswords ducking and rolling playing on repeat in his head. Had his parents undergone training like that? Could his mum really use a Spellshooter to battle big green monsters? He had an easier time believing in a flying horse.

— CHAPTER ELEVEN —
Dark Elves

Ben couldn't imagine anything topping the Spellsword Department and his opinion was reinforced when they reached the next set of double doors on the floor below.

"Department of Diplomacy?" Ben said, giving Natalie a dubious look. Beneath the title was a symbol of a crown. "Is that as boring as it sounds?"

"It sounds interesting to me," Charlie said. He was too busy trying to see beyond the doors that he missed the smile Natalie gave him.

Interesting it was not, when compared to the excitement of the previous floor. There were lots of lavishly appointed meeting rooms where negotiations between the Institute and many of the Unseen Kingdoms took place. There were bigger briefing rooms that reminded Ben of lecture halls and there were a couple of café areas, which only made his stomach growl.

"The King of Treem was here last week," Natalie said. "He had over a hundred people in his retinue. The apprentices were responsible for looking after them; it was mad."

Charlie started to ask a question, but Natalie gave a little gasp and stopped, thrusting her arms out to stop them. Ben heard it a fraction after she did – voices coming from round the corner. The language was foreign, unlike anything he'd ever heard.

"Backs to the wall," Natalie whispered urgently, slamming her own back so hard it made a slapping noise. "Stare at the floor, *quickly.*"

Ben and Charlie did so just in time. From the corner of his eye, Ben saw a small group approaching. He strained his eyes to get a better view. There was a man wearing a black suit with five blue diamonds hovering above his shoulder, but it was the others who caught Ben's eye. They were tall but slender and walked gracefully, each with a sword strapped to their waist. Their faces were so pale they were almost white, their ears were pointed and their shoulder-length, silver hair was tied back. They wore a purple uniform, except for the one in the middle. He wore a cloak that seemed to blend in with the background.

Charlie gasped loudly and Ben saw Natalie grimace from the corner of his eye.

The fabric! Ben felt it in his pocket. The properties were identical. Ben resisted the urge to look up, instead straining his eyeballs until they ached. Closer they came, until they were within touching distance and stopped just as they were about to pass by.

There was a small intake of breath and a clicking of the tongue.

"Well, well, what's this? A Greenwood? Let me look at you."

The voice was soft but compelling and Ben found himself looking up at the speaker. His eyes were purple and seemed to glow. His skin was so tight he looked skeletal.

"You didn't tell me their son was here, Colin," he said, not taking his eyes off Ben.

"We didn't think it relevant, Elessar," Colin replied. His voice reminded Ben of royalty, pronouncing every syllable with exaggerated clarity. He was impeccably dressed in a tailored suit and reminded Ben of a banker or a lawyer.

"Not relevant? You have the son of the traitors who have brought our two great empires to the brink of war. He may have knowledge that could aid our search."

"The Executive Council is meeting this evening to establish exactly that," Colin said.

"Good," Elessar replied. Ben's head was starting to hurt from the purple stare; it seemed to bore into his skull. "However, I fear our methods of extracting information will be more fruitful than your own. We can delve into the very deepest subconscious and still leave the subject mostly intact."

Ben felt his anger bubbling. He wanted to speak, but he couldn't get his vocal chords working.

"We can discuss such matters at the Executive Council after our own investigation," Colin said. His face was calm, his response unhurried.

Elessar nodded and finally turned away, directing his intense gaze upon Colin.

"I report to my king tonight. You must understand the dilemma I am presented with. My king is not unjust or vengeful, but he will wonder at young Greenwood's freedom, given the tragic fate of my king's son."

Free of the purple stare, Ben found his voice again. He was about to give Elessar a piece of his mind, but Natalie squeezed his wrist.

"I understand your predicament," Colin said, with what sounded to Ben like genuine concern. "Let us discuss it further in the meeting. I'm sure we can come up with something."

Elessar and Colin walked side by side and the others fell in behind. Ben watched as they filed into one of the meeting rooms. There was a click as the door shut behind them.

"That was close," Natalie sighed. "Sorry for grabbing you, but if you had backlashed it would have been a diplomatic nightmare. Things are really tense right now with the dark elves and it doesn't take much to insult them. The Department of Diplomacy has given all apprentices an exact code of conduct so we don't accidentally mess things up. It generally consists of keeping our heads down and speaking as little as possible."

"Who was the fellow with the strange cloak?" Charlie asked.

"Elessar. He is the General of King Suktar's army. He is a dark elf of great power. I have never seen him close up before."

Despite Natalie's warning, Ben felt a strong urge to burst into the room and ram his fist into Elessar's face. Instead he pulled out the piece of fabric and handed it to Natalie.

"I found this in my parents' house the day they disappeared."

Natalie stared at the cloth. Her mouth slowly opened as its significance dawned on her.

"Before we jump to conclusions, do you know if anyone else uses those camouflaged cloaks?" Charlie asked.

"No," Natalie said softly, as if the elves might hear them through the thick walls. "The dark elf officers are famed for them."

"Well, that's one mystery solved," Charlie said. There was a sudden energy about him and he looked as if he wanted to start pacing around the hallway. "We know it was a dark elf officer, possibly this Elessar, who came after your parents."

"We should get out of here so we can speak freely," Natalie said, casting an anxious glance at the meeting room door.

Charlie and Natalie had to grab Ben and drag him back to the relative sanctuary of the staircase.

"I know what you're thinking," Natalie said, twirling a lock of hair with her finger. "But this doesn't change anything to do with your parents."

"Why not?" Ben asked, louder than he meant to. "This proves that they came after my parents."

"True," Natalie said. "But I bet the Institute already knows that. The dark elves probably claim they came looking for your parents to bring them to justice."

Ben ruffled his dishevelled hair and kicked the ornate banister to vent his frustration. "This is so unfair, it's a joke."

"We know that, Ben. Wren said she is convinced your parents are innocent and I believe her. But the Institute can't prove it yet."

Ben didn't share Natalie's confidence in the Institute. Charlie, however, had a small smile on his lips.

"Ben, you may not have realised it judging by your mini tantrum, but this is actually good news."

Ben looked at him, confusion suppressing his anger.

Charlie punched his fist into his hand. "We have a lead," he said, trying to contain his excitement. "For the first time, we have something to go on."

Charlie's enthusiasm was infectious and Ben's anger started to fade.

"A lead?" Natalie gave them a serious look. "I know this might seem like a game, but this is serious Institute business."

Charlie was taken aback, but Ben met her stare with his own. "This is my family we are talking about."

Natalie softened. "I'm sorry. I know how much this means to you and, of course, you want to do everything you can. But you must trust the Institute. However well-intentioned your help may be, it will only interfere with the Institute's search for your parents. Please promise me you won't get in their way."

Ben gave her his most sincere smile. "We promise," he lied.

Natalie seemed to buy it. "You should show that fabric to Wren. It might help them somehow."

"Good idea," Ben said, slipping the fabric back in his pocket. He would have to watch what he said in front of Natalie from now on. Would Wren also expect them to sit back and do nothing? He hoped not. He had a feeling fooling her would be a good deal harder than Natalie.

Natalie led them down the stairs to the next set of double doors, which read "Department of Trade" with a picture of a gold sovereign below.

"This department will take your mind off the dark elves, I promise," she said.

The statue in the hallway beyond the doors was of a pretty woman by the name of Charlotte Rowe. She had a Mona Lisa smile and held a small pouch.

"A woman," Charlie said. He immediately turned bright red when he realised what he had said. "Which isn't bad, quite admirable, in fact; I just thought in the sixteenth century..."

"You're right, it was unusual," Natalie said, putting an end to Charlie's flustered explanation. "But remember, it was Queen Elizabeth who appointed the first directors. Charlotte Rowe was a unique woman. She was the first to learn Elvish and established many valuable contacts."

Charlie looked ready to continue the boring history lesson so Ben walked quickly to the nearest door, which read "Trading Centre".

"This is where most of the action happens," Natalie said. "You can wander round by yourself. The only rule is: never stop. If you stop, they assume you are listening, which is forbidden. It might be difficult, but keep moving, no matter how slow."

They opened the door and Ben was immediately hit with a wall of noise. Voices of every pitch and volume clashed with an energy that set Ben's hair on end. The place was packed with people seated at huge wooden tables spanning the entire room. Everyone seemed in an animated discussion with the person opposite. It looked like a busy lunch room but instead of food there were documents and papers on the tables. On one side were Institute members, identified by the yellow floating diamonds on their shoulders. On the other side was the most fantastic array of people Ben had ever seen. There were elves – Ben was getting used to them – but he never realised they came in such variety. All had the pointed ears, smooth skin and delicate features, but the similarities ended there. Some were tall and big as men with loud voices and fiery eyes; others were slender and spoke so softly Ben could barely hear them. Some wore earthy green garments that looked like someone had hand-knit them, others wore expensive uniforms and wore beautiful jewellery. There were small, stocky dwarves and lumbering giants, towering over everyone and making the benches creak. There were fairy creatures, fluttering their wings while talking with every bit as much gusto as those around them. For the most part, English was spoken, but there were other languages that the Institute members seemed equally fluent in.

Ben walked slowly, trying to make out bits of conversation within the mayhem.

"...that's the going price of sugar, my friend, take it or leave it..."

"...magic has been going up consistently, look at the figures..."

"...yes, we like your spices, but not enough to bankrupt our nation..."

"...these earthquake spells have been extensively tested, they will bring the house down, trust me..."

Ben wanted to listen to every conversation, but if he stopped too long he started getting looks, so he always moved on. He lost himself in the energy of the room and marvelled at the way the Institute members bartered – to a man they looked like seasoned salesmen undaunted by the opposition no matter how peculiar or intense the debate was.

He wasn't sure how much time had passed before he'd seen enough. It took him a moment to spot Charlie and Natalie. They were by the door talking in hushed voices with somebody. It was Wren, Ben realised in surprise. Surely it hadn't been three hours already? He hurried over, the fascination of the trading tables evaporating.

"Ben," Wren said, smiling at him with a pervasive calm. "I am sorry to barge in like this – you looked like you were enjoying yourself. Fascinating, isn't it? Our best traders can sell ice to an Eskimo, as the saying goes."

"Is everything okay?" Ben asked, seeing the sombre expressions from Natalie and Charlie.

"Everything is fine," Wren said. "Unfortunately, I am going to have to cut your tour short. Draven, in his fanatical obsession to move things along, has managed to convene everyone quicker than I anticipated. They are now upstairs, awaiting your presence."

— CHAPTER TWELVE —
The Executive Council

Ben, Charlie and Natalie were once more heading down the staircase. Wren had ordered Ben to get some food as she said he would need the energy. A sombre silence had descended, broken only by the rhythmic pattering of feet echoing on the marble stairs.

While touring the Institute Ben had managed to put thoughts of the meeting aside, but now everything came rushing back. He could deal with the questions and was looking forward to seeing if his parents really had cast any spells on him. It was the Memory Search that worried him, the idea that people would be able to see inside his head. *It will replay in your mind as if it's happening again.* Would he have any control? What would he see?

Natalie led them through a set of double doors that read "Department of Apprentices" with a symbol of a tree below. Ben's troubles receded momentarily as they walked through the hallway into a large room that looked a bit like the sixth-form campus at school. There were a dozen people, most not much older than him, sitting on couches and chairs that were sprawled haphazardly. Books lay everywhere – on the couches, on small desks and even on the floor. Most were reading, but a few were tinkering with their Spellshooters.

Ben felt several curious eyes on him and a few jealous looks from some of the guys. He was in no mood for introductions and thankfully Natalie led them straight through to an adjacent dining hall. It looked like the trading room minus the craziness. There were two wooden tables and benches either side of them. At the end of the room stood trolleys with piping hot food creating a pleasant aroma.

Ben barely paid any attention to the chicken casserole he served onto his dish. He didn't feel like eating, but forced the food down, barely aware that it tasted delicious. Before he knew it he was bussing his tray and they were making their way back up the stairs to the very top floor. Occasionally someone overtook them, but Ben was happy with the slow pace; it gave him a few more minutes to prepare and helped Charlie to keep up. When they passed the Department of Spellswords, Ben felt the first shiver of nerves.

"Have you ever had a Memory Search?" Ben asked Natalie. She had been unusually quiet, twirling her hair round her finger.

"No, but I have studied a bit about it," she said. "There is no physical pain in the spell, but re-experiencing the memory can be unpleasant if it's not a nice one. Try not to worry too much, they will look after you."

Ben hoped she was right. In no time at all they were walking along the hallway of the lavishly appointed Executive Floor. Outside the door that said "Executive Council" was Wren waiting for them with a smile. Her flowery red dress and piled-up hair were as flawless as ever, but Ben thought he detected tiny wrinkles of concern.

"Take Charlie back to my office," Wren said to Natalie. "We will come down as soon as we are done."

"Good luck! You'll be fine. Just let them do their jobs," Natalie said, somehow sounding enthused. Charlie gave him an encouraging smile and they both turned to leave.

Wren made no move to open the door. Instead, she put a hand on Ben's shoulder and gave him a long look.

"Inside are nearly all the senior members of the Institute. You have met Draven, Colin and me. Now you will meet two others. It is important you realise that everyone, even Draven, is on your side."

"Nearly all the senior members?" Ben asked, frowning.

"Our most senior member is not here. Now, no more questions, you need to focus."

Ben nodded, suppressing his curiosity.

"Remember, there is a lot we don't know. We are trying to find out where your parents are and why they thought it best to hide rather than seek the sanctuary of the Institute. Most importantly, we need to prove your parents' innocence and that they had nothing to do with the death of Suktar's son. It's crucial you remember that, as there may be moments when it gets uncomfortable."

Ben bit his lip and nodded again. For a moment he thought about revealing the fabric, but it didn't seem like the right time.

"I understand. Let's get on with it."

Wren smiled and for a moment he thought she was going to say more, but she just squeezed his shoulder and opened the door, ushering him through.

Four sets of eyes stared at him as he entered. They were seated in plush leather seats around a circular table.

"Please stand on the spell circle," Wren said, as she sat herself down.

It was clear what she was referring to. Ben walked to the back of the room and stood on a large, blue circle that had been painted on the wooden floor. His heart was thumping, but he met the directors' stares without flinching. The five sets of coloured diamonds floating above their shoulders were strangely impressive.

Draven was there, eyebrows furrowed, his constant scowl even more prominent, watching Ben like a hawk. Wren's warm glow countered Draven's. There was one other woman in the room. She was tall and slender, with as many curves as a pencil. She had long, brown hair and glasses that magnified her eyes to scary proportions. Her frumpy, grey jumper clashed horribly with her lime-green trousers. Next to her was Colin. His black suit was just as spotless as before. He sat as if he had a pole inside the back of his jacket, with his hands folded neatly on the table. Ben was struck by the size of his eyebrows – they looked as big as moustaches. He didn't blink, bat an eye or make the slightest response when Ben looked at him. Beside him was a man Ben instantly warmed to. He wore a Jedi-styled, blue, hooded cloak and had wavy hair, bright eyes and lips that seemed creased in a permanent little smile. He was leaning forward, resting his elbows on the table. A small gold coin ran over and under his fingers with stunning dexterity. When Ben made eye contact, he gave a little nod and a wink.

"Alright, let's get on with this," Draven said, slapping his hand on the table. "I have called the Executive Council for an emergency meeting to discuss Greg and Jane Greenwood's son, Ben, who stands before us. I am proposing we cast two spells on Ben. The first is a Memory Search, to see if Ben has any memories hidden by magic. The second is a Search Spell, which will search for any enchantments or charms his parents may have placed on him. Any questions?"

"Who will cast the spells?" Wren asked.

"I will do the Memory Search," Draven said. "I have the most experience. You, Wren, will do the Spell Search."

Ben groaned inwardly. He hoped Wren would object, but though she pursed her lips, she said nothing.

Draven stood up and produced his Spellshooter, which he proceeded to inspect.

Ben felt a shiver run through him and he took an involuntary step back. Suddenly, he wanted to stall, somehow, anyhow.

"Is this going to hurt?" he asked, hating the way his voice trembled.

"There is no pain," Draven said. The usual gruffness in his voice lessened a fraction. "I've cast this spell hundreds of times. You should sit down and try to relax."

There was a loud knock on the door just as Ben was about to take a seat. The Council turned around in surprise. Draven stood up and marched to the door, ready to fling it open and unleash hell on the person who dared interrupt their meeting.

"We're in session!" Draven said.

The door swung open suddenly, almost hitting Draven in the face. A tall man stood in the doorway. He wore a black cloak and was sopping wet with rain and mud. But there was power and grace in his posture. Ben couldn't stop looking at the man's eyes; there were peculiar flecks of gold in them.

Draven stepped back and the rest of the Council rose as one.

"Your Highness," Draven said, with an awkward bow. "I apologise. We didn't realise you were back."

Ben frowned. Your Highness?

"Calm yourself, Draven," the man said in a deep voice. "I had not expected to return so soon." He entered the room and the Council immediately gave him the centre chair.

"Ben Greenwood?" the man asked, taking a seat. The rest of the Council followed and suddenly Ben was again the centre of attention.

"That's right."

He sensed curiosity in those peculiar, dark, gold-flecked eyes, but the man's expression remained impassive.

"My name is Robert. I am Commander of the Royal Institute of Magic."

Ben wasn't surprised, given the way the Council was behaving. He looked the part despite his appearance. But why had Draven called him "Your Highness"?

"I don't have much time," Robert said. "I came here to see the Memory Search. Let us proceed."

It took a second for Ben to realise what Robert meant until Draven stood up, Spellshooter in hand.

"Sit down please, Ben," Draven said. The word "please" sounded odd coming from him.

Ben sat down, careful to stay within the circle. He had almost forgotten about the spell, but now it came flooding back. He looked anxiously at Wren and she smiled.

"If you are in any difficulty we will cancel the spell," she said. Ben couldn't help noticing Draven's doubtful expression.

"Get ready," Draven said. "You're going for a ride."

He aimed his Spellshooter at Ben and fired.

— CHAPTER THIRTEEN —
Spells and Memory Lane

The world disappeared and everything went black. There was no floor beneath his feet. He had no feet. He was a floating entity in a void of darkness.

An image of Wren standing outside the meeting materialised. It was a picture from his memory in perfect 3D, with every perception just as clear as the original incident. It felt like he was watching an IMAX movie of his own life filmed through his eyes.

The scene froze. He started walking backwards, away from Wren, as if someone had hit rewind. He was going back in time, he realised. At first, it was slow enough to decipher, but it quickly became a blur. Occasionally he could make out a scene from school or home. Each time the world looked a little different; he was getting smaller, so everything started looking bigger as the months and years cycled back.

Eventually the "movie reel" slowed. Ben's heart jumped at the scene before him. He was playing football in the garden with his dad who was smiling at him as he went in for a tackle. Everything was so real: the bearded stubble, the thin moustache, even the sparkle in his eye.

The scene stopped and blurred again.

Fast forward.

Ben was walking down the road towards his house. His dad's Mini was sandwiched between two police cars parked on the curb at the base of the hill.

Despite having no perceptible body, Ben shivered.

He was watching the moments before he learned of his parents' disappearance.

Thankfully, the scene blurred.

Forward and back they went, honing in on a memory, before fading out and then blurring to something else. Ben wasn't sure how long it went on, but it made him feel queasy unless he stayed focused.

The stabbing head pain came from nowhere.

"There!"

Ben was only dimly aware of the voices in the room.

The memories stopped and reversed, slower this time. He could see bits and pieces – a house, his parents, the car.

Then he saw it. A black spot amongst the colour of his past; a gap in his memory where nothing existed. Staring at it made his head throb. As soon as he looked away the pain eased. He glanced at it again and his head immediately started aching.

"That's the one." Draven's voice. "Focus and you will pierce it."

Ben was trying, but it hurt. His head was pulsing. He was dimly aware that he was squeezing his temples and groaning.

"Draven, that's enough. Release him from the spell." Wren's voice came from afar.

"No, this is it."

"You could damage his mind."

"He's nearly got it. Fight it, boy. Fight it!"

Ben was on the verge of collapse, but the anger in Draven's voice fuelled his own. With a cry of pain and defiance, he summoned every ounce of willpower he had and forced himself into the blackness.

A flicker of light pierced the darkness. Ben focused on it and the light started to expand. Within moments it had grown from a pinhole to something he could fit his hand through. Ben saw colour; behind the darkness was another memory.

Ben attacked the remainder with such energy he was barely aware he was screaming. The last of the blackness vanished and with it the pain. Ben found himself staring at a memory he had forgotten existed.

The scene sharpened and he felt himself being sucked into the picture. In front of him was a kitchen door, ajar. Its handle was at eye level. He turned and saw his reflection in a mirror. A small boy stared back at him with mischievous, blue eyes and messy, blond hair. The smell of roast chicken came from the kitchen and the hallway carpet felt soft beneath his feet.

He was re-experiencing the moment as if he were there. He *was* there. The memory became an all-encompassing reality.

"Absolutely not – I refuse!"

Ben was about to head upstairs, but the anger in his mum's voice made him stop. It came from somewhere in the kitchen. His mum had told him many times how rude it was to eavesdrop, but that didn't stop him from tiptoeing up to the kitchen door to get a better listen.

"Now is the time, Jane." His dad's calm voice was in stark contrast to his mum's. "The longer we delay, the more dangerous it becomes. Suktar will soon come for us again."

Ben's interest was now well and truly piqued. What danger was his dad talking about?

"I will not leave Ben – he is too young," his mum said.

Ben's eyes widened. He resisted the urge to barge in, knowing the conversation would end the moment he did.

"You won't leave him. I will begin the search myself."

There was a pause. Ben inched closer to the door. He could picture his parents facing each other.

"You won't find them by yourself, Greg. You need me."

"Ben could stay with Anne."

Ben slammed a hand over his mouth to muffle his protest. To his relief, his mum sounded just as outraged.

"Are you mad? I'd rather send him to a foster home."

His dad gave an angry grunt. "Well, I'm open to suggestions."

His mum's reply was so soft he barely heard it. "What about the Institute? They could help."

"No." His dad was firm. "They will ask too many questions. And that would involve Ben. The Greenwood relationship with the Institute ends with us."

"If you won't use the Institute, then we wait until Ben is sixteen."

"Suktar may come for us before then. We can fool him only so long."

"That's a risk we'll have to take," his mum said. She threw something down on the counter.

Ben heard footsteps.

His mum was coming! Ben turned away, but he was too slow.

The kitchen door opened.

His mum was staring at him, her eyes wide.

"Ben! What are you doing here?"

"I live here, don't I?" Ben replied. Always best to go on the offensive.

His dad came hurrying over. Ben lost his nerve a little – his dad, normally so calm and relaxed, wore a stern frown. He had never seen his dad angry before.

"How long have you been here?" his dad asked.

"*Only a minute.*"

"*Did you hear anything?*"

"*Not much,*" Ben answered. But curiosity got the better of him. "*Mum's right, I'd rather stay in a foster home than at Grandma's. Where are you going?*"

"*Nowhere,*" *his parents replied. They looked at each other for a moment.*

"*No,*" *his mum said.*

His dad shook his head. "I'm sorry, Jane, on this there is no debate."

Before Ben could work out what they were talking about, his dad pulled a peculiar toy gun from behind his back.

Ben gaped.

His dad pointed it at him and fired.

Blackness.

The world around him faded and there was a flash of white light.

He was back with the Council. Six sets of eyes were staring at him intently.

"Well, that was interesting," Alex said, a small smile on his lips. The coin was still running through his fingers.

"I don't see how," Draven said. "We didn't learn anything that would help us locate the Greenwoods."

"No," Victoria said, staring at Ben thoughtfully. "But we learnt something else: Greg and Jane knew Suktar would come for them again."

"Again? He's come for them before?" Ben asked.

Nobody was listening to him. No – that wasn't true. Robert was watching him closely. His expression was impassive, but those dark, gold-flecked eyes were thoughtful.

Robert rose suddenly; the others immediately followed.

"Colin," he said, turning to the immaculately suited man. "I want a report of this meeting, including results from the Spell Search."

Colin nodded and Robert turned to the others. "Wren and Draven, I would like to see you in my office." Finally, Robert turned to the pencil-thin lady.

"Victoria, you and Ben Greenwood are the main reason I returned to the Institute. I am searching for an old colleague of yours and I believe you might know where he is. Please find me once this meeting is over."

Victoria nodded and gave an awkward curtsey.

They waited a good thirty seconds after Robert left before returning to their seats.

"Well, that Memory Search doesn't change anything," Draven said, breaking the momentary silence. "In fact, it only reinforces what I suspected, that Greg and Jane had a long-standing issue with the dark elves."

There was a noise that sounded like something between a sigh and a snort of laughter. Everyone turned to the hooded man staring at them innocently.

"Sorry, did I say something?" he asked.

"No, Alex, but I fear you would like to," Victoria said evenly.

"Well, the whole thing's a load of rubbish really, isn't it? But I may have expressed my thoughts already."

"Yes, you have – so shut up unless you have something useful to say," Draven said.

"I'm far from happy with the logic and there is clearly a lot we don't know," Victoria said. "But until Greg and Jane turn up, we cannot prove the dark elves are lying to us."

Ben snapped. "That's completely unfair," he said, with such anger and pent-up emotion the Council finally turned to him.

He had their attention.

"This Suktar – isn't he the bad guy? Yet you're taking his side over my parents'?"

Draven leant forward onto the table. "You have no clue what's going on, so keep your trap shut."

"Draven is right. There are many different elements and factors that you are unaware of," Victoria said.

"Personally I'm with Ben," Alex said, flicking up his gold coin absently.

Ben had had enough. His hand flew into his pocket and he produced the peculiar fabric that matched the dark elf cloak.

"See this?" he said, thrusting the fabric at them. "I found this at our house the day my parents disappeared."

It didn't produce the response he had expected. Only Alex showed the slightest bit of surprise at the fabric.

"The dark elves were trying to bring your parents to justice," Victoria said in a perfectly calm voice.

"You knew that?" Ben asked, taken aback.

Colin nodded. "Of course. There is a lot we know that you don't, Mr. Greenwood, particularly when it comes to your parents' past."

"What about my parents' past?"

"Such debate serves no purpose right now," Wren said, her voice cutting through the argument. "I will have a proper conversation with Ben after the meeting. Let's move on."

Ben wanted answers now, but he took a deep breath and nodded. They would come later.

Wren stood up. "I am going to cast a Search Spell, Ben. You will feel a light tingling, but it is not unpleasant and won't last long."

Despite Wren's calm reassurances, Ben ran a weary hand through his messy, blond hair. He felt reluctant to be the subject of any more spells after the last one. But his trepidation was offset by curiosity. She had no Spellshooter. How was she going to cast a spell?

Wren raised a hand and extended her forefinger; the tip suddenly turned white. A jet of sparks arced towards Ben and showered him from head to toe. They grew into tiny stars and floated around him. Some made his skin tingle, but they didn't hurt; quite the opposite, it felt strangely relaxing.

The Executive Council were watching him closely. Ben desperately wanted the spell to find something. The thought that his parents had an eye on him was so uplifting it made his heart ache. But when the stars started disappearing, so did the Council's interest and Ben's shoulders sunk.

And then it happened. One of the stars hovering above his head exploded and ballooned into a silver ball the size of a pumpkin, pulsing gently.

"What is it?" Draven asked.

Wren was a picture of concentration. She narrowed her luminous eyes, lips parted.

"I cannot tell yet."

Nobody, not even Draven, interrupted her as she continued to stare at the silver ball.

Suddenly, the silver ball disappeared, making Ben jump. Wren lowered her hand, but continued to stare a few inches above Ben's head where the ball had been.

"The spell isn't one of ours," she said.

There was a collective murmur. Draven cursed and thumped his fist on the table.

"If I ever see those Greenwoods again," he muttered. "Can you tell us anything about the spell or are you going to be completely useless?"

Wren tapped a finger on her pursed lips. "Its power and complexity are considerable. It may have been cast by the wood elves. We know the Greenwoods are friendly with them."

"Can you tell us what the spell does?" Colin asked.

Wren shook her head. "I cannot say."

Ben had been listening intently and yet, to his immense frustration, understood nothing.

Before he could ask a question, Draven stood up. "We're done here."

"What about Mr. Greenwood?" Colin asked.

"What about him?"

"It's not safe for him to be wandering around. I call a vote to keep him in the Institute."

"Within Taecia," Wren said. "He's not a prisoner."

"Those in favour of keeping Ben in Taecia?" Draven asked. All hands were raised except Alex's.

Ben watched in astonishment as they voted on his fate as if he weren't there. He was still trying to work out what had happened when the Council filed out, leaving him alone with Wren.

— CHAPTER FOURTEEN —
Commander of the Institute

Ben hoped Wren would explain what had transpired, but she led him out of the meeting room moments after the others.

Questions buzzed round his head, but one demanded an answer above all others.

"What about my parents' past were they talking about?"

Wren put a finger on her lips. "Not here."

With some difficulty, Ben saved the questions for later, but that didn't stop him thinking about them. What were his parents searching for? Why were they trying to end the Greenwood relationship with the Institute? It occurred to Ben that Wren might not know the answers to all his questions.

They went back down the stairs to Wren's office. Ben suddenly became aware of how tired he was. His legs wobbled and he had to grip the banister to prevent a nasty fall.

"The Memory Search spell is a real energy-sapper," Wren said, slowing her pace. "You're doing really well. Many have to be carried afterwards."

Ben found speaking difficult when so much effort went in to putting one foot in front of the other.

"Why did Draven address Robert as 'Your Highness'?"

"Good question," Wren said. "Robert is a direct descendant of Queen Elizabeth I. His full title is Prince Robert, Commander of the Institute of Magic."

Ben rubbed his heavy eyes. "My history isn't great, but didn't Queen Elizabeth die childless?"

"You're right. The classrooms teach you that Queen Elizabeth died without an heir. But that isn't true: she had a son."

Ben ran a shaky hand through his hair. "Why didn't he become king when Elizabeth died?"

"By that time Elizabeth was more interested in the Unseen Kingdoms than the British Empire. So James VI of Scotland became king of England, and Henry, Elizabeth's son, became the new Commander of the Royal Institute of Magic. Since then her descendants have continued to rule the Institute."

Ben's weary mind needed a moment to take it all in. "I don't want to sound like Charlie, but how is that possible? Wouldn't somebody notice if she were pregnant?"

"I'll put that question down to your mental and physical fatigue," Wren said with a smile. "A simple spell could easily disguise her state."

"Of course," Ben said. "I forgot about that. So does Robert really rule the Institute? He doesn't look like the sort of person who would sit in meetings all day." Ben recalled the wet cloak and muddy clothes. "He came in last, left first and didn't take part in any of the Council's decisions."

"Well observed." She became momentarily distant and Ben thought he saw concern in her face. "The last few commanders have spent much of their time away from the Institute."

Now her concern was plain to see.

"Doing what?"

"Travelling. To where and for what purpose, I can't be sure," Wren said, unconvincingly. "But whatever the reason, the Commander has left governing the Institute almost exclusively to the Executive Council."

There was definitely a story behind why Robert and his forefathers spent their time travelling rather than ruling, but Ben's sluggish mind was in no shape to work it out; he needed Charlie. So he changed the subject.

"How did you fire a spell without a Spellshooter?"

"I do not need one."

"Are you an Unseen?"

Wren nodded. With her pointed ears and abundance of grace, Ben was hardly surprised. She was far more elf-like than

Natalie. He wondered how many other Unseens worked at the Institute.

"Why did you vote to keep me in Taecia? Alex didn't."

"Voting is done on majority," Wren said. "I knew Colin, Draven and Victoria would vote to keep you here, so there was nothing to be gained by voting against them. By voting with them I keep their trust and confidence."

"So why did Alex vote against them?"

"Alex speaks and votes his mind because he doesn't give a hoot what the Executive Council thinks about him. In return, his voice carries little weight outside his department. In truth, he's probably the least-suited director in history."

"I quite liked him."

Wren smiled. "That doesn't surprise me. He is very close friends with your parents, especially your dad. After they disappeared it took Draven several weeks before he was satisfied that Alex wasn't secretly in touch with them."

Ben found his affection for Alex growing. Had he more energy he would have asked Wren where he could see him again, but they were already approaching Wren's office and the thought of collapsing on her couch was overpowering.

Two contrasting faces greeted them as they entered Wren's office. Natalie was standing by the door, her green eyes wide with concern, hands playing with her hair. Charlie, by contrast, looked surprisingly calm. Despite Ben's weariness, he could have sworn he saw a flash of disappointment on Charlie's face before it yielded to curiosity. Of course, it wasn't often Charlie got the exclusive attention of a pretty girl. Ben almost felt bad interrupting them.

He made a beeline for the couch and collapsed on it with a groan of bliss. He wanted to shut his eyes, but knew if he did they wouldn't open again.

"Drink this."

Natalie was holding out a glass filled with green liquid.

"Is this one of those magic drinks that tastes great and rejuvenates me instantly?" Ben asked, sitting up.

"No, it's vegetable juice made from spinach and cucumber."

Ben took the glass reluctantly. "Don't those magic potions exist then?"

"They do," Charlie said, "but apparently they aren't as genuinely healthy as the vegetable option."

Natalie nodded in confirmation.

Ben took a sip and almost gagged. "Did you tell Natalie that I don't care which one is genuinely healthier? Especially if one tastes nice and the other tastes like grass."

"He did actually, but I chose the healthy option anyway, so drink up. The nutrients start to lose their effectiveness after twenty minutes."

"I'm afraid I have to go," Wren said. "It's late and the Commander is expecting me."

Ben looked at her in surprise. "Already? I have questions."

"I know you do, Ben," Wren said. "And tomorrow I will answer them. You will find my answers far more useful with a clear head and a good night's rest."

Her calm reassurance coupled with Ben's exhaustion staved off his protests. She turned her attention to Charlie. "Are you planning on staying the night or returning home?"

"I'm staying," Charlie said to Ben's relief.

"Good. Natalie, could you book them a twin bed at the Hotel Jigona please? The Institute will cover the costs."

Natalie left immediately to make the arrangements, leaving just the three of them alone in the office.

"Natalie will be back shortly," Wren said. "I will meet you here tomorrow after breakfast."

Her flowery red dress swirled as she turned and left.

Ben lay back down, resting his hands behind his head. He allowed himself the luxury of closing his eyes.

"Aren't you going to tell me what happened?" Charlie asked.

"We should wait for Natalie. There are a few questions I need to ask her to try to understand everything myself." Ben opened one eye and focused it on Charlie. "How about yourself? You looked like you were enjoying yourself with Natalie."

Charlie's face suddenly resembled a tomato and Ben knew he had hit the mark.

"We were having some interesting discussions about the history of the Unseen Kingdoms. She is really quite smart, you know, unlike some of the pretty girls you hang out with at school."

"That's not fair. What about Amy?"

"Are you serious? Have you heard some of the answers she gives Mr. Barlow in maths? It makes me cringe and I don't even like her."

"Fine, Amy wasn't the greatest example. What about Hannah?"

"You're missing the point. I was able to talk to Natalie like I talk to you." Charlie waved a hand and puffed his cheeks in frustration. "Oh, forget it. I can't explain it."

Ben gave him an even look, cutting through Charlie's embarrassment. "You feel comfortable around her."

"Is that strange?" Charlie asked.

"Not at all," Ben assured him. "She is very easy to talk to."

Though Ben didn't show it, he was concerned. They had only met Natalie hours ago and she had already penetrated Charlie's considerable female shield. Was that the Institute's plan – to get someone close to them? Was that Wren's plan? Or was he just being cynical?

Before Ben could debate the matter further, Natalie re-entered the room with a cheerful smile.

"Everything's arranged. You're lucky, you normally have to book well in advance to get into the Jigona – why are you both looking at me like that?"

Ben smiled casually at Natalie, his mind working quickly. "It's a bit embarrassing, but since you asked – we were wondering what we were going to do about spare clothes. I could really use some different underwear for tomorrow."

It was Natalie's turn to blush, while Charlie suddenly felt compelled to examine the desk at the back of the room. But Ben's lie seemed to do the job, deflecting Natalie from their private conversation.

"We can go shopping tomorrow," Natalie said, recovering far quicker than Charlie. "Wren has instructed me to watch over you and be your guide, so I'm afraid you'll have to put up with me for a while longer. I am also staying at the hotel. You'll like it there, it's really unique."

Charlie's pleasure was obvious, but Ben's smile masked his misgivings. Did the Institute really need to watch over him so closely to warrant Natalie staying with them at the hotel? But as much as he hated to admit it, he liked her company and he needed her knowledge.

Ben struggled to his feet. The vegetable juice had helped to wake him up, but his legs still felt like they had weights attached. He was eager to get to the hotel while he was awake enough to question Natalie.

Natalie disappeared into the little side room and came back with a small suitcase.

Noting the slight grimace Natalie made as she carried the suitcase down the stairs, Ben motioned to Charlie, who looked back at him with blank confusion. With a sigh, Ben took the suitcase off a surprised Natalie and, despite his weakness, carried it down the staircase.

"The place looks empty now," Ben said.

"It's past 7pm now, remember?" Natalie said. She tapped her wrist and Ben saw a sparkly watch masquerading as a bracelet. "The Institute is only open from 8am to 6pm so most have gone home."

"Do people commute here every day on that dragon train thing?"

"The Dragonway, yes, unless you are wealthy or important enough to warrant an animal you can fly home."

Ben was dreaming about how he could get his hands on such an animal when they reached the lobby. There were a couple of boys sweeping the wooden floors and chatting happily amongst themselves.

"Queen Elizabeth," Natalie said, pointing at the statue standing in the centre of the room that was surrounded by the great galleries above. Ben had never given the statue a proper look before, but he did so now. A lady in armour held a sword and shield, surrounded in a protective circle by four men and a woman. Everyone was white marble except the lady in the centre; she was made of a silver that shone so brightly Ben suspected magic at work. On her breastplate was the familiar coat of arms. The armoured lady's regal expression and posture left Ben in no doubt to her sovereignty.

"That is Queen Elizabeth's royal coat of arms," Natalie said, pointing at the breastplate. "You will see it a lot around here."

"Who are the men and woman surrounding Elizabeth?" Ben asked.

"They were the founding directors. You may have seen some of them as we passed through their respective floors. Within the Institute they are almost as famous as Queen Elizabeth. They were instrumental in helping Elizabeth grow the Institute in its formative years."

Ben knew it could just be the artist glamorising them, but they looked a nobler bunch, barring Wren and possibly Alex, than those today. Each stood tall and proud, trim and fit, with a cloak and sword.

"Michael James," Natalie continued, pointing to one of the figures, who happened to be the only one smiling, "was the first Director of Spellswords. He is credited with helping thwart King Suktar's first and only invasion of Taecia."

"Suktar?" Ben said, giving Natalie an odd look. "The same dark elf who wants my parents?"

Natalie nodded. "Elves live a long time, especially one as powerful as Suktar. It is said he faced off with Michael James and Queen Elizabeth herself in the heat of battle. There are hundreds of different stories of how the fight unfolded, but it is generally accepted that Suktar was sorely injured – I doubt he experienced such pain before – and it swung the battle against his army."

Ben never had much interest in history at school, but he was captivated by Natalie's story. He was staring so intently at the statue he didn't notice Natalie and Charlie head for the exit until they called him.

It seemed as though they had entered the Institute days ago so much had happened, but less than six hours had passed since they had first entered the grand building. The sky was turning pink though there was still some daylight left. Ben felt the mild air on his face and sighed with pleasure.

As they passed the noticeboard Ben couldn't resist one more look at his parents' photo. The words "High Treason" plastered above their faces set his blood curdling and he was tempted to rip the whole thing down.

"Your diamond is gone," Charlie said.

Ben's attention was drawn away from the noticeboard to Natalie's shoulder; sure enough, the single colourless diamond had vanished.

"We can make it come and go at will," Natalie said. "Generally we only display it inside the Institute or while on official duty."

They passed the manicured garden with its water fountain and through the gated exit between the mighty walls. Soon they were heading back down the hill along the cobbled path that was lined either side by trees and torch lamps.

"Don't worry, it's not far," Natalie said, glancing at the suitcase Ben pulled.

They turned off the main road and started walking across the hill rather than down it. The timber-framed buildings were larger than usual, uncluttered and detached. Some had stables, others had hitching posts and a few even had car parks. Ben watched with amusement whenever a strange car zoomed by, making a great racket. They reminded him of the old two-seater sports cars and seemed to be favoured by the dwarves, wearing helmets and goggles. Ben recognised several makes by their badges, including several Jaguars and a few Caterhams.

When he was not looking at cars or people, he was staring at the pubs, shops, restaurants and houses. It was Saturday evening and it was fascinating to see what the Unseens were doing. Many of the elves were dressed fashionably and tended towards the restaurants or coffee shops. The pubs seemed full of dwarves, wearing smocks or jeans, most of them smoking. Then there were the goblins, all elbows and knees, who had congregated in small groups around certain unsavoury take-out joints. Of course, there were always exceptions, such as the elderly goblins dressed in pinstripe suits heading to a fancy restaurant or the homeless elf strewn across the cobbled road.

With all the looking, Ben forgot his weariness and the suitcase he was pulling, but his neck started to ache with the constant twisting and turning.

"Aha – here we are!" Natalie said. "Hotel Jigona. You're going to love this place. Queen Elizabeth used to stay here when she visited Taecia. I guarantee you'll never want to leave."

— CHAPTER FIFTEEN —
Hotel Jigona

The hotel exterior wasn't as impressive as the Institute, but it was just as fascinating. It was a skyscraper version of an old Tudor inn. The architecture was similar to neighbouring buildings with the addition of a thatched roof. A sign protruded from the wall proclaiming itself "Hotel Jigona: Official Taecian Residence of Queen Elizabeth I".

Attached via a walkway was a huge car park and stable. The bottom levels were filled with antique cars and the upper levels populated by animals Ben had seen at the top of the Institute. There was an open shaft in the centre enabling the animals to fly in and out.

"Shall we check in?" Natalie asked with a smile.

A set of large oak doors, similar to the Institute's, was open, allowing a view into a welcoming reception area. The Royal Institute of Magic, though magnificent, could never be described as cosy or welcoming, but the hotel was both. A series of grand candle-lit chandeliers hung from the high, beamed ceiling. A crackling fire set within an ornate brick hearth was surrounded by several people in armchairs enjoying the warmth; a few young kids had sticks with marshmallows thrust into the flames. The smell made Ben's mouth water.

Natalie was talking to a man in a black tuxedo standing behind the reception desk.

"Master Greenwood and Master Hornberger," the man said, dipping his head as they approached. His accent reminded Ben of the royal family as he rolled his "R"s with ridiculous enunciation. His hair was jet black and shone from liberal amounts of gel.

"Welcome to Hotel Jigona. My name is Travis. I am the deputy manager and your point of call if anything is not completely to your satisfaction during your stay."

He spoke with perfect civility but with a confidence that implied nothing ever went wrong.

"Thank you," Ben said.

"I know you have only one suitcase, but allow me to take it straight to Miss. Natalie Dyer's room."

Before Ben could intervene and assure the well-spoken Travis that carrying a small suitcase was no trouble, the sound of thundering footsteps cut him short.

From the end of the room came a hulking, seven-foot troll. He had a huge nose, big flapping ears and, quite bizarrely, wore a black tuxedo. Ben didn't know if it was the suit or the genteel brown eyes, but the troll somehow looked harmless. He ambled over, crossing the lengthy reception room in just a few strides. He bowed to each of them with an air of elegance Ben wouldn't have believed possible.

"Thomas!" Natalie said and threw her arms round his waist. It looked like someone trying to hug a giant Redwood.

"Hello Natalie," Thomas replied in a voice two octaves lower than Ben had ever heard before. "How have you been? I missed your witty banter at the craft night last week."

"I know, I'm sorry. It's been mad at the Institute recently. I'm here with friends today – this is Ben and Charlie."

"Pleased to meet you," Thomas said. Ben was surprised how gentle his handshake was. "Forgive me if I'm wrong, but are you new to Taecia?"

"We are."

The troll nodded. "I hope you are enjoying your first visit. It can be quite an eye-opener."

"You said it," Ben said, giving him a smile.

"Well I hope your time at Hotel Jigona is as pleasant as the weather we've been having. Now, may I take the young lady's bag please?"

Despite the troll's soft nature, Ben wasn't ready to defy him so he handed over the luggage.

The troll gave one final bow and started backing away.

"I owe you a crochet lesson," Thomas said, pointing his big finger at Natalie. "I am determined to teach you – it's such a marvellous craft."

"Next week, perhaps," Natalie said, with a fond smile.

The troll turned and headed towards a set of stairs Ben hadn't noticed by the entrance.

"If you'll follow me, I'll show you to your rooms," Travis said. He rounded his desk and they followed him through reception.

"Right before that conversation with Thomas, I thought I was starting to get used to this place," Charlie said.

At the end of the reception were two doors. On one was a sign that said "Lift entrance", the other said "Lift exit – DO NOT ENTER". Travis turned the handle of the entrance door and pulled it open.

"What on earth is that?" Ben asked.

He was pointing at the jets of pink gas coming from the top of the doorway, spraying anyone who walked through. The spray was concentrated enough to conceal the lift beyond.

"Levitation. It's really easy, follow us in," Natalie replied.

Travis and Natalie passed through, oblivious to the pink spray that covered them. Ben followed, Charlie close on his heels. The spray felt warm and made his skin tingle. Ben frowned as soon as he made it to the room beyond. They were not in a lift, but a small room with no ceiling, enabling them to see up to the roof of the hotel.

"This is not a lift," Charlie said, too bemused to realise he was stating the obvious.

Natalie gave him a mysterious smile. "Isn't it? I'll see you up there."

And with that, she levitated off the ground and started floating up and away. Ben and Charlie watched in astonishment until Travis cleared his throat.

"The key is simply to will yourself upwards. It's a very simple but responsive spell, so have a care not to will yourself up too fast."

Travis started rising smoothly and with such nonchalance he looked as though he wasn't even aware of it.

"That sounds simple enough," Ben said, rubbing his hands together.

The ceiling was a long way up, which meant there was a long way to fall, but Ben put that out of his mind. It was a spell, so hopefully he could control his movement both up and down.

Ben looked up and imagined lifting off.

The effect was instantaneous. He left the ground – one feet, two feet, five feet. Ben whooped, wiggling his legs and marvelling at the freedom from gravity.

With another thought, he stopped his ascent and steadied himself at a comfortable six feet off the ground.

"Come on, Charlie, it's easy!"

Charlie looked excited yet nervous. He grabbed hold of a wooden beam that ran up the wall and shut his eyes.

"I'm doing it! I'm floating!" Charlie said.

Sure enough, when Ben squinted he saw a sliver of light between Charlie's shoes and the ground. Charlie ascended slowly, a hand always on the beam, until he reached Ben.

"Are you ready?" Ben asked. Charlie had taken so long Ben was concerned the spell might fade and they would fall; a concern he didn't mention to Charlie.

Charlie pried his fingers away from the beam so he was floating free. His fear finally disappeared and he smiled, flapping his limbs like someone making a snowflake.

Ben rose higher and they passed two more wooden doors, labelled "Floor 1 Entrance" and "Floor 1 Exit – DO NOT ENTER". Travis and Natalie had already ascended further, so Ben accelerated, his stomach momentarily staying behind. Doors whizzed by and it was only when he caught up with a floating Natalie and Travis that he came to a reluctant stop by the eighth floor entrance.

"Excellent work," Travis said. "Please note only go through the door marked 'entrance' when entering the lift. Otherwise you will enter without being sprayed with the spell."

They followed him through the door and into a luxuriously appointed corridor. The vanilla carpet was so plush Ben longed to sink his feet into it. Doors appeared left and right at regular intervals, each numbered. Travis stopped at number 816 and pulled out three large silver keys.

"Here we are," Travis said, handing a key each to Ben and Charlie. "You are staying in room 816." He turned to Natalie and gave her the remaining key. "You are in 823, just down the hall. Breakfast is served from 7:30 to 9am or you can have it delivered to your room if you prefer?"

"Room service for us," Ben said, after conferring with Charlie. "At 8:30am would be great."

"Wonderful," Travis said, after Natalie agreed she would like the same. "In that case I shall bid you good night."

He bowed again and left the three of them alone outside the room. Without Travis or any other distraction, Ben was eager to relay his story to Charlie and Natalie. He inserted the skeleton key and stepped into their hotel room.

A small candle-lit chandelier hung from the ceiling, illuminating two generous-sized single beds that Ben eyed longingly. There was a suite of comfortable, brown chairs arranged neatly around a stone hearth where a fire crackled merrily.

"I know it's only 8pm, but if you're too tired, I can go to my room and we can meet up tomorrow after breakfast," Natalie said, catching Ben's repeated looks at the bed.

"No, I'm fine. I want to ask you some questions, but they will only make sense after I have explained what happened during the meeting."

He took his shoes and socks off, digging his tired feet into the lush carpet and made straight for the couch. Charlie and Natalie took the remaining chairs.

Ben took a deep breath and recounted everything, downplaying only the pain in his head, which still hurt to think about. By the time he finished, Charlie was practically bouncing off his seat with excitement. Natalie, however, looked worried.

"Remarkable!" Charlie said, springing up and pacing the room. He stared at the carpet intently, hands behind his back. "Greg and Jane knew Suktar would come for them. They *knew*. The question is – why?"

Ben felt dizzy watching Charlie pace. "I don't know, but I wonder if it has anything to do with the search my dad kept mentioning."

Charlie nodded, his eyes squinting. "That seems to be the key. Who would your parents be searching for? And why?"

"I'm sure the Institute will know," Natalie said, giving Ben a reassuring smile. "I know it's really hard, but try not to worry about it too much. The Institute are doing all they can to find your parents."

Ben didn't believe that for a second, but he pretended to look reassured. "When I protested my parents' innocence, the Council said there were elements about my parents' past I was unaware of. Do you know what they were talking about?"

Natalie shook her head.

"Who might know?" Charlie asked, stopping his pacing.

"Either Wren or someone in the Department of Scholars," Natalie replied. "They know the Institute's history inside out. I have a couple of friends who could help should we need it."

"Good." Ben stifled a yawn. "Now, what about these 'wood elves' – what are they?"

"They are the oldest type of elf. While many have adapted to modern civilisation and diluted their bloodline by bonding with humans, the wood elves are pure, one hundred percent elf. They live in forests and many of them only speak Elvish. Their magic is the strongest in the Unseen Kingdoms, but the Institute hasn't been able to use it."

"Why not?"

"The wood elves won't let us near them," Natalie said. "We have sent countless diplomats out there, but the elves told us to stop coming. In our eagerness for their magic, we persisted. Last year we sent a large party, including some of our best diplomats. They never came back."

"Where are these wood elves?"

"I'm not sure," Natalie admitted. "With the destruction of forests, they are becoming an endangered species."

"Where could we find out?" Ben asked casually. He saw Charlie's pointed look from the corner of his eye, but Natalie gave no visible reaction to the question.

"The library," she said. "I was going to show you that floor anyway as you've not seen it yet, so that will give us something to do down there."

Ben turned to Charlie. "I was expecting one of your rants when I mentioned that Robert is a descendant of Queen Elizabeth."

"Natalie already told me," Charlie replied. "I did have a mini rant, but then I realised if I can accept dragons pulling underground trains to magical islands, I should be able to deal with Queen Elizabeth secretly having a son."

Another yawn escaped Ben's lips before he could stop it and Natalie stood up immediately.

"You look exhausted. I will let you sleep."

Another gigantic yawn prevented Ben from protesting. Natalie wished them good night and left.

It was all Ben could do to stumble over to his bed. "You have to get under the covers," Ben said, spreading himself and groaning with pleasure at the softness.

"I'm not tired," Charlie replied. He was sitting on his bed, cross-legged. "You wouldn't be either if they hadn't cast that Memory Search spell. It's only 8:30pm."Charlie gave Ben a sudden calculating look. "You want to track down these wood elves."

Ben, still in his spread-eagle position, turned his head to face Charlie."I had a feeling you'd worked that out. Thankfully Natalie seems clueless."

"She doesn't know you for the raving nutcase you are," Charlie said. "Didn't you hear what Natalie said? Hunting down those wood elves is suicide."

"It's the obvious thing to do," Ben said, stifling another yawn.

Charlie looked at him as if he'd sprouted wings. "Are you mad? If we found the right group of wood elves who know your parents, it could be useful. However, set against that already slim possibility is the much larger probability of being killed."

"Don't be such a pessimist," Ben said. "I know it's a long shot, but the longer I'm here the more I feel that the answers to my family's disappearance lie outside the Institute, not within it. We have two leads: the dark elves and the wood elves. Given that the dark elves are trying to hunt my parents down, I think we have a better shot with the wood elves, despite their unfriendly response to the Institute."

"Unfriendly? They killed them."

"We don't know that," Ben said. "Natalie just said the diplomatic party never returned."

"Good point. Perhaps they liked the forest so much they decided to stay."

"I'm just saying we can't be sure what happened. I don't believe my parents would be friends with the wood elves if they really were evil. I also want to know about the spell they cast on me."

Charlie's eyes became distant at the mention of the spell. "Natalie won't go for it."

"I know," Ben said with a sigh. "We will have to sneak off without her."

Charlie's face pained at the thought, but he offered no argument.

"It would have been nice to have her – for her knowledge I mean," Charlie said, a little hurriedly. "We will have no idea where we're going or what we'll be up against."

Ben saw Charlie's embarrassment but ignored it. "She would have been a real help. But don't worry – the two of us will work it out. I have a plan."

— CHAPTER SIXTEEN —
Elizabeth's Legacy

Ben woke to the sound of Charlie's voice. The morning light streamed through the windows and the clock said 8am. Ben felt wonderfully refreshed. His recurring dream had not surfaced, enabling him to sleep right through the night.

"Very clever," Charlie said.

Charlie was talking to himself unless there was somebody else in the room.

"I see what you're doing," Charlie continued. "But did you expect me to do this? I don't think so!"

Ben turned his head. Charlie was not in bed. He sat up and saw Charlie sitting on the couch. His hair was wet and he had a fluffy white towel about his waist, supported by his belly. He was leaning over the table staring intently at what looked like a game of chess, with several noticeable differences: the pieces weren't familiar, the board was bigger and it had three layers with ramps connecting each one.

Charlie appeared to be playing against an invisible enemy, for as soon as Charlie had moved, one of the opposing pieces (a figure shaped like a wizard) slid forward of its own accord, taking one of Charlie's pieces.

"What? You can do that?" Charlie asked aghast. He grabbed a heavy manual next to him and hurriedly flipped through the pages. A moment later he cursed.

"Morning," Ben said.

Charlie was so engrossed in the manual Ben had to repeat his greeting several times before Charlie turned around.

"Ah, you're up! You were sleeping so deeply I thought maybe you'd gone into unconsciousness."

"What is that game you're playing?"

"It's called 'Captains of Magic'. It's a bit like chess, but way cooler." Charlie frowned down at the set. "I told my opponent to play easy, but I'm still being annihilated."

"What opponent?"

"It's magically operated," Charlie said, with such nonchalance that for a moment Ben suspected the real Charlie had been abducted. "I have it on the difficulty level of a Lemming. Unfortunately, it seems even a Lemming is too good for me."

Ben ran a hand through his scruffy hair in bemusement. "You're taking all this magic surprisingly easily now," he said.

Charlie lifted the big manual he had been reading. It was a hardback book with an expensive, red-leather cover. On the front it said "Hotel Jigona Guide" scrawled in elegant hand.

"I've spent about three hours reading this between last night and this morning. I can see why Natalie was so excited about this place. Did you know this was the first four-star hotel to run purely on magic? I'm beginning to see how they survive without science. Once the Unseens have infused an object with magic, anyone can use it as long as you know how."

Charlie pointed to the chandelier hanging from the ceiling; its flames were flickering dimly, the morning light making it surplus to requirement.

"Check this out," Charlie said.

The flames on the chandelier suddenly flared with such vigour they created a hanging fireball. Ben shielded his eyes, his hand warming from the heat. A moment later the candles dimmed and returned to normal.

"How did you do that?" Ben asked a grinning Charlie.

"It's simple, just focus your attention on the chandelier and will it to the level of light you desire."

Ben caught on quickly and spent the next five minutes amusing himself by turning the light on and off. They had a battle of will, with Ben trying to turn it on and Charlie attempting to turn it off. It was as if someone were going crazy with the dimmer, but eventually, with Ben straining every sinew, the chandelier burned brightly.

"It's the same with everything," Charlie said, wiping his perspiring brow with a white handkerchief. "You can tint the windows, control the hot water and a dozen other things I haven't read about properly yet."

Ben spent the time before breakfast indulging himself in a luxurious bath. There was even fresh underwear Ben assumed was complimentary. When he was clean and dressed, he felt better than he had in a long time. Only his stomach had anything to complain about.

"I wonder what breakfast in bed will be like," Ben mused. "Is there anything in there about it?"

Charlie was still engrossed in the manual searching for an answer when 8:30am arrived.

Ben looked towards the door in anticipation, but a noise from the hearth made him turn. The fire, which was still dancing merrily, suddenly flared. Through the flames two young girls materialised and stepped through carrying silver trays filled with breakfast. They had wings like a butterfly, fine silver hair and innocent, angelic faces.

"Breakfast in bed, 8:30am as ordered," the faeries said in union. They placed the trays on the low-lying table. "Is there anything else we can get for you?"

"We're fine, thanks," Ben said, recovering from the surprise first.

The faeries curtseyed and disappeared back up the fireplace, immune to the heat.

Ben took one look at the breakfast and promptly forgot about the manner in which it was delivered. There were eggs, bacon, sausages, hash browns, beans and piping hot tea. He had never seen anything so delicious.

"I wonder how they knew we weren't vegetarians," Charlie mused.

Before Ben really had time to appreciate the food, he had devoured most of it and was lounging back, cup of tea in hand, patting his stomach with great contentment.

"That was amazing," Ben said.

"The cook is a wizard," Charlie agreed.

With a full stomach and a proper night's sleep, Ben felt ready to take on the world. But with a clear head, he also became alarmingly aware how risky yesterday's idea to find the wood elves was. There was the Institute, who had ordered him to stay in Taecia. There was their "babysitter", Natalie, who was sticking to them like glue. Then there was the small matter of finding the right group of wood elves and hoping they didn't kill them like the Institute's diplomatic party.

Ben sipped his tea. He might need to make a proper plan for once. He started brainstorming when somebody knocked on the door.

He got up and let Natalie in.

"Good morning," she said brightly.

She had changed into a green dress, which highlighted her eyes; her dark brown hair fell over one shoulder. But it was her waist that caught Ben's attention. She wore a Spellshooter in a discreet leather holster.

"I have practice today," Natalie said, seeing Ben's look. "Are we ready? You both look well fed and rested."

They left the hotel room and headed towards the lift, but they had barely made it halfway when Ben stopped as if he'd hit a brick wall.

At the end of the corridor was a small group filing through the lift door. Their long silver hair, pale faces and shining swords were unmistakable.

Ben cast Natalie a stunned look, but she didn't look surprised.

"The dark elves always stay here when visiting the Institute," she said softly. "I didn't want to tell you and create unnecessary tension when I knew we'd probably never see them."

Ben said nothing. Half of them had already disappeared through the lift door. The leader with the shifting cloak wasn't there, but he may have already taken the lift.

At the back of the group was a younger elf. He would be the last to go through the door, which meant that for a split second, he would be alone.

Ben's eyes narrowed. The dark elves were the key to all this. If he could learn the real reason they were after his parents, he might not need to track down the wood elves after all.

"Bad idea," Charlie whispered. "Terrible idea."

From the corner of his eye, he could see Charlie's alarm and Natalie's confusion.

Ben's blue eyes locked onto the young elf like a tractor beam. As he was about to pass through the door, Ben gave a very loud, very obvious cough.

The dark elf stopped. His mouth opened in surprise when he recognised their faces.

There was a moment's hesitation. The elf looked at the lift door and then back at them.

Ben gave the elf the sort of impudent grin that frequently earned him detention; he coupled this with a cheeky wave.

The elf forgot about the lift and started walking towards them.

"What have you done?" Natalie asked, her hand going to her mouth. She went from confusion to shock, and then horror in the blink of an eye.

Ben was momentarily taken aback – he had never seen such raw emotion from Natalie before; it threatened to breach his confidence. "Don't worry, I have a plan. We're just going to talk."

"Ben, this is not what you think," Natalie said. Her voice was tense and she spoke quickly, for the elf was quickly bearing down on them. "He might look young, but he is a dark elf. A pack of hungry lions would be less dangerous."

Natalie's analogy was hard to fathom. The dark elf was smaller than his fellows, though he was still a good head taller than Ben. His walk lacked a touch of the usual grace and Ben could see a few subtle pimples on the elf's face. But Ben had no doubt the elf could still use the sword strapped to his waist. He had an ugly, hooked nose, cruel eyes and a sneer that seemed to be his default expression.

"Good morning, Aryan," Natalie said, stepping forward. Ben was amazed to see how quickly she concealed her fear behind a gracious smile. "I hope you are well?"

"I was well," Aryan said in a slimy voice. "I was heading down for breakfast minding my own business when I spotted a human sneering at me. Imagine my surprise when I realised it was none other than the Greenwood boy."

"He is new to the Unseen Kingdoms and completely unaware of the politics, culture and respect your people are accustomed to."

"That is no excuse," Aryan sneered. "Your Institute is already in deep water thanks to the Greenwoods and now their son shows disrespect to the very people he should be trying to appease? I should report this to my general. With the treaty on a knife edge, a diplomatic blunder, no matter how small, is the last thing your Institute needs."

This time Natalie shifted uncomfortably under the dark elf's onslaught.

Ben had had enough. "I wasn't smirking, I was smiling. I'm sorry if you can't tell the difference."

Aryan looked as though he'd been slapped and for a moment appeared at a loss for words. Ben had a fraction of a second to decide the best approach to take. He gambled and focused on the elf. His intense, blue-eyed stare had opened many secrets before, but never with a volatile, sword-bearing dark elf. "Why are you after my parents?"

Aryan turned and Ben felt the full force of those strange purple eyes. There was anger there. Ben wanted anger.

"Your parents are wanted for treachery," Aryan said, his voice dangerously soft. "For the murder of Prince Ictid, the king's only son."

"Oh, I know that," Ben said, maintaining his intense stare. "I'm talking about the real reason you are after my parents, not the ridiculous cover story."

There was a gasp from Natalie and a groan from Charlie. Aryan heard neither; his purple eyes were focused on Ben like daggers, his smirk transformed into a snarl.

"You do not know how close you are to danger," Aryan said. His hand made a subtle movement to his sword.

Ben did know. He could see it in Aryan's eyes; he remembered Natalie's warning and he could sense the power radiating off the elf despite his youth.

Aryan was on the edge. Ben needed him to step over it.

"You're afraid of my parents, aren't you?" he said in a teasing voice, narrowing his eyes.

Ben knew immediately he had gone too far. Aryan's eyes lit up and he hissed, his arm shooting forward. Ben was ready, but Aryan was faster and stronger than he anticipated. Aryan grabbed him by the neck, rammed him back and pinned him against the wall.

Aryan smiled and squeezed his hand. "It's time you learnt some manners."

Ben started to choke. He grabbed the elf's arm but couldn't move it. Ben kicked out with an urgency borne of panic. Several blows found their mark, but though the elf winced, his grip didn't yield.

A flash of colour flew across the room. Ben's vision was blurred, but he could have sworn it was a large cannon ball. With a mighty crunch it smashed into Aryan and sent them crashing onto the vanilla carpet.

Ben rolled and rose in one smooth motion, finding himself between Natalie and Charlie, Aryan picking himself up a little slower half a dozen steps away.

Charlie's lip was bleeding. He looked dazed, but there was a steely glint in his eye.

The cannon ball had been Charlie.

"The little fat boy wants a lesson as well?" Aryan asked. He raised a hand, his palm pointing at them. "My father told me humans have a remarkably poor tolerance for pain. Let's find out, shall we?"

"Aryan, please!" Natalie begged. "These boys are under the Institute's protection. If you injure them, I will have to report you."

Aryan smiled. "You can't get me in trouble. Now, watch as I make your friends cry."

Aryan's palm started to glow purple until it was engulfed by a pulsing ball of energy. Ben tensed himself. A streak of purple lightning shot from Aryan's hand. Ben never came close to dodging it; he barely had time to thrust his arm up in a futile act of self-defence.

A shimmering crescent shield materialised in front of Ben and deflected the lightning bolt into the wall.

There was a moment of shock as everyone stared at the scorch marks along the hallway.

Aryan turned to Ben as if seeing him for the first time. "Elizabeth's legacy," he whispered. "So it is true."

"Sorry?" Ben and Charlie said in synchrony.

Aryan drew his sword with a flourish. "I wonder, does Elizabeth also protect you from the lick of a blade?"

Ben raised his hands in surrender. He didn't like the confident manner in which the elf held his sword. "Okay, I think we should all take a deep breath. Surely you wouldn't kill me just because I smiled at you?"

"Who said anything about killing?" Aryan said, a modicum of annoyance in his voice. "Pain is all I want, as punishment for your insolence. A bit of blood will suffice."

Aryan stepped forward, sword raised.

"What is Elizabeth's legacy?" Ben asked.

Aryan didn't respond or halt his advance. Ben cast a desperate sidelong look at Charlie and Natalie. They were making subtle nods towards the lift door. Could they outrun the long-limbed dark elf? Ben doubted it, but what other options did they have? He certainly couldn't rely on the elf's sword being deflected as his spell had.

Ben was still mulling over the options when Aryan attacked.

The sword thrust at him like a lizard flicking his tongue. Ben side-stepped and the sword grazed his side, ripping into his shirt. Aryan seemed surprised that his sword had not found its target, but Ben knew the next thrust would be harder to dodge; the elf now had a measure of Ben's reflexes.

Aryan feinted, throwing Ben off balance and then struck again. The blade was a blur. Ben twisted as hard and fast as he could, but he knew this time he was too slow.

A mighty crash came from Ben's right and a nearby door burst open. Thomas the troll was still wearing his tuxedo, but the genteel look was gone. With speed to match Aryan's blade, Thomas grabbed the elf by the scruff of the neck and held him aloft.

"What's this?" Thomas said, in his trombone-like voice. "A hotel guest trying to kill another hotel guest? That's not polite."

"Put me down, you lumbering oaf," Aryan said. He tried to strike the troll with his sword, but Thomas held him at such a distance that the sword only swished air.

"Happily, once you remove that murderous look and stop trying to kill your fellow guests," Thomas said reasonably.

"I wasn't trying to kill them. I was teaching them a lesson." Aryan was starting to sound like a spoilt child.

"Wonderful. I also enjoy teaching, though I'm unfamiliar with the technique of running at pupils with a sword."

"I was provoked."

Thomas nodded. "I'm sure you were. If I catch you brandishing your sword in this hotel again, regardless of the provocation, you will pack your bags. Are we clear?"

Ben hoped he would protest so that Thomas might bash him about a bit. Unfortunately, Aryan nodded and was released.

"This isn't over," Aryan said, pointing a finger at Ben. "Watch your back."

Aryan disappeared through the door to the lift.

"That was good timing," Ben said, turning to Thomas.

"I can smell magic. I came as soon as I caught a whiff of the spell."

"You saved us," Natalie said, giving Thomas a radiant smile.

"Always glad to be of assistance to my guests," Thomas said with a bow. "I shan't ask what happened here because I don't particularly want to know and I expect you would be reluctant to tell me. Don't worry about the damage to the wall, I'll fix that. And now I think I will get back to work, please excuse me."

He bowed and left through the door from which he had come, which Ben assumed must lead to a staircase.

Natalie turned back to the scorch on the wall and put a hand in front of her lips. "We just fought a dark elf," she said softly, speaking to the wall.

After repeating the statement half a dozen times, the colour in her face started returning.

"I hope you won't get in trouble," Ben said.

"What? No, Aryan is far too arrogant to relay such a humiliating experience to his superiors."

"So what's the problem?"

Natalie shook her head. "You don't get it, but how could you? This is all new to you. One of the first things parents teach their children about the Unseen Kingdoms are the rules of conduct towards a dark elf: never talk to them; never make them angry; and never fight them."

"That seems a bit cowardly," Charlie said.

"It's for protection. If we leave them alone, they leave us alone. The Institute cannot afford another war. We have been fighting them on and off for over five hundred years."

"So we broke a few rules. Is that all you're worried about?" Ben asked, feeling slightly miffed.

"Yes – I mean, no." It was the first time Ben had seen Natalie lost for words. She was looking at him with a peculiar glint in her eye. "How did you deflect that spell?"

"I have no idea. Do you think it could have been the spell the wood elves put on me?"

"I'm not sure," Natalie said, curling a lock of hair round her finger, looking bemused.

"You both seem to be forgetting something."

Ben turned towards Charlie. He was practically bouncing off the walls with an energy that could only be attributed to the detective work going on inside his head.

"Two words," Charlie said, sticking a couple of chubby fingers out. "Elizabeth's legacy."

Charlie was right. Ben clearly recalled those words uttered by Aryan in response to his deflected spell.

"How does Elizabeth's legacy relate to the way I blocked that elf's magic? Is there another spell on me completely different to the wood elf one?"

Charlie tapped his chin thoughtfully. "There must be. I don't see how the wood elf spell could have anything to do with Elizabeth's legacy. The problem is we haven't the faintest clue what Elizabeth's legacy is."

"Let's go see Wren," Natalie said. "I'm sure she will have answers."

She didn't sound quite as certain as yesterday.

— CHAPTER SEVENTEEN —
Ten Great Dwarf Recipes

Conversation was muted as they made their way back to the Institute. Travis had reserved their room for another night and Ben realised the hotel was to be his home for the foreseeable future. He would have been delighted if the dark elves weren't staying there.

Natalie's green eyes were troubled and she curled a lock of hair around her finger, lost in thought. Charlie was staring at the ground, also deep in thought. Ben considered the questions he wanted to ask Wren. Did she know anything about Elizabeth's legacy? He still recalled the shock on the dark elf's face the moment the spell was deflected. Most important of all, what did she know about his parents?

Ben was so wrapped up in his own thoughts he barely noticed they were passing the wall surrounding the Institute and the manicured gardens within. It was only when Natalie opened the great oak doors did Ben realise they were back.

Though it was Saturday, the place was still a hive of activity, with people scuttling across the lobby or up and down the stairs. Ben marvelled again at the small coloured diamonds hovering above their shoulders; Natalie's had appeared the moment they had crossed the threshold.

"I really think they should consider installing an escalator," Charlie groaned, as they headed for the familiar grand staircase.

They set a good pace and even Ben's legs were aching when they reached the Department of Spellswords. Natalie led them round the corridor to the office. She turned the handle, but to her dismay it didn't move.

"Locked. Which means she's out or busy," she said.

Natalie produced her ID card and pressed it just below the handle where a lock would have been. There was a click; she tried the handle again and this time the door opened.

The office looked just as they had left it and there was no sign of Wren. Natalie disappeared into the little side room and returned with several notes in her hand and a worried look on her face. She handed one of the notes to Ben and another to a surprised Charlie.

With a funny feeling in his stomach, Ben opened the letter.

"Dear Ben,

"I'm sorry I am unable to meet you this morning. Something unexpected has come up. You have questions that deserve answers, not least the insinuations from my colleagues last night about your parents' past. I would prefer to talk to

you about this personally because most (though not all) in the Institute do not know the full story. Indeed, I do not know everything, but having worked with your parents for many years, I know of their honesty and integrity.

"I hope to meet you this evening when I can enlighten you properly.

"Best wishes,

"Wren"

Ben looked up and saw Natalie and Charlie watching him.

"What did yours say?" Charlie asked.

Ben handed him the note, which Charlie read and then passed to Natalie.

"Intriguing, yet cryptic," Charlie said with a glint in his eye.

"Do you know where Wren is?" Ben asked, his voice betraying his impatience.

Natalie tapped her own note. "Dragon raid on Riardor, a country not far from here. She had to lead a group of Spellswords to repel them."

"And she'll be back for dinner?" Charlie asked doubtfully.

"If she says she will be, she will."

Ben took his note back and scrunched it up. His frustration was starting to boil over. He knew how important Wren was and what demands there must be on her time, but it still seemed unfair to ask him to wait for her. He wanted answers now.

"So what do we do?" Charlie asked.

"Whatever you want," Natalie said. She tapped her letter again. "Wren has instructed me to look after you until she returns."

Ben's mouth twitched at her babysitting reference, but he tried to ignore it. "I would like to find out where the wood elves live."

Perhaps he could have been subtler, but Natalie's bright smile indicated she was still clueless regarding his plan to find the elves. She might be pretty and friendly, but Ben was starting to doubt her intelligence.

"We should be able to find that at the library, in the Department of Scholars," Natalie said. "I know it sounds boring, but I think you'll like it."

As they went back down the staircase, Ben's mind drifted back to Wren's note. There was an ominous undertone. What had his parents done in the past?

"Please don't worry about it," Natalie said. So she wasn't completely unobservant; Ben hadn't realised he looked so concerned. "Wren will explain everything as soon as she returns."

Ben ruffled his hair and turned to Charlie. "What do you think?"

"It's just my opinion," Charlie said, "but it seems like your parents have been in trouble before."

"That's just Charlie's opinion," Natalie said, giving Charlie a meaningful look.

"Charlie's opinions are normally pretty accurate."

Ben had been thinking the same thing. Could they have done something wrong in the past?

"Here we are," Natalie said. "The Department of Scholars."

They passed through the double doors and the statue beyond and headed round a distinctly musty corridor. It smelled of old books. Shelves lined the corridor, sometimes on both sides, making walking a bit of a squeeze.

Natalie led them to a door marked "Library". Ben noticed Charlie rubbing his hands together. He found it hard to share Charlie's excitement, but his eyes lit up the moment he entered.

It was much more than a library. There were the obligatory book shelves creating a maze of corridors, but Ben's attention went straight to something far more interesting. It was a big open room that reminded him of the Science Museum in London, only cooler. There was a huge globe floating in the centre of the room, circling slowly. Like the map in Wren's office, the globe included the Unseen Kingdoms. Running along the walls were colourful illustrations detailing a timeline of the Institute's history. Then there were dozens of exhibition stands showing things like the evolution of Spellshooters, various animals and foods found in the Unseen Kingdoms, and charts showing every type of spell with its composition of elements.

"Uh, Ben, wrong way."

Ben had drifted away from Natalie and Charlie into the centre of the museum room. He was tempted to tell them to go find the books on wood elves by themselves.

"We can come back here later," Natalie said, dragging him back into the labyrinth of book shelves.

Thankfully, it wasn't as boring as Ben had imagined. The shelves were clearly marked and the subjects ranged from spells and enchantments to the climate and cultures of the Unseen Kingdoms. Ben wasn't a big reader, but even he felt like taking out a handful of books. Occasionally they stopped and Natalie, aided by Charlie, pored over a certain book. Ben passed the time by browsing nearby titles for the most outlandish subject. He had just spotted a book called *Ten Great Recipes for a Dwarf Vegetarian* when Natalie gave a little shout of joy.

"Well done, Charlie – this is the one!" she said.

They were both on the floor, poring over a small, open book called *An Elf Census 2012*.

"Borgen has a large population," Charlie said. "Over two thousand, it says."

"Wow, there are less than ten thousand wood elves left," Natalie said. "Half the amount of five years ago."

Ben could see the chart they were reading, but it was useless to him because he didn't know anything about the countries listed. He needed to know which one would be best to visit, but how could he ask Natalie without arousing suspicion? Any moment they would shut the book and move on. He was going to have to risk it and hope Natalie's record of delightful ignorance remained untarnished.

Several familiar voices interrupted his scheming.

They all perked their heads up like deer sensing danger. The voices were near, perhaps two or three shelves away, but they were moving. For a brief moment, Ben could make them out.

"...the Commander leaves today on another of his ridiculous journeys and Wren's not here, so that's two thorns out the way." Draven's voice.

"Regardless, protocol must be carefully followed," Colin said. He sounded anxious, his normally perfectly enunciated words slightly off.

"Do what you must," a softer, more compelling voice said. It was Elessar, the first dark elf he had seen, Ben realised, with a ripple of fear. "But it must be done tonight. My king grows impatient and I can appease him only so long."

The voices faded as they moved out of earshot.

There was a moment of silence as Ben, Charlie and Natalie stared at each other in shock.

Ben moved first. He picked up the book and made to put it back on the shelf, but with a sleight of hand slipped it under his top. Neither Natalie nor Charlie noticed anything.

"Where are you going?" Charlie asked, as Ben set off.

"To follow them. Come on."

This time it was Ben's turn to lead, toward the general direction the voices had originated, through the small alleys created by the shelves. Occasionally they passed small, open spaces with a table and chairs where people could read. Ben was just starting to fear he had lost them when he heard the unmistakable voice of Draven.

They were now in an older section of the library. Many of the books looked ready to crumble and the light struggled through the dust that powdered the shelves and permeated the air.

The voices led them to a small reading room, empty except for a couple of chairs and a table piled with books. At the back was an open doorway, but it was guarded by someone.

"Oh no, it's Josh," Natalie whispered. They had stopped in the small room unable to proceed further.

"So you *are* still here," Josh said, showing a set of sparkling white teeth as he smiled at Natalie. "We thought you'd been released or buckled under the strain of the apprenticeship and left."

Josh looked a year or two older than Ben and perhaps a head taller. He had expensively styled hair, tanned skin and a self-satisfied smile. His yellow polo shirt and Bermuda shorts looked like they'd left the Ralph Lauren shop five minutes ago. Strapped to his shorts was a holstered Spellshooter.

The voices they were chasing were already getting fainter and Ben was desperate to keep moving. He was tempted to barge his way past, but that could cause problems, especially as Josh was armed.

"I'm still here," Natalie said. She smiled, but Ben thought it lacked a touch of its usual warmth.

"Indeed," Josh said. "Well, I should let you know you're falling behind. I'd be slightly concerned if I were you. Even Graham, with his IQ of a dormouse, has overtaken you. He just finished the Level 1 diplomacy course. Personally I think he cheated. How can someone who can barely speak the English language display even the smallest crumb of diplomatic tact?"

"Well I'm happy for him," Natalie said.

"Oh, so am I," Josh said, not looking the least bit jovial.

Just as Ben was suspecting that he and Charlie must be invisible, Josh turned to them.

"Aren't you going to introduce us?" Josh said, flashing his white, toothy smile at them.

"Sorry," Natalie said. "Josh, this is Ben and Charlie. They are guests here and I've been looking after them."

Josh shook their hands and he stared at Ben curiously.

"Not Ben Greenwood of the infamous Greenwood family?"

"That's right," Ben said, with barely masked impatience.

Josh gave him a sympathetic smile. "I'm sorry to hear about your parents."

"What do you mean?" Ben asked. He kept his voice mild, his expression neutral, but there was something in Josh's voice that annoyed him.

"You seem like a decent guy, but having a mum and dad of such poor character will reflect badly on you. I've seen it with many other apprentices – those who have strong, successful parents often do better. Take myself as an example."

Ben felt Natalie's hand on his shoulder, but it did little to calm his growing anger. "The treason my parents have been accused of is nonsense."

Josh nodded. "Supporting your parents is admirable. It is just unfortunate that their criminal records count against them."

"What criminal records?"

"You don't know?" Josh said, with mild surprise. "I thought the Institute would have told you of all people. Perhaps they didn't want you to suffer."

Ben started clenching and unclenching his fists in an effort to stop them from throttling Josh.

"My parents don't have criminal records," he said.

Josh gave him a look like a mother breaking the news to her son that Santa doesn't exist. "I'm afraid they do. Unlike your parents' current predicament, this one is a matter of historical record."

Ben wanted to deny it, but something unpleasant had settled in his stomach. "For what?" he asked.

Josh smiled and tapped his nose in a friendly manner. "I don't think it would be right to say, do you? If you haven't been told by now, it's clear the directors don't want you to know."

For a moment, Ben was too angry to do anything except concentrate on not hitting Josh. He was probably sixteen and looked like he worked out, but Ben was confident that he could take him down, especially if Charlie pitched in like he did against the dark elf.

"Josh, that isn't fair," Natalie said, but her pleading only seemed to delight Josh.

"I'm sorry, but it just wouldn't be right," Josh said. "Look, I can already see Ben's lip quivering; let's move on before he gets too upset. A few of us are going to the Horse and Groom for a few drinks. Unfortunately, Ben and Charlie look too young to join us, but I'm sure I could get you in."

"No, thank you," Natalie said curtly. "It's time we got going."

Josh, however, did not move from the open doorway despite Natalie's obvious intent to walk through.

"I'm sorry," Josh said. "The Director of Diplomacy, Colin Seymour himself, told me to stand guard and not let anyone through. He is holding an important meeting and needs some privacy."

Natalie gave him a dazzling smile that made Ben's skin tingle despite not being the recipient. "We just need to get to the Victorian history section," she said. "We'll only be a second."

"No can do," Josh said, with an uncaring shrug. He smiled, showing his sparkling teeth in a manner he clearly thought charming. "My offer still stands for drinks tonight though, if you tire of looking after these two."

Natalie turned to face Ben and Charlie with a helpless look. Charlie looked angrier than Ben could remember. His fists were balled and his cheeks were red, however, he did nothing but give Josh an evil look.

Little thought went into Ben's plan – partly because he didn't have the time, but mostly because he was angry and itching to do something.

He lunged forward and in one smooth movement pulled Natalie's Spellshooter out of her holster and aimed it at Josh.

Josh's eyes widened in surprise. He seemed unaware Ben had no clue how to use a Spellshooter or perhaps he was too scared to realise it. His tanned face suddenly looked significantly less brown.

"What are you doing?" He looked at Ben and clearly didn't like what he saw, for he turned to Natalie. She looked as startled as Josh but said nothing.

"As I have the Spellshooter pointing at your face, I will ask the questions," Ben said, relishing the fear in Josh's eyes. "Let's talk about my parents. What crime are they accused of?"

"I don't know," Josh said. He was looking down the barrel as if there were a snake inside. Ben made a show of readying his trigger finger on the Spellshooter and Josh let out an involuntary moan.

"I swear it!" Josh said. "The only thing I know was that your parents pleaded guilty and spent a year in jail. It happened many years ago, before you were born."

"They pleaded guilty?"

Josh nodded, slightly frantically. "Yes, that's what made the court case so strange. The Institute was prepared to defend them, but they declared their guilt and were offered a lenient penalty in return."

Ben's head started to swim, but he forced his questions aside and inched the Spellshooter forward until Josh was looking at the barrel cross-eyed beneath his nose.

"It's the truth," Josh said. "You can look at the records in the Justice section for proof."

Ben glanced at Natalie who nodded. He hesitated for a moment. He desperately wanted to look up his parents' court case, but it would mean missing the meeting between Colin, Draven and Elessar. Even now they might be too late.

"Get out of here," Ben said.

Josh looked like such a pathetic wreck that Ben lowered his Spellshooter. The instant he did so, Josh's face transformed. The fear vanished and he raised his own Spellshooter with a look of triumph.

But Ben was quicker.

He aimed his Spellshooter like a seasoned cowboy. The instant he touched the trigger time seemed to blur. In his mind he could see with crystal clarity, down to the finest tone of colour, the coloured pellets floating in the orb. He could see the elements they were made of, their strengths and exactly what each one did. The advice from the Spellshooter teacher came back to him. *If you concentrate and command it well enough, the spell will obey.* Ben focused on a tiny yellow pellet with every ounce of willpower he had, casting aside any doubts it might not work.

He pressed the trigger and fired, a fraction of a second before Josh.

Ben had visions of a ball of energy hurling towards Josh and knocking him off his feet. What he got was a tiny yellow ball so insubstantial it looked like it might splutter into nothing. It curved erratically and hit him on the arm.

Josh's face glazed over and he fell to the floor, breathing but unconscious. Ben nudged him with his foot; he didn't move.

"Not quite what I envisioned," Ben said, inspecting the Spellshooter.

"Did the job though," Charlie said.

He handed the Spellshooter back to Natalie, but she made no move to retrieve it. She was staring at him with such astonishment her green eyes seemed to take up half her face.

"You fired the Spellshooter," she said.

"It was pathetic," Ben said, Natalie's astonishment making him slightly uncomfortable. "It almost disintegrated before it reached Josh and he was only standing about a foot away."

Natalie shook her head. "Most people can't fire anything for at least a month and it takes double that for the spell to do anything effective."

"I'm a fast learner," Ben said. He was looking at the doorway, eager to get going. Natalie finally took back the

Spellshooter. She looked down at the unconscious Josh and aimed her Spellshooter at him. Before Ben could ask what she was doing, she fired. A small silver bullet hit him with a soft pop and Josh disappeared.

"We don't want anyone seeing him lying there," Natalie said. "Both those spells should last about half an hour."

Ben led them though the doorway back into a maze of bookshelves. It was dark and musty, but it was his ears, not his eyes, Ben was relying on. After a moment of walking as quickly as he dared through the shelves, Ben picked up the sound of familiar voices. He slowed to a crawl, the voices slowly getting louder until he had to stop for fear of turning a corner and running right into the meeting.

All three of them strained their ears to listen. Colin was speaking, an edge of concern in his voice.

"...to more important matters: who will pick up Ben Greenwood tonight? This procedure must be carried out as quietly as possible."

"I will," Draven said. "He's a slippery one, but I know how to deal with him."

"Unharmed," Elessar said. "We need him in perfect condition for the Memory Search."

Ben bit his lip to stop from crying out.

"How will he cope with the stress of the spell?" Draven asked.

"There are many variables. We delve much deeper into his subconscious than you, but every effort will be made to retain his sanity."

There was a moment's silence. Ben prayed that Colin and Draven were having second thoughts.

"I want a full and immediate withdrawal from Burnstad," Colin said. "I also want an official cessation of hostilities towards the Institute."

"We will withdraw from Burnstad. I am not authorised by my king to grant your other request."

"I suggest you obtain authorisation," Colin said. "Otherwise we do not have an agreement."

There was a faint hiss. "You ask a lot for a boy my king feels is owed to us anyway."

"I could never explain this to the Council for anything less," Colin said.

"I agree. Those are the terms," Draven said, his rough voice cutting through the book shelves. "King Suktar can take them or leave them."

"I will speak to my king," Elessar said. "I hope, for your sake, he does not take offence."

There was a sudden shuffling of feet and the sound of footsteps approaching.

Ben, Charlie and Natalie retreated as quickly and silently as possible, past the small room where an invisible Josh lay and back into the relative comfort of the main library.

Ben needed to get outside. His heart was racing. He knew he was in no immediate danger, but he couldn't shake the feeling that Draven was just around the corner, ready to spring out and catch him. Ignoring questions from Charlie and Natalie as they hurried behind, Ben kept walking, leaving the library and hurrying down the grand staircase and through the main lobby.

The sun on his face and blue sky above gave him a feeling of freedom he had never really appreciated before. He hurried along the Institute's grounds and only stopped when they had exited the gate.

There was no going back to the Institute now, with the plans that had been instigated in Wren's absence. Part of him wanted to scream at everything they had just witnessed. Someone should be able to help them, someone who could expose the obvious wrongs being perpetrated.

He took a deep breath and turned around to face a perplexed Natalie and a huffing and puffing Charlie. The time had come to lose Natalie, unless he could persuade her to help. Would she agree to his plan? Last night he would have said no, but everything had changed. Would she still side with the Institute or could he make her see reason? The prospect of finding the wood elves without her knowledge of the Unseen Kingdoms was daunting.

"Is there somewhere safe we can talk?" Ben asked. "I have a plan. It will take some explaining."

— CHAPTER EIGHTEEN —
Natalie's Surprise

Natalie led them back to the hotel. Ben wasn't happy about the proximity to the dark elves, but he reluctantly agreed this was the best place for a bit of peace and quiet.

This time they went to Natalie's room. It was just as welcoming with one king-size bed instead of the two twins. Ben, Natalie and Charlie sat on the chairs surrounding the fireplace, nibbling on biscuits that had been placed on the table for them.

"So, what's this plan?" Natalie asked.

This was it – the moment of truth. To include her in his mad plan or to blow her off? He had agonised over the decision the moment they fled the library, but he was no closer to an answer. Natalie was looking at him with inquisitive green eyes and a strange smile. Ben had no idea what she found funny, but it highlighted one of her assets – she was beautiful. A pretty girl was always useful, especially one as chatty as Natalie. More importantly, she also knew her way round the Unseen

Kingdoms; she was born there. But her blind allegiance to the Institute meant if he did reveal his plan, she might just report them to the Institute; after all, the Executive Council had ordered him not to leave Taecia. Additionally, she didn't seem to be the brightest lamp on the street; given the obstacles they might encounter, this was another strike against her.

"Hello?" Natalie said. "You mentioned something about a plan?"

Why was she smiling at him? He was trying to concentrate and it was distracting. Charlie was looking at him anxiously, but offered no words of encouragement. Ben wished he could have gotten Charlie's advice, but there had been no time.

Ben grit his teeth. He knew what he had to do.

"I bet I can guess your plan."

Ben looked at Natalie in surprise. Her eyes sparkled with mirth.

"You want to track down the wood elves that put the spell on you."

Ben's jaw dropped. He cast an accusing look at Charlie. "You told her!"

"No, I didn't," Charlie said. He too was staring at Natalie, mouth agape.

"Nobody told me. I figured it out. It wasn't difficult really, with your constant questions about the wood elves and where to find them."

Ben was speechless, which only seemed to delight Natalie further.

She pointed a finger at him. "You thought I was an airhead, didn't you? You assumed I was too dim to work out what you were up to."

"What? No, I—"

"I'm not insulted," she said. "I have to admit, I did play along a little. By dismissing me as an idiot you seemed less cautious about what you said."

Ben stood up and paced the small hotel room. His head was a whirl with emotions. He couldn't work out whether to be angry that she had duped them or ashamed that he had dismissed her so easily.

"It was Wren who tipped me off," Natalie continued. "She said you might take matters into your own hands. But it was only after that conversation we overheard with Colin, Draven and Elessar that I realised you would want to act now."

Ben spread his arms in a helpless shrug. "Well, now that you know our plan, what do you think?"

"I think you're brave, but completely mad," she said matter-of-factly with a sweet smile to soften the blow.

"Those are the hallmarks of all Ben's plans," Charlie said.

Ben wasn't sure whether to be encouraged by Natalie's calm demeanour or put off by her sentiments. He was still confused by this new Natalie.

"The dark elf will get permission to cast his own Memory Search spell today," Ben said. "Given that it will probably make me go crazy, I cannot return to the Institute."

Natalie's humour subsided. "Wren will stop it."

"Wren isn't here."

"No, but she is due back this evening."

"I can't risk that. I know you said she was reliable, but the moment King Suktar agrees to the Institute's terms, Draven will come for me. This hotel isn't even safe; the Institute knows we are here. Wren might be able to help me, but unless she is constantly by my side, I can't rely on her."

"What about the other members of the Council?" Natalie asked. "Victoria or Alex are both as senior as Colin and Draven."

"Alex would help me, I think. But I don't know where he is and Wren said he carries little authority outside his own department. I don't know about Victoria, I haven't worked out which side she's on, but I wouldn't gamble on her."

"What about the Commander?" Charlie asked. "He has more power than any of the Council members and he of all people might know something about Elizabeth's Legacy."

"That's not a good idea."

Natalie's firm voice caught Ben and Charlie by surprise.

"Nobody but the Executive Council is allowed to address the Commander of the Institute."

Ben gave a dismissive wave. "I don't care about rules."

"It's not just that," Natalie said. "There's something peculiar about him. Instead of leading the Institute, he spends his time travelling to the most obscure places in the Unseen Kingdoms. It was the same with his father; in fact, the last three commanders have all died while travelling."

"They must have a reason for travelling so much."

"Maybe, but no one knows why. It gets worse as they get older, until they are so obsessed they barely have time for the Institute."

"That is a little odd," Charlie admitted.

Ben wasn't convinced. "Are you saying he's crazy?"

"Not yet, but I would say he's irresponsible, uncaring and the last person I would go to for help. Even Wren thinks he's strange and she knows the Commander as well as anyone. Trust me, asking him is a bad idea."

Ben recalled those dark, gold-flecked eyes. There was no doubt there was something peculiar about the Commander. He seemed sensible enough at the meeting, but there was an intensity about him that even Ben found a little daunting.

"If the Commander is out of the question, then it has to be the wood elves. I know it's a long shot, but we have no other lead. My parents trusted them. They will know something, I'm sure of it," Ben said.

Natalie didn't say anything for a moment. She appeared to be composing her own line of defence, playing with her hair as she did so. There was an intelligence in her eyes Ben hadn't noticed before.

"I know you are aware of the dangers of the wood elves," Natalie said, "but I don't think you get how scary they are. The diplomats we sent knew their culture, customs, habits and even their language. Despite all that they didn't return."

"I know," Ben said, seeing Charlie's growing look of unease. "But my parents made it, didn't they?"

"Yes, your parents made it. But assuming some of them are friendly towards your family, we have absolutely no idea which colony of elves that is. There are half a dozen possibilities, most of them I can't even remember."

Ben pulled out the small library book he had taken and placed it on the table. "We will have to make an educated guess."

Natalie stared at the book for a moment and then looked up at Ben, her eyes serious. "Would you really take such a risk?"

"I don't have a choice," Ben said. "It's that or go back home. But what do I have there? A step-grandma who likes her TV more than me."

Natalie chewed her lower lip, doubt playing across her face for the first time. "I'm supposed to be watching over you, not sending you on crazy missions."

Ben leant forward, putting every ounce of conviction into his voice. "That's why we need you to come with us. Our chances of success go from impossible to unlikely with you guiding us."

Natalie turned to Charlie. "You are willing to go with Ben?"

Ben was impressed with the way Charlie held Natalie's green-eyed stare.

"I don't think we have a choice. It might be risky, but it's less dangerous than heading back to the Institute into the hands of the dark elves or waiting for them to kidnap Ben back at his grandma's."

"What about your parents, Charlie? You've been gone a day already. Aren't they going to get worried? If we leave, we won't be back for a while."

Ben cursed. "I hadn't thought of that."

Charlie, however, was unconcerned. He pulled out a folded note from his pocket and handed it to Ben.

"Dear Charlie,

"I am sure your parents will soon be wondering where you have got to, especially as you will obviously not be answering your phone. However, Ben may be stuck here for a while and I am sure he would benefit from your company. There is a Warden working near your area and I have taken the liberty of instructing him to cast a very mild Forgetfulness Spell on your parents, should you not return home. There is no harm in the spell; it only lasts a short period of time. The Warden can re-cast it until you are back.

"I hope we will speak soon.

"Best,

"Wren"

"I would like to return home soon, but this is more important," Charlie said.

Natalie sat with her hands on her lap, staring into space. Ben wished there were something else he could say to convince her, but he was out of ideas.

"I will go on one condition," she said.

"Whatever it is, we'll do it."

"Ignore Charlie," Ben said. "What condition?"

"I want you to trust me," Natalie said. Ben started to protest, but she raised a hand. "I know you think I trust the Institute too much, and maybe I do, but this crazy plan is only going to work if we can rely on each other. I'm the only one who knows anything about the Unseen Kingdoms."

Charlie agreed even before Natalie had finished speaking, but it was Ben she focused on. An hour ago he would have fobbed her off with false assurances. Now he wasn't even sure that would work. Could he trust her? Not if she was asking for the type of trust he had in Charlie, that was borne of a lifetime of friendship. But he could certainly stand to open up a little.

"It's a deal," Ben said.

Natalie looked far happier than he expected, given their crazy mission.

"Let's see the library book," she said, extending her hand.

Ben grinned and handed over the book; Natalie put it on her lap.

"There are six countries that have wood elf colonies, but only two of them are realistic options," she said, after studying the book for a while. "There is no way your parents would have travelled to the others. They are either against the Institute or located on the other side of the world."

"What are the two?"

"Borgen and Algete. Algete is just off the coast of Spain. My family has been there a couple of times on holiday; it's really beautiful. Unfortunately, there aren't a huge number of wood elves there and the book isn't very precise as to their location. The other option is Borgen, which is located close to Norway. It has the largest population of wood elves in Europe and the book gives several detailed locations of them. It's also a shorter journey and easier to get to."

"Seems like an obvious choice," Ben said.

Natalie cringed. "There is a small catch: they have recently been conquered by King Suktar."

"Algete it is then," Charlie said. "I prefer the sun anyway."

"It's not that straightforward. Just because the dark elves occupy the country doesn't mean visitors are outlawed. The changes are mostly to do with politics. For most people life goes on pretty much as normal – except for the patrols that sometimes roam the streets."

Ben ruffled his hair in thought. "Which country would my parents have been more likely to go to?"

"I would say Borgen," Natalie said, with an apologetic smile at Charlie. "It's the obvious choice if you're looking for wood elves. Plus, your parents would have visited the country before the dark elves invaded, so that wouldn't have been an issue."

"Borgen it is then," Ben said, thumping his fist on the couch.

Charlie sighed. "I suppose one more insurmountable obstacle doesn't really matter to a mission that is already verging on impossible."

"That's the spirit." Ben grinned. "So, what now? Do we take that underground dragon train to Borgen?"

"The Dragonway, yes," Natalie said. "But first, there are a few things we need to get if we're going to last in Borgen."

"What things?"

Natalie cringed. "You're not going to like this."

— CHAPTER NINETEEN —

On the Run

"You're kidding."

Ben had repeated himself half a dozen times in the last minute. They'd checked out of their rooms and were standing outside the hotel in the late morning sun.

"Ben is right," Charlie said. "It's too risky. If he thinks your plan is dangerous then it must be suicidal."

"Would you both stop worrying? It's you they're after, Ben. As long as I go by myself I'll be fine."

"I'm not worried," Ben said, sounding a little insulted. "I'm simply telling you that going back to the Institute is mad."

"It will take me less than ten minutes to get in and out. There are a couple of things we need from the Institute that we can't get anywhere else."

Ben ruffled his hair. "I wanted to get straight on the Dragonway. Draven's cronies could be watching us right now."

His warning had Charlie glancing around nervously. Ben had already checked the area as soon as they'd left the hotel. There were a few people on the streets and the odd car or horse passed, but nobody paid them much attention. Occasionally something sped by overhead, clearly not interested in them. Yet the Institute knew they were staying at this hotel, so Ben was eager to get going.

"We won't survive in Borgen without certain equipment," Natalie said. "Don't worry about the Institute – we'll be fine as long as we stay in Taecia. It's leaving that will be a problem. The Dragonway will be guarded."

"How will we get past the guards?" Ben asked.

"I have an idea, but to make it work there are a few things we need to buy when I get back."

"Fine," Ben said, conceding defeat. "Where shall we meet?"

"The food court at Taecia Square," Natalie replied. "I'll be there in half an hour."

She gave them directions, which Ben ignored – Charlie was listening and he had a far better sense of direction. Then she waved goodbye and headed back to the Institute, leaving Ben and Charlie alone outside the hotel.

They set off in the opposite direction to Natalie. After less than five minutes they forked left, down the steep hill.

"Just the two of us again," Charlie said, stretching his arms in an act of freedom.

"Yeah."

"I wasn't expecting cartwheels of delight, but I thought you'd be slightly happier."

Ben peered into a pub they were passing. "I don't think we're as safe as Natalie thinks."

"Why? Have you seen something?"

"No."

"But?"

"It feels like we're being watched."

Charlie groaned. "Any chance your eerie sixth sense could be off for once?"

"It's possible."

As they continued on Ben began to think maybe he was just being paranoid. The more they distanced themselves from the Institute, the better he felt. They came to the bottom of the hill and Ben heard the roar from the Dragonway. The pavement began to get busy as they neared Taecia Square.

And then the Warden materialised on the corner of the street. Ben almost missed him. There was a split second of eye contact before he slipped away.

"Oh crap," Ben said calmly, not wanting to draw attention to himself.

"I hope that's a good 'oh crap'," Charlie said. "As in, 'oh crap, I just found twenty pounds in my pocket'."

"Not quite. It's 'oh crap, I just saw a Warden spying on us'."

Charlie ran a hand over his face. "Are you sure?"

Ben nodded. "It's the same guy who was watching us yesterday at Starbucks. Those lanky legs and pointy chin are hard to miss."

"What do you think he wants?"

"I don't know. Just try to act normal and don't look round."

Charlie immediately looked round, staring anxiously at everyone he could see.

"I said *don't* look round."

"Sorry. Where is he? I didn't see him."

"That's because he's hiding. Calm down and keep walking."

"What are we going to do?" Charlie asked, a note of despair in his voice. "If he spies on us he'll know exactly what we're up to."

Ben thought for a second and then smiled. "Let's lose him."

"Lose him? This isn't a Hollywood movie, Ben. We need to—"

Ben took a sudden right down a small alleyway, cutting off Charlie's protests and leaving behind the hustle and bustle of the main pavement.

"I'm not sure this is a good idea," Charlie said, breathing heavily. Ben had increased his pace and they were now speed walking. "In fact, I *know* it's not a good idea."

"Did you have a better one?"

"I did actually," Charlie said. "But it relied heavily on the Warden accidentally falling over and crippling himself."

"Brilliant. Why didn't I think of that?"

The alleyway split two ways and turned out to be the perfect place to make an escape. It was a little maze, with roads splitting off at all sorts of angles. Some roads doubled back, others were dead ends.

"Could we rest a second?" Charlie asked. They had been walking and running for the last five minutes and Charlie was panting. "We're not all future Olympic athletes. Have we lost him yet?"

They paused at the corner of a street and Ben peered round. Ten seconds passed and nobody came. Twenty. Forty.

Just as Ben was beginning to relax, the Warden appeared.

He was closer now and in full view, giving Ben the chance to take a proper look at him. Taller than Ben remembered, he had a really gangly stride and a chin that probably entered rooms a good second before the rest of his face. Ben's eyes went to the holstered Spellshooter and his stomach lurched.

"We need to keep moving," he said.

The Warden was proving particularly good at tracking them, considering he rarely had a line of sight. Ben grit his teeth and doubled his efforts. They jumped over walls, climbed through open windows, slipped in and out of houses and created false trails by doubling back.

"I can't take any more," Charlie panted, sagging against an old brick house. "You keep going, I'll risk the Warden. If he's still tailing us, he's some sort of tracking god."

Ben stared grimly down the narrow path. "He's still tailing us."

"That's not possible," Charlie gasped.

"Must be magic," Ben said. He grabbed a protesting Charlie and hauled him to his feet.

"I wasn't joking when I said I can't go on."

"Change of plan," Ben said, ignoring Charlie's protests. "This Warden could probably find us if we hid under a rock on planet Narg. Let's head back to Taecia Square. At least we'll be safe in the crowd."

"As long as we stop with the obstacle course. Lead on."

"Lead on? You're the one who got directions to Taecia Square."

"Yes, from the hotel, not the middle of nowhere."

"So we're lost?"

"Of course we're lost," Charlie said, exasperated. "Have you seen where you've been taking us? A skilled ranger with an iPhone and a pet bloodhound would be lost."

"Point taken," Ben said. He put an arm around Charlie's waist and half walked, half dragged his exhausted friend onwards. They had to keep moving.

The Spellshooter was now in the Warden's hand and he was getting closer, walking just that bit faster than them. Ben increased his pace despite Charlie's protests, but the Warden did the same and the gap kept narrowing. Even if they ran, the

Warden would probably be that bit quicker. Ben had a feeling they were being toyed with.

They were now taking every turning they came across so the Warden wouldn't get a clear shot. The roads were getting really narrow and Ben was concerned they would hit a dead end.

"I just thought of plan C," Ben said. He was now breathing hard as well; Charlie was not light. "We—"

He stopped. Voices! A distant murmur coming from somewhere ahead. The road split before them. Which way? No time to pause and debate.

"Left," Charlie said, in a voice that left no doubt that he too had heard the voices.

The noise became louder with every step. A different noise came from behind. Pounding footsteps.

The Warden was running right at them.

"Run!"

With a surge of energy fuelled by pure terror, Charlie let go of Ben and put in one last dash. Ben followed, hoping they ran into someone soon as Charlie was already slowing after his initial burst. The road forked again, but this time they were close enough that even Ben could hear which way to go.

He rounded the corner and ran headlong into a mob of people in some sort of marketplace. Stalls lined both sides of the street and the colourful scene dazzled his eyes just moments before the aroma hit him. Sweets. Chocolates. Ice cream. All shapes and sizes. There were boys and girls everywhere, eyes like saucers as they walked from stall to stall, and many followed by haggard parents. A large banner fluttered overhead reading "Taecia Sweet Market.

"Blend in," Ben said, tearing his eyes away from the stalls.

They walked until they were safely in the heart of the market. Ben scanned the crowd searching for the lanky Warden, but there was no sign of him. He took a deep breath and relaxed. Even if the Warden had entered the market, he would never try something in this crowd.

"Now what?" Charlie asked, eyeing up a strawberry tart.

"We need to get directions back to Taecia Square."

They started searching for a vendor who wasn't occupied; most of them were trying to serve half a dozen kids at once. Eventually Charlie spotted a stall selling multicoloured toffee apples that was momentarily empty.

Ben was so focused on getting to the idle apple vendor, he almost missed the Warden slinking behind the stalls. Ben stopped, slapping an arm out to halt Charlie.

"What was that for?" Charlie asked, rubbing his chest.

He didn't answer. It wasn't the Warden after all. This man was tall and well proportioned, not lanky like the Warden. He wore a hooded black cloak that concealed most of his face, but Ben could just make out gold flecks in his eyes.

It was Robert, Commander of the Institute.

"I don't see him," Charlie said, following the line of Ben's pointed finger.

"There!"

Most of the vendors seemed oblivious as the Commander passed behind their stalls. Those who spotted him did nothing more than casually shift aside.

"I see him!" Charlie said finally. "Wow, how did I miss someone that big?"

"I don't know. Let's follow him."

They continued down the centre of the market, almost parallel to the Commander. There were so many people around, it was easy to blend in.

"I wonder what he's doing here," Ben said.

"Maybe he's got a sweet tooth."

Unless Ben kept a good eye on the Commander, he lost sight of him easily. As Charlie led the way, Ben put a hand on his shoulder so he didn't have to worry about where he was going and could focus on their target.

"Sorry, my mistake!"

Charlie came to a halt and bent over to pick up a bag of sweets he must have knocked over. Ben was only distracted for a second, but it was enough. He lost sight of the Commander. He scanned the stalls, but there was no sign of him. It took him a moment to guess where the Commander must have gone.

There was a gap between the stalls ahead. Through that gap he could see a small, dilapidated shop. The sign above it read Irvine Rainwater Boks. There was a missing letter in the last word, which Ben assumed was supposed to spell "books".

The Commander must have walked inside. Ben thought he could detect a whiff of dust coming from the recently opened door.

"Not the most welcoming book shop, is it?" Charlie commented, as they looked over the store front. It was dull compared to the vibrant colours of the surrounding market. The books in the window had accumulated so much dust Ben couldn't read the titles and people passed the shop as if it didn't exist. Surely the Commander was the first customer the shop had seen in some time.

"I wonder what he's doing here," Charlie said.

"Well, he's in a book store. I know it's a long shot, but could he be looking at some books?"

"You know what I mean," Charlie said, with a roll of the eyes. "There must be a million books in the Institute library. Why come here? It probably has fewer books than my bedroom."

"Maybe he's not looking for a book. Maybe he's looking for someone."

Charlie followed Ben's gaze to the sign. "Who? This Irvine Rainwater bloke?"

"During the Executive Council meeting, the Commander asked Victoria, the Director of Scholars, if she knew where a colleague of hers might be. What if that person was Irvine Rainwater? If he runs a book shop he could easily be the scholarly type."

Charlie tapped his chin thoughtfully. "You could be right. But what does that prove, other than your detective prowess?"

"Nothing," admitted Ben. "But I don't think the Commander is as strange as Natalie claims. I wonder if he could help us."

"No way," Charlie said, shaking his head vigorously. "Remember what Natalie said? Even Wren thinks there is something odd with him. I know he looks normal enough, but you've only met him once. Wren knows him far better. I think we should trust her."

Charlie had a point, but Ben still wasn't convinced. He eyed the shop door. What did they have to lose by approaching the Commander? They might not get another chance. Ben recalled those strange eyes within the cloak. They had looked determined, thoughtful, not strange. But a peculiar doubt tugged at him and it took him several minutes before he could work out what it was. The Commander could remove that ridiculous declaration of treason on his parents with a click of his fingers. But he hadn't, which meant he was either clueless or thought Ben's parents were guilty. Neither scenario was good news. Yet, there was something about him Ben couldn't ignore. He held answers, Ben was certain of it.

He was still lost in thought when the Commander re-emerged from the shop and continued on his way.

What to do? He had to act *now*.

"Let's do it," Ben said. He grabbed Charlie's arm, anticipating the usual protest.

But Charlie wasn't there. He looked around desperately and saw him standing by a bright yellow market stall some twenty paces away.

"Charlie!" Ben said, waving at him furiously.

Charlie waved back enthusiastically, oblivious to Ben's urgency.

"Good news! These guys are heading to Taecia Square and they said we can follow them."

Ben cursed. The Commander was disappearing down the street. Ben considered running after him, but he didn't. He watched until he could no longer see the black cloak and then he turned reluctantly towards Charlie.

— CHAPTER TWENTY —
Taecia Square

They followed the family through the market back to the small, winding lanes. Ben was relieved to find a growing number of people taking the same route; that would deter the Warden. The main road kept getting wider until there was enough room to land a 747. A mighty arch came into view, towering above the buildings. On the front it read "Queen Elizabeth's Taecia". It reminded Ben of a holiday to Paris where he saw a triumphal arch.

As soon as they passed underneath, the pavement opened up to a square surrounded on all sides by timber-framed shops. In the middle was a throng of people, many walking with shopping bags, others basking in the sun or drinking coffee at one of the many outdoor cafés.

"I guess this is Taecia Square," Ben said, raising his voice above the hum of activity.

It looked like Oxford Street in London on a Saturday. Twice already he had been barged into with a subsequent apology.

"Natalie said to meet her at the food court," Charlie said.

They made their way to the tables in a corner of the square. Surrounding them were pastry shops and cafés, and the smell of bread and coffee filled the air. They sat down at one of the few empty tables. It was easy to relax amongst all the people, the delicious smells and the balmy weather, but Ben still kept an eye out for the Warden.

"Did we make it here within half an hour?"

"Incredibly – yes," Charlie said, after asking a stranger the time. "Natalie should be here soon."

Five minutes passed and Ben was starting to get concerned, when Charlie spotted her. She had changed into a jumper and jeans but didn't appear affected by the summer heat. On her arms were two jackets and over her shoulder was a backpack.

"Mission accomplished," Natalie said with a smile. "I got into a bit of trouble with the apprentice in charge who had a go at me for missing this morning's classes." She showed them the jackets. "But it was worth it for these."

"Did you notice anyone following you?" Ben asked, searching the crowd.

Natalie rolled her eyes. "Of course not. I told you, we're safe unless you try and leave Taecia."

"Tell that to the Warden who's been following us for the last half-hour."

Natalie gasped, her hand covering her mouth. "What happened? Are you okay?"

"Yeah—"

"Other than my lungs and legs, which won't recover until next week."

Ben recounted the last half-hour, omitting only the bit about almost approaching the Commander of the Institute. By the time he had finished, Natalie was also scanning the crowd, fiddling with her hair.

"I don't think I was followed," she said. "At least, I didn't notice anyone, but I wasn't paying that much attention."

"I think we're okay for now," Ben said.

Natalie joined them at the table. "I can't believe the Commander was out and about; he's normally so reclusive. I've only seen him half a dozen times and always inside the Institute."

"Have you heard of the book shop 'Irvine Rainwater'?" Charlie asked.

"I've never been to the shop, but I recognise the name."

Ben leant forward. "Who is he?"

"He used to be the Scholar Director at the Institute. When he got too old, they demoted him to a less stressful job teaching apprentices the history of the Institute. He's a history fanatic. He retired from the Institute last year. I didn't know he had set up his own book shop, but it makes sense. He was a super bookworm."

Ben tapped his fingers on the table. "I wonder why the Commander went to see Irvine Rainwater. It must have been important to go during the day if he's normally so reclusive."

"I really don't know," Natalie said. She didn't seem that interested either.

Charlie, however, was nodding and tapping his chin thoughtfully. "I bet it had something to do with the Institute's history."

"Not necessarily," Natalie said with a perfectly straight face. "Irvine Rainwater was also famous for making a superb cup of tea. Maybe the Commander was just craving a good cuppa."

Ben and Charlie opened their mouths, but no words came out.

"That was a joke," Natalie said. "Clearly not a very good one, though."

Charlie cleared his throat. "Actually it wasn't bad."

Natalie smiled and held out the jackets. "These are for you."

It was obvious Natalie's opinion of the Commander wasn't going to change. Ben was still convinced the Commander was a mystery worth solving, but since he was unlikely to get another chance at meeting him, it hardly mattered right now.

"Green isn't really my colour," Charlie said, looking at his jacket doubtfully.

Ben filed the conundrum away and looked over his own jacket. "Will they be warm enough? You said it was cold in Borgen and these look more like spring jackets."

Natalie smiled. "They have an all-weather enchantment."

"What does that mean?"

"Put them on and see."

Ben was already a little hot and the thought of wearing a jacket was distinctly unappealing. But the moment he slipped it on his entire upper body cooled down and he let out a sigh of relief.

"Pretty cool," Ben said, leaving his jacket on.

Natalie stood up. "There are a few other things we need to get, but those we have to buy. First, we need to draw out some money. Follow me."

Ben gave Charlie an apprehensive look at the mention of money, but Charlie was too busy staring at everything they passed to notice. So concerned was Ben, he didn't spot the familiar red sign until they were on the building's doorstep.

A flame came out of a white oval on a red background. The red signage was fit snugly above the door.

It was a Santander bank.

"I know I shouldn't be saying this after everything we've been through – but this cannot be possible," Charlie declared.

Ben silently agreed, but Natalie just smiled and pulled a Santander card from her pocket. It looked identical to the ones at home.

"You have to register the card with the bank to have it work here," she said, as if that explained everything.

Natalie approached something resembling a cash machine next to the bank's door. It had no keypad or buttons of any sort and instead of a display area, there was an empty black hole and an over-sized card slot, which Natalie placed her card into. A small hairy hand reached out from inside the machine and grabbed it.

"What was that?" Charlie asked in alarm.

"The cashier – watch."

A small figure materialised from the blackness of the display. He was chubby, with a well-kept ginger beard and ruddy cheeks. He sat on a stool wearing a crisp, black suit and red tie.

The cashier studied Natalie's card for a minute. When he found what he was looking for, he gave a little sigh and a curt nod.

"Good morning, Ms. Dyer," he said in a bored voice. "How can I help you?"

"Good morning. Could you tell me how much I have in my current account?"

"You have five hundred and twenty-eight pounds, forty-four pence," the cashier droned.

Natalie drummed her hand on the cash machine. "I would like to take out five hundred pounds please."

Ben could have sworn the cashier winced. His hands went into the blackness and drew out a small wad of cash, which he counted exactly into Natalie's hands.

"Anything else I can help you with?" the cashier asked, clearly hoping there wasn't.

"No, thank you."

"Would you be interested in joining our Super Saver?" Though the cashier spoke with civility, Ben could almost visualise him staring at his nails. "To qualify you need to deposit five hundred pounds a month."

Natalie declined and the cashier bid them goodbye, descending slowly back into the blackness.

"The richer you are, the nicer they act," Natalie said. "They treat Wren like a goddess when she draws out money. They are supposed to treat everyone equally, but it's difficult. Dwarves love money."

"Why don't they hire someone else?"

"Because dwarves are geniuses when it comes to arithmetic."

Ben couldn't help staring at the big wad of cash Natalie had drawn out. Five hundred pounds was way beyond anything he could get his hands on.

"Are we really going to spend all that money?"

"Yes, but don't worry," Natalie said, seeing Ben's concern. "I plan on getting it back from the Institute once this is all over."

"Does everyone use the English pound here?"

Natalie nodded. "Elizabeth introduced it in the sixteenth century when her armies first discovered the Unseen Kingdoms. Since then it has become the accepted currency."

"So, what are we buying?" Charlie asked, looking around eagerly.

"You'll see," Natalie said. "Follow me."

Ben didn't share Charlie's excitement for shopping because he was usually broke. Natalie led them past several familiar shops meshed in between others that were unique to Taecia.

"How do all these shops exist here?" Charlie asked. "It looks like half the retail industry knows about the Unseen Kingdoms."

"Not quite," Natalie replied. "The Department of Trade at the Institute is responsible for establishing relationships with high street shops. Only a handful of top executives from the shops will know about the Unseen Kingdoms."

Ben attempted to walk with his head turned so he could stare at the passing shop windows, trying to dodge the throngs using peripheral vision. It worked until he came upon a store that made both him and Charlie stop, causing a near pile-up.

Westminster Armoury was clearly a popular shop, attracting a great deal of attention from passers-by. It reminded Ben of a Ferrari store he once passed in London that cast a hypnotic spell upon every passing male. Ben and Charlie plastered their faces against the window while Natalie continued on her way, oblivious to the fact that she was now alone.

Nearly everyone was staring at the same thing – a shining silver breastplate, embossed with Queen Elizabeth's royal coat of arms. Below it was a sign that said, "Official replica approved by the Royal Institute of Magic: £9,999."

Ben stared in astonishment at the price tag, but that was apparently not much of a deterrent.

"...sold out in three hours I heard," an excited onlooker said, whose face was also plastered to the window.

"I've got an uncle whose sister's husband has a contact and apparently he's top of the waiting list."

"Does it make you invincible like the original?"

"Of course not. Anyway, the original didn't make Elizabeth invincible, that's just made up."

"Still, look at those enchantments it comes with. I'd feel invincible wearing that."

"For that money I'd rather buy a second-hand car or even a griffin."

Elizabeth's replica breastplate wasn't the only item on display; there were swords, shields, spears, crossbows and other weapons he'd never seen before.

"Ben, Charlie!"

Natalie picked her way through the crowd and dragged them both away. "I should have known you'd get hypnotised by that shop."

Ben was so busy trying to get a last look at the armoury he didn't see Natalie stop and bumped into her.

"Here we are," Natalie said after Ben had apologised.

Ben hadn't expected anything to top the armoury shop, but he was wrong – very wrong.

The shop signage extending from the wall was a wizard's hat, cast in silver with the letter "W" imprinted on it. There was no shop name Ben could see, but that wasn't affecting custom; there was a queue to get in.

"They pride themselves on service so they don't like it crowded inside," Natalie said. "Do you still have the Institute ID cards you used to get to Taecia?"

When they nodded she led them to the head of the queue to a man whom Ben strongly suspected was a half-giant guarding the entrance door. Natalie presented her Institute ID card, which the giant man peered at, then nodded and beckoned her enter. Ben and Charlie did likewise and they entered the shop, ignoring the envious stares of the waiting crowd.

"Perks of the job," Natalie said with a smile.

Ben didn't know where to look first. There were three rows of varnished oak tables that ran the length of the store. On top of the tables, mounted on small stands, were Spellshooters of every conceivable design. There were other items too – orbs, staffs, shimmering cloaks and many more objects Ben couldn't even identify.

"Who makes all this stuff?" Charlie asked, staring at the tables.

"They are manufactured by the Unseens, especially the elves. They package their magic and sell it to humans."

Ben noticed the majority of customers were men and women. "Sounds like good business for the Unseens."

Natalie nodded. "Even before Queen Elizabeth and her Institute arrived, the Unseens made good money dealing with humans within the Kingdoms. When Elizabeth arrived, business exploded."

"If you can buy magic, aren't the richest people the most powerful?" Charlie asked.

"Not necessarily. The best spells can only be cast by those with extraordinary willpower and concentration."

Ben was so glued to the items that it took him a moment to realise someone had walked up to them.

"Can I help you today?" a friendly voice asked.

The enquirer had pointed ears and shoulder-length, brown hair. He wore a tunic and breeches, with leather boots and a cloak. Everything was coloured in earthy greens and browns except for the small silver badge on his tunic, which read "Wizard".

There were dozens of such elves scattered around the store, assisting people, instructing them on an item or just standing there looking helpful.

"We're looking for spells," Natalie said.

"Second floor," the elf wizard said. "My colleagues upstairs will be happy to help you with any questions you have."

Natalie had to use physical force to pry Ben and Charlie away from the tables and up a spiral staircase located in the centre of the room.

The second floor consisted of rows of shelves so tall they touched the ceiling. Ladders were placed everywhere to help customers reach the upper levels. Each shelf was filled with glass containers and in them were spell pellets of every size and colour, creating a rainbow glow that permeated the room. Hanging from the ceiling above each shelf were signs like "Fire" and "Water/Earth", which Ben assumed indicated the elements of the spell.

"First, we need pouches," Natalie said.

"Pouches?" Ben said, exchanging a confused look with Charlie.

Natalie led them to a shelf filled with hundreds of different pouches of varying colours. She picked out a red one and started inspecting the stitch.

"What are these for?" Ben asked.

"To carry the spells," she said. "We are going to buy you and Charlie a few basic spells so you can protect yourselves."

Ben stared at the pouch. They looked a bit feminine for his taste. "We can cast spells with this?"

"Very basic ones. The spells are no way near as powerful as those fired from a Spellshooter, to say nothing of the range, since you are throwing instead of shooting. But they are still useful and it's very easy to learn."

Natalie picked up another pouch, this one green. "The trouble is there are so many pouches to choose from. Each one has different properties; some make spell casting easy but sacrifice the spell's power; others retain the full force of the spell but are difficult to use."

Natalie picked up another pouch; this one had a chequered pattern. As far as Ben could see, each of the pouches she had chosen cost about twenty pounds.

"These are the three contenders," Natalie said. She juggled the three in her hands and with a completely serious face said, "All of them come with the standard vanishing spell, so they disappear if anyone searches you. The problem is, I can't decide which fabric to go with. The red one has a nice feel, but I don't like the style, whereas this chequered one, while ugly, has a much nicer stitch. What do you think?"

Ben was about to tell her he couldn't care less, but thankfully Charlie stepped in.

"I think you should go with the chequered one," Charlie said, examining them carefully. "This red one looks like it will fall apart in a week."

Natalie nodded and smiled at Charlie. "We should go shopping more often," she said, putting the other pouches back and taking two chequered ones.

Ben was relieved when Natalie directed them away from the pouches back to the shelves full of coloured spell pellets. They headed towards an overhead sign that said "Fire/Air".

"These two elements are the best combination for spells that stun and paralyse. They also have some good basic attacking spells."

Each box on the shelf had a label of the spell, its strength, numbered from One to Five, and its elements. Ben cast his eyes over the spells and felt like dancing with childish delight. There were fireballs, air blasts, stun (both fire- and air-based), levitate, and dozens of others. The weakest spells (grade One) ranged from as little as five pounds up to twenty pounds. The grade Four spells were hundreds of pounds each and the grade Five ones were padlocked; they simply said "Price on application".

"We have about two hundred and fifty pounds left. We still need to get a few other things so let's try to spend less than a hundred pounds. Pick what you want, but don't take anything stronger than a Two as the chances of successfully casting it are too slim."

Ben rubbed his hands – he hadn't felt this excited since his tenth birthday when his parents took him to Toys R Us. First, he picked out everything that looked interesting, but before he knew it he had a dozen spells in his hands totalling more than three hundred pounds. He examined each one thoroughly and after much deliberation ended up with six of the finest spells he could afford.

"Are we ready?"

Natalie and Charlie were watching him impatiently. Charlie had his spells in his pouch.

"How did you go so quickly?"

"He didn't. You were just incredibly slow," Natalie said.

By the time they had paid, Ben's stomach was growling and he was pleased when their next stop took them to a bakery where they stocked up on sandwiches and bottles of water. Back on the street, they found a free table in the open seating area and sat down. Ben tore into his baguette and for a few minutes they were too busy chewing to do any talking.

"This seems like some trip," Charlie said eventually, having downed his food the fastest. "Will we be gone long?"

"I hope not, but I don't want to take any chances," Natalie replied.

"Aren't there any hotels or places to stay?"

"There are, but we can't afford them. Anyway, this food is for the forest. We might be in there for a while searching for the elves and there are certainly no hotels there."

Ben had never considered the ramifications of their journey and he was now doubly glad they had Natalie.

"So what's your plan for getting past the guards and onto the Dragonway?" Ben said.

"We will need to be invisible so we can get on unnoticed."

"Great idea," Ben said. "Will you use your Spellshooter to hide us?"

To his surprise, Natalie shook her head. "The only invisibility spell I have isn't strong enough to deceive the Wardens. Even if I had the right spell, I'm not competent enough to cast it."

"So what do we do?" Charlie asked.

"There are people who will cast the spell we need, for a fee. It's called 'Spell Service' and it's a big industry."

Ben didn't like the way her voice went soft as she spoke, as if she were scared of being overheard.

"Is there a catch?"

Natalie checked over her shoulder to make sure nobody was listening and leant across the table. "It's not the most respected business in the world. You don't always get what you pay for."

Ben had a vision of someone asking for super human strength and being turned into a baboon.

"Is there another option?" Charlie asked, massaging his forehead with concern.

"This is our best chance of evading the Wardens, unless you want to risk charging onto the train before they can stop us," Natalie replied.

With the crowd in the station to hide amongst, Ben would have given that option a go, but not with Charlie and Natalie. Thankfully, Charlie didn't seem keen on this option either, tapping his little belly subconsciously.

"What will the Wardens do if they catch us?" Charlie asked.

"Let's not worry about that," Natalie said.

Ben slapped his hand down on the table. "I agree. Let's go and get some spells cast. I want to get out of here."

— CHAPTER TWENTY-ONE —
Sognar's Spell Services

"Is that horse manure?" Charlie asked.

"Not just horse," Natalie said. "There are some disgusting animals around here."

"Just what I need after a big lunch," Charlie mumbled.

They had left Taecia Square some time ago and travelled east, keeping an eye out for anyone following them. The further they went, the worse the place became. The streets were narrow and felt cramped. Many of the houses were in disrepair, some with broken windows, others missing doors. The pavement had turned to dirt and Ben was constantly watching his step to avoid walking in crap. The people seemed to reflect their environment; they looked run-down and some eyed him suspiciously.

"Where are we?" Ben asked.

"It's called the East End," Natalie said. "We're almost there."

The road split and they took a right turn.

"Oh wow."

Ben raised a hand to block the glare. Every house was painted in bright colours. Many of them looked like a child had attempted his first work of art, doused in every colour of the rainbow. The vibrancy was in stark contrast to the dereliction they had walked through just moments before. Colour didn't seem to be the only subject of competition; size also seemed to matter, though not in the traditional sense. It was all about who could best defy gravity. The houses were misshapen, with extensions sprouting out at all angles. Ben saw one that resembled a mushroom, a sprawling upper level built on a tiny ground floor. Other houses sprouted upwards like a tree, constantly twisting and turning to catch the sunlight.

"Clearly they are in need of some decent architects here."

There were plenty of people about, but the more Ben looked, the more he realised the three of them stood out like a sore thumb. They were the only humans.

"Ben, look," Charlie said.

He was pointing at a dirty road sign, partially covered by green moss. The sign read "Goblin Avenue".

It was like stepping into a fairytale; there were goblins everywhere. It hadn't been immediately obvious because they wore normal clothes – shirts and trousers, some even in jeans. They had green skin, large ears and a pointy nose. Most of them were wiry and no taller than Ben's shoulder. Ben spotted a few carrying their shopping, with small goblin children running by their sides.

"I've always wanted to come here, but the Institute discourages it," Natalie said, staring in delight at the houses.

Ben masked his surprise; the old Natalie would never have dreamed of going against the Institute's wishes.

"Why do they discourage it?" Charlie asked.

"Goblins are great thieves. I know someone who came here during the winter markets. It wasn't until he felt the cold that he realised they had stolen everything but his underpants."

Charlie gave a furtive glance left and right and patted his pockets.

"Don't worry, they normally prey on individuals. As long as we stick together, we'll be fine. Follow me. It's not far from here."

They had been walking only a few minutes when Ben pointed at one of the more ordinary-looking houses. It was painted in red and green stripes, and there was a big wooden sign out front that read "Precious Spell Services Inc.".

"No, that one is too expensive," Natalie said.

They kept walking and Ben soon realised every second building, big or small, offered some form of spell services. Some specialised in a certain element (Blazing Spell Services, For all your fiery needs) while others were family run (Grynchek's High Quality Spell Services).

They passed several that looked promising, but Natalie kept walking. The shops were becoming less frequent, when Natalie finally stopped.

"You're joking," Charlie said, giving Natalie a disbelieving look.

Ben had to agree. They had passed some strange stores, but this topped the lot. It was a red circus tent complete with stakes in the ground and a flag at the top that read "Sognar's Spell Services".

"This one was recommended, which is important when you've heard as many stories as I have."

They approached the tent flap, but Natalie stopped just before they entered. There was an unmistakable look of excitement on her pretty face, which caught Ben by surprise. Was she actually enjoying herself?

"Goblins like to bargain," she said softly. "In fact, they love it and they tend to be quite good."

"I'll keep my mouth shut then. I'm hopeless at negotiating," Charlie said.

Ben said nothing, but there was a little smile on his lips as they pushed the flap aside and walked through.

He wasn't sure what to expect upon entering, but he had certainly not expected an office. There was a large desk in the centre piled high with papers and several empty bottles.

A goblin wearing a suit several sizes too big slept in a reclining leather chair, his feet up on the desk next to the empty bottles. He was snoring so loudly the tent walls rippled.

"It's not too late to sneak out," Charlie whispered, staring at the little goblin like he was rabid.

"Mr. Sognar," Natalie said in a firm voice.

The little goblin jumped, his backside getting a good few inches of air. The chair, already unbalanced, promptly fell backwards, but the goblin displayed remarkable dexterity in landing, rolling and jumping up in one smooth motion.

"I paid me bills! Whaddya want?" the goblin asked. His eyes had a dazed look and his voice was croaky with sleep.

Charlie took an involuntary step back and even Ben felt startled.

"We require your services, Mr. Sognar," Natalie said with a smile.

Sognar blinked and rubbed his bald, green head. He seemed to see the three of them for the first time and gave a little sigh of relief.

"Just a bad dream," he muttered. "Must cut down on the chocolate."

The goblin gave Natalie a salesman's welcome, flashing his uneven, yellow teeth.

"Certainly!" he said, surprising Ben with his sudden enthusiasm.

Sognar sat back down at the desk and attempted to tidy it up by sweeping folders and bottles onto the floor. There were no chairs for them to sit down on, but he beckoned them forward with a spidery finger.

"What can I help you with? I have a very good deal on grade Three Levitation this week — cheapest in Goblin Avenue, guaranteed."

"No, thank you," Natalie said. "We need a grade Three Shroud."

"A Shroud, eh?" Sognar said, rubbing his hands. "Not the easiest, nor the cheapest spell. Is this for all three of you?"

"Yes."

Sognar opened a drawer, pulled out a pencil and paper and started scribbling down some figures.

"I have some good news," the goblin said. "Ordinarily a grade Three Shroud retails at £149.99, but I can offer you a bulk discount and give it to you for £99.99."

Natalie was clearly a little taken aback by the price, but Charlie dug his hand into his pocket, a triumphant smile on his face. Charlie had money, Ben realised, and he was planning to come to Natalie's aid to make up the difference. Sognar had noticed it and he licked his lips, sensing the sale.

Ben cleared his throat and in a loud, clear voice said, "We'll give you £25, no more."

Sognar turned towards Ben, noticing him for the first time.

"£25? Are you trying to insult me?"

Charlie's hand froze in his pocket.

"You came recommended," Ben said, "and we would like to use you, but we have already had several offers below yours."

Sognar narrowed his eyes and Ben thought he saw a flicker of a smile. "£85," he said.

"Oh please," Ben replied, rolling his eyes theatrically. "Let's get out of here."

He turned to leave. Charlie followed, as did Natalie a moment later. They were almost at the tent flap when the goblin called to them.

"£65," he said, with the slightest trace of desperation in his voice. "You will not get a better offer than that."

Ben paused, counted to five and then turned around.

"I'll give you £40," he said. "Not a penny more."

Sognar's eyes were glittering. "£60," he said, leaning forward.

"£45."

"£50." Sognar was practically salivating.

Ben clapped his hands. "Done!"

Natalie produced the money and Sognar leapt off his chair to grab and count it, before pocketing it in one of his saggy jacket pockets. He was so eager Ben wondered if he should have held out longer.

Sognar rubbed his green hands together. "Good, good. Do you want the spell now? Remember, it will only last one hour."

"Yes, please," Natalie said.

Sognar took a deep breath and instructed them to stand together. His green eyes, which had been wild with glee moments earlier, suddenly focused on a spot on the floor. A green glow materialised and started swirling round him, accompanied by a faint humming noise. The glow intensified until it was difficult to see the goblin.

"Don't move," Natalie said, stopping Charlie from shuffling backwards.

The green glow expanded and Ben watched with a mixture of fascination and alarm as it enveloped them. Soon it was circling the whole room, slowly at first and then faster, with Sognar at the centre of the storm. The mist felt cold against Ben's skin. Streaks of green energy like forks of lightning flashed within the mist and some struck Ben, though he felt nothing. It became so intense Ben found it hard to keep his eyes open.

"Ben, look at you!"

Ben could just make out Charlie's astonished eyes through the swirling mist. He looked down and gasped.

A white glow was surrounding his body as if he were radioactive. Every time the sparks hit the glow they would sizzle. Before Ben could ask what was happening, there was a loud bang and the green mist receded into Sognar's open mouth, sucked up like a vacuum cleaner. As soon as the mist went, so did Ben's glow.

Sognar looked up panting slightly and gave Ben an accusing stare. "Why didn't you say other spells have already been cast on you?"

"I didn't think it mattered."

"It might have," Sognar said. "Goblin magic isn't too different to dark elf magic, you know."

Ben felt his pulse quicken. "What do you mean?"

"Your spell protects you from dark elf magic. It's strong – really strong – I thought it might reject my spell. Lucky for you we got away with it."

Ben spread his arms to examine himself. He didn't look or feel any different. For a moment he thought they had been cheated.

Then Natalie faded away.

Ben stared at the spot she had been in a moment earlier. He was still gaping when she faded back with a smile on her face.

"It's perfect," she said, giving Sognar a glittering smile.

"The spell will last an hour, starting from now. Remember to recommend Sognar's Spell Services to your friends and family," he said as they bid him goodbye and left the tent.

"Dark elf magic," Charlie said as they started back down Goblin Avenue. "That makes perfect sense! Your parents must have taken measures to protect you knowing the dark elves were a threat."

"Charlie's right," Natalie said, looking only marginally less excited than Charlie. "It explains why the dark elves never captured you after your parents disappeared. They may have tried but given up when their magic failed."

Ben nodded. "But is that because of the wood elves' spell or due to Elizabeth's legacy thing?"

The question stumped them and they eventually conceded that, without more information, it was impossible to know.

"So, how do we disappear?" Charlie asked.

"It's simple, just will yourself to disappear."

Charlie looked at her dubiously. He closed his eyes and scrunched his face in concentration. Just as Ben was beginning to doubt Charlie's method, he faded away. If Ben squinted he could just about make out a Charlie-like outline. He had blended with the background like a chameleon.

"That's brilliant," Charlie said, fading back in.

"Great. Let's hope it's enough," Ben said. He gave a determined stare down the street. "We've got an hour to get to the Dragonway, find the right platform and make the train without the Institute noticing. We should probably pick up the pace."

— CHAPTER TWENTY-TWO —
Fight and Flight

Ben paid little attention to the smelly and filthy surroundings during their journey back through Goblin Avenue to the Dragonway.

Armed with the shrouding spell, he felt quietly confident they could avoid the Wardens and make the train. Charlie, however, was not in such good shape. He kept rubbing his forehead and was so pre-occupied he had already stepped in several different types of poo without noticing.

In no time at all Natalie had guided them along Goblin Avenue, through the hustle and bustle of Taecia Square and within sight of the Dragonway station. Ben could hear the distant roars of the dragons as they embarked on their journeys.

"This is it," Natalie said as they stopped just short of the station's entrance. She took a deep breath. "Are we really doing this?"

"Of course we are," Ben said, rubbing his hands together, feeling a surge of adrenaline fuelled by anticipation.

"What is the plan?" Charlie asked. He was shuffling from foot to foot.

"Simple," Ben said. "We use the spell to shroud ourselves and make it to the train without bumping into anyone."

"Which train are we getting on?"

"Platform twelve. There is a direct train to Borgen that goes regularly," Natalie replied.

Charlie took his handkerchief out and dabbed his forehead. "If we are shrouded, how will we see each other once we make it to the train?"

"At the end of the platform is a set of chairs. Let's meet there," Natalie said.

Ben took his small pouch of spells from his pocket. "What about these bad boys? How do we use them?"

"In the same way you fired the Spellshooter," Natalie replied. "Once your hand is in the pouch you will feel each spell and should be able to pick out the one you want. Then it's just a matter of throwing it at your enemy with as much willpower and concentration as you can muster."

"Sounds easy enough," Ben said, pocketing the pouch again.

Natalie raised a finger and gave them a stern look that was mostly directed at Ben. "Do not use them unless it is an absolute emergency."

"Don't worry," Ben said, giving her a lopsided smile. "So, are we ready?"

Charlie shook his head, looking anxious. "Not really. How will we recognise Draven's Wardens?"

"Just try to avoid anyone who has a Spellshooter," Natalie said. "The station guards may also be on the lookout for Ben so watch out for them too."

"Wonderful," Charlie said.

Ben could see the nerves in Charlie's face. He clapped him round the shoulder. "Just think of this as an obstacle course like in gym class at school."

"I hate gym."

"I forgot about that," Ben admitted. "Okay, think of it like a video game. The train will take us to the next level."

"If we get caught, can I load the set-up screen and press restart?"

"You're not going to get caught," Natalie said. She put a hand on Charlie's shoulder, which seemed to help more than Ben's efforts. "Remember, it's Ben they are looking out for. Just walk normally and don't let anyone bump into you. You'll be at the platform before you know it."

Ben grinned at them. "Are we ready?"

Two nods. Both Natalie and Charlie suddenly faded away.

Ben willed himself to be invisible and felt his skin tingle. He watched his arm meld into the background until he could only see it by wiggling his fingers in front of his face. He gave a little sigh of relief; so Sognar had been right, the spell hadn't affected the shroud.

Ben headed towards the station entrance. Almost immediately someone bumped into him and looked about in surprise. Ben apologised by habit, which only caused further confusion, and quickly moved on. The station was busy, with people constantly coming and going and Ben had his work cut out dodging people. He tucked in behind a suited ogre and followed in his wake. To his left were the crossroads and the sign that had originally directed them to the Institute up the hill. It was hard to believe that was only yesterday.

The ogre he was following took a left up the hill and Ben was suddenly without a buffer to deflect the people ahead. He quickly found someone else and was soon walking under the large sign that said "Taecia Dragonway". He went up the stairs that led to the gangway and risked a glance at the station below. He counted twelve platforms, half of them occupied by squat dragons pulling carriages. One began to depart, breathing a mighty flame into the black tunnel so that for a second Ben could see the track's gradual descent as it headed underground.

He reached the top of the stairs and hugged the barrier to avoid people while he got his bearings. There were numbers at regular intervals hanging from the ceiling with stairs leading down to the corresponding platforms. Unfortunately, platform twelve was at the very end of the gangway.

There was a Warden holding a Spellshooter at the top of each set of stairs. They stood at ease, but Ben caught the keen looks they gave the passing passengers.

He cursed silently. It was time to put the shroud spell to the test. The gangway was narrow, causing congestion, which made avoiding people even harder.

He started walking. It felt like a dance game on the Nintendo Wii, dodging, side stepping and occasionally backtracking, to make sure nobody bumped into him. Ben risked a sidelong glance at the Warden as he approached the first platform stairs. There was no reaction; the Warden's gaze slid right by him. Ben allowed himself a moment's relief, before he continued to slip and slide down the gangway, until he reached platform twelve.

There was a dragon there already. Ben felt his heart flutter – it could be leaving any minute. He hurried down the stairs, risking a shoulder glance off a lady, and onto the platform. The dragon was blowing steam out of his nose onto the platform making visibility poor, which gave Ben an excuse to barge past people without his usual caution.

Near the front of the platform, adjacent to the first carriage, were three chairs currently occupied by elderly gentlemen.

The finish line.

Ben resisted the urge to make a final sprint. He walked cautiously to the chairs and stood directly behind the middle one, careful not to disturb the gentlemen seated.

"Guys?" he whispered. Nobody replied. He glanced left and right, but saw no shadowy outlines of Charlie or Natalie.

Ben wasn't surprised they hadn't arrived yet, as he'd made good time. He glanced up at the platform board.

Platform 12 Departures

Borgen 15 Minutes On time

Borgen 45 Minutes On time

Fifteen minutes was perfect, even Charlie should have no trouble making that. They had about forty minutes left of the shroud spell, which meant if they had to get the following train, they would do it without cover. With all the Wardens around that would be risky. Such a scenario wasn't worth thinking about because they would make this train.

Plenty of time.

Ben amused himself by watching the drivers seated in saddles on the dragon's nape. They were tucking into sandwiches and each had a hot drink balanced on his lap. Ben marvelled at the way they were able to talk and joke, ignoring the slow, rhythmic breathing of the dragon, seemingly unaware they were sitting on a beast that could cook and eat them in a heartbeat.

Ben's attention drifted back to the platform board.

Twelve minutes.

He started watching the stairs and the gangway, knowing it was a pointless exercise because Charlie and Natalie were shrouded; he wouldn't see them until they were by his side.

Ten minutes.

Ben whispered their names again just to make sure they weren't nearby. It had taken him about ten minutes to make the journey; they had now been fifteen minutes. There was nothing to panic about, nevertheless, he started making regular glances up at the platform board.

Eight minutes.

The men in the chairs stood up and boarded the train.

Ben squeezed the back of the chair. Why hadn't they discussed a contingency plan in case one of them didn't make it? Ben had assumed everything would be plain sailing.

Seven minutes.

Ben heard the soft sound of footsteps and he turned his head so fast his neck cracked. He sighed with relief when he saw a familiar curvy shadow standing by his side.

"Natalie, thank god. I was starting to get concerned. Did you stop off for coffee or something?"

Without warning, Natalie released the shroud spell and materialised before his eyes.

"What are you doing?" Ben asked in an urgent voice. "There are Wardens all over the place. There are still several minutes before the train leaves and Charlie has not..."

His voice trailed away.

Natalie's eyes were wet. There was a tear running down her cheek.

"It's over, Ben," she said, her voice a whisper. "I'm so sorry."

Ben felt his mouth go dry. "What are you talking about?"

"They caught us. They had a Warden who could see through our shrouds."

"I don't understand. I'm here. You're here."

"They let you go. Draven's orders. They caught Charlie and me. I was sent over here to retrieve you."

Ben didn't want to believe it. "Why would Draven let me go?"

Natalie wiped the mascara running down her face. "He thinks you won't leave without Charlie."

Ben closed his eyes as the pain of acceptance hit him. Deep down he knew it had been too easy. He bit his lip until it hurt. They should have come up with a different plan. But what? There was no other way to board the train.

He looked up at the gangway, but saw nothing unusual, just the usual hustle and bustle.

"They are on platform six, not up there," Natalie said.

Ben cursed loud and long. Several people turned around in disgust and confusion when they only saw a tearful Natalie.

Ben ran a hand through his hair and glanced once more at the platform board.

Three minutes.

"What will they do with Charlie if we get on the train?"

"I really don't know," Natalie said. She took a deep breath and composed herself. "I know this will sound completely awful, but the sensible thing to do would be for us to jump on the train without him."

"You're right," Ben said, staring across the platforms, searching for Charlie and his captors. "The sensible thing would be to get on the train."

"But you're not going to," Natalie said, the resignation in her voice contrasting with the admiring look she gave him. "Draven was right."

Ben couldn't bring himself to get on the train, no matter the cost. He wouldn't abandon Charlie.

"What are you going to do?" Natalie asked.

"I'm going to rescue him."

"Are you mad?" Natalie asked, shock washing away her despair. "If you think you have any chance of springing Charlie from the Wardens and making off with him, you're in fantasy land."

Ben glanced at her, his face serious. "What about your speech to trust each other? It works both ways, you know."

"It's not a matter of trust," Natalie said through gritted teeth. She looked ready to lay into him, but stopped and took a deep, calming breath. "You're right. I asked you to trust me, so I should do the same. I just hope Charlie is up to escaping."

Ben turned to her in surprise. "What do you mean?"

"He was sobbing. He was trying to hide it from me, but I could hear him. I think this is all too much for him."

Charlie was crying? Ben's eyes resumed their fruitless searching with greater urgency.

"You won't see them," Natalie said. "Platform six is—"

A sudden noise came from the gangway. Voices cried out in surprise and anger.

Ben saw movement. Rapid movement.

There was a flash of light and a loud bang; more voices, these ones louder, edged with fear.

Charlie came belting down the stairs like the devil himself was on his tail.

He was halfway down when four Wardens appeared at the top, Spellshooters in hand. They hadn't Charlie's low centre of gravity, but they made up for it with long strides, taking three steps at a time, shouting at Charlie to stop. They took aim, but Charlie seemed to sense it and he blended into the stairs. A white bullet whizzed by the space where his head had been.

Ben heard a thump and assumed it was Charlie leaping the final few stairs onto the platform. A second later Charlie released the shrouding spell and re-appeared, screaming at the top of his voice for people to get out the way.

Natalie's face was pale, her hand covering her mouth. "I don't believe it," she whispered.

Ben glanced again at the platform board.

One minute.

"All aboard!" a voice shouted.

The sound of doors shutting filled the air.

Ben stepped forward, waving encouragement. "Come on, Charlie, run!" he shouted.

Charlie was pumping his arms like a man possessed. Ben could see the fear and exhilaration in his eyes.

"The train!" Natalie cried.

The dragon roared, blowing smoke and fire, signalling its departure. The Wardens were closing fast, their Spellshooters trained on Charlie's back. Ben knew with sickening certainty Charlie wasn't going to make it.

"Hold the door open," Ben shouted over the cacophony to Natalie.

He stepped forward, his hand going to the pouch in his pocket. Natalie screamed at him, but he ignored her. As soon as his fingers made contact with the pouch he saw the spells in his mind's eye. They seemed dull compared to the vibrancy of those in Natalie's Spellshooter, but it made them easier to control. He focused on a white one and it came to his fingers.

Ben threw the small pellet with everything he had at the nearest Warden, hitting him full in the chest. The spell ignited, creating a hammer blast of air that lifted the Warden off his feet. He collided with the Warden behind him and they both went down in a heap.

Ben's elation was short lived. A terrible creaking noise came from the carriage's wheels.

The train was departing.

"Ben, hurry!" Natalie said. She was holding a door open, walking alongside the train. It was moving down the track, slowly picking up speed.

From the corner of his eye Ben saw a flash of red. He dived to the ground and a ball of flame sailed over his head, singeing his hair. He was still cloaked by the shroud, but throwing his own spells was giving away his position. Ben rose smoothly and launched another pellet with venom. It hit the third Warden on the arm and he clutched it in agony, halting his charge.

Ben released the shrouding spell the moment Charlie reached him collapsing onto the platform in exhaustion.

The final Warden, seeing Ben's sudden appearance, had stopped running. He was taking careful aim with his Spellshooter.

Ben hauled Charlie to his feet and turned back to the train. He let out a cry of despair. The train was moving too fast and was about to enter the tunnel. There was no way Charlie, already exhausted, could catch it. Natalie had gotten on board, unable to keep pace from the outside. She was leaning out of the open door, her Spellshooter aimed at the Warden behind them. She was screaming something, but Ben couldn't hear her over the sound of the train.

Natalie fired.

The Warden fired.

Ben knew instantly that Natalie had got her spell horribly wrong. It was heading right at them instead of the Warden. Ben had no chance of dodging both spells, one from either direction.

The Warden's spell was a glowing red boomerang that came soaring at him in an arc. Natalie's spell was a thin silvery rope, darting towards him like a snake.

A rope.

Ben grabbed Charlie by the waist and dove into Natalie's spell, narrowly avoiding the Warden's boomerang in the process.

The silver rope hit Ben in the chest and looped around him. It yanked him so hard he fell and nearly lost hold of Charlie. Ben flew forwards with such pace the platform around him blurred.

They soared into the open door and landed in a crumpled heap on top of each other inside the train. The door closed behind them with a click and the train disappeared into the tunnel.

— CHAPTER TWENTY-THREE —
Ratlings

"Ow, that's my arm."

"This is awkward, sorry," Ben said.

He untangled his limbs from Charlie's and sat down. They were getting odd looks from the passengers, but thankfully the train was half empty.

Charlie clambered onto a seat just as the conductor's voice came echoing through the carriage.

"Ladies and gentlemen, please brace yourselves."

The bar fastened to the back of the seat in front slid forward until it pressed down gently on their laps.

Charlie barely had time to grab the bar before the train took off like a rocket. The wind whistled in their ears and the carriage jumped as its wheels left the track. The popping sound came just as the train grazed the top of the tunnel, blocking out the wind and steadying their ride.

Once the train had settled down, Ben and Natalie turned their attention to Charlie.

"I saw you sobbing," Natalie said slowly. She was staring at Charlie with a mixture of confusion and disbelief.

"Ah, yes, my sobbing," Charlie said with a proud smile. "As Ben can testify from school, drama class is one of the few artistic subjects I'm good at."

"He was excellent in *Great Expectations* last year," Ben said, nodding.

"But why put on such an act?"

"Did you see the way the guards stopped watching me?" Charlie said, his expression turning serious. "Who is going to suspect a sobbing, fat little boy of attempting an escape?"

Natalie shook her head; it wasn't sinking in.

"Brilliant," Ben said with a grin, giving Charlie a pat on the shoulder. "Utter genius. So how did you escape?"

"It was all about timing. I waited for the right moment when the fewest number of Wardens were facing me. An old lady dropped her purse, distracting a couple of them; that's when I ran. I must have been twenty yards away before anyone noticed."

"And then what?"

"They wasted a few seconds thinking I would stop if they ordered me to come back," Charlie said. "I turned round and threw one of the spells from my pouch; it created a mist, which gave me a few more seconds. Then I ran for my life."

Natalie was curling a lock around her finger, unable to take her eyes off Charlie. She was looking at him as if she'd never seen him before.

Charlie seemed to relish the attention; his cheeks were a rosy red and there was a smile on his lips that wouldn't go away. Ben's good mood faded a little as he stared into the blackness of the tunnel. "I don't think we'll be too welcome back in the Institute."

"We will be okay with Wren," Natalie said, a steely determination in her voice.

"But not without her," Charlie said.

Natalie didn't argue.

Ben couldn't help marvelling again at the change in Natalie since she had guessed his plan to find the wood elves. Just a few hours ago he thought her dedication to the Institute unwavering; yet here she was escaping with them. More importantly, she had trusted him despite his crazy intention to rescue Charlie. Ben wouldn't forget that.

The journey to Borgen was about two hours, according to Natalie, so they tried to relax. Ben closed his eyes, figuring it would be a good idea to rest while they could.

It seemed like minutes later when he felt a nudge from Natalie. The train was ascending slowly towards sunlight spilling in at the end of the tunnel. He felt a cold breeze on his face, but his enchanted jacket absorbed the chill.

"Remember, be on your guard," Natalie said. "There are dark elves on patrol. They have no reason to stop us—"

"Unless they have been told to look out for Ben—"

"They won't have," Natalie said, giving Charlie a look.

"Charlie's got a point. Will the Institute try and re-capture me before Elessar works out I've disappeared? Or will they let the dark elves loose on me?"

"Either way, the next train from Taecia doesn't arrive for half an hour, which means we have a bit of time before anyone here knows we escaped. So let's try not to worry about it," Natalie said.

It took a second for Ben's eyes to adjust to the sunlight as they exited the tunnel. The air was incredibly fresh and he took several deep breaths, soaking in their new surroundings. Everything was made of timber, from the platforms to the small gangway and even the houses beyond. Everything appeared remarkably vibrant, as if the trees hadn't died when they had been turned into timber.

In the distance, Ben could make out vast, rolling hills covered with pine trees. The station was smaller than Taecia; Ben counted just four platforms, but the structure was similar.

As they pulled into the station Ben searched for any sign of the purple-uniformed dark elves. He didn't see any, but he did notice something just as striking.

"The Borgen natives are half-elves," Natalie said, seeing Ben and Charlie's looks.

They all had pointed ears and flowing hair, but it was so subtle he only noticed it because of its prevalence. With a hat on they could walk through London without a second glance.

"Where are we going?" Ben asked as the doors opened and they filed off the train. He couldn't help noticing how far away the forests were. Suddenly, the food in their backpack seemed meagre.

"Follow me," Natalie said.

They walked up the gangway and exited the station, spilling out into the town. The pavement was made of wood inlaid with intricate patterns of flowers and leaves. The road was also constructed from a darker wood, with planks so large he could only wonder at the size of the trees they came from. There were no cars but plenty of horse-drawn carriages. Quaint wooden cabins lined the street, reminding Ben of his only ski holiday with his parents.

"It's not far from here," Natalie said as they started down the street.

"What isn't far?"

"Taxis. They are the best way to travel around."

Ben and Charlie exchanged glances. Given their limited budget it seemed like an expensive way to get to the distant forests.

They hadn't gone far when Ben noticed an oddity amongst the residents. They seemed pre-occupied, with a distant, troubled look on their faces.

"They've recently been conquered. Their country is no longer their own. It must be hard for them," Natalie said.

Was that why Ben was feeling uneasy? Was he just feeling their pain? No. It was something else. He had felt on edge the moment they stepped off the train.

"Something isn't right," Ben said. He spoke calmly, in contrast to the way he was starting to feel.

"You're being paranoid. Everything is fine," Natalie said.

Charlie, however, started checking over his shoulder. "What should we do?" he asked.

"Charlie, don't let Ben spook you."

Charlie shook his head. "You don't understand. Ben has a Spiderman sixth sense that borders on scary."

Natalie wasn't convinced, but Ben did see her take one or two furtive glances behind as they walked.

"How much further?" Ben asked.

Natalie pulled a small book from her jeans. "Not more than five minutes. We need to take the second right."

The streets were like grids with regular perpendicular intersections. They came to their first such junction and Ben stared down the street they crossed.

A unit of soldiers was being led by a purple-cloaked dark elf.

Any chance of remaining inconspicuous was ruined by Charlie, who gave such a start – only a swift hand from Ben prevented him from stumbling.

"What on earth are they?" Charlie said.

It was obvious he was referring to the soldiers. They looked like huge, walking rats dressed in rags, which partially concealed their fur. They held spears in their claw-like hands and walked hunched forward. Their long noses were constantly twitching as they sniffed the air.

Ben dropped his gaze, hoping they hadn't noticed him.

"Ratlings," Natalie whispered. "They used to have their own little empire before Suktar conquered them. Disgusting things; you can smell them from here."

"That's them? I thought it was a sewage problem."

"Just keep walking. I told you they have patrols around. It's nothing to worry about."

"Nothing to worry about?" Charlie said in a faint voice. "There are a dozen mutated rat-men behind us. I hate rats."

"Stop panicking," Natalie said. "They're not following us."

Charlie was trying very hard not to look back. "Why rats? What's wrong with rabbits or cats? Catlings – I could handle those."

The ratlings, led by the dark elf, would be approaching the junction any moment now. Ben glanced back.

"Damn. They turned towards us."

"We're in trouble," Charlie moaned.

"It doesn't mean anything," Natalie insisted. "They just happen to be marching down this street."

Nevertheless, Ben was relieved when he reached the next intersection and the three of them took a right. The road was narrower here and Ben noticed few people were about.

"Third road on the left and we're there," Natalie said.

Ben was glancing back every ten seconds. Less than a minute passed when his eyes widened. "They've turned down this road."

Unable to take the tension, Charlie looked for himself. "Is it me or are they closer than before?"

"They're closer," Ben said.

The ratlings were less than fifty yards behind. They weren't actively chasing, but their steady march seemed to have picked up.

"Let's walk faster."

Were they being followed? Had the dark elf leading the ratlings somehow recognised him?

"If we split up, head to the train station and get back home," Ben said.

"Home?"

"I saw trains running to Croydon and London. It's the safest place for now."

"We are not splitting up," Natalie said.

"Not intentionally, but after what happened at the station in Taecia we need a back-up plan."

He wouldn't be returning home if they split up, but Ben kept that quiet.

"We don't need a back-up plan, we are almost here," Natalie said. "The taxi station is just round this corner."

Ben wondered what the taxi station would look like. He was prepared for cars, horses or even something more exotic.

He got dark elves and ratlings. Lots of them.

— CHAPTER TWENTY-FOUR —
Taxi Chase

The ratlings formed a blockade along the road. In front of them were three dark elves, but it was the one in the middle who made Ben's stomach churn. His glowing purple eyes and sunken face were unmistakable.

The taxi station, a stone's throw away, was agonisingly out of reach.

"Perfect timing. I was beginning to get impatient," Elessar said.

Ben was speechless and not just from fear. How could *he* possibly be here?

"You didn't really think the Institute was the only one watching you?" Elessar asked. There was no smile, no humour in his demeanour, and Ben could sense satisfaction reeking from the elf.

"How did you get here so fast?" Ben asked, finding his voice. He didn't expect Elessar to answer, but he needed to buy time to get his sluggish mind into gear.

"We have quicker methods of travelling than the Dragonway. I was notified as soon as you boarded the train. You are looking for wood elves, I assume?"

Ben didn't answer, but clearly Charlie's or Natalie's expression gave the game away.

"I expected you to travel here as soon as you discovered the spell they have on you. I am glad you managed to escape the Institute's clutches. They cannot meddle with us here."

Elessar looked calm and relaxed. He assumed the chase was over, Ben realised.

"What is Elizabeth's legacy?"

The question came out as a squeak from Charlie. Ben wasn't sure if he was trying to help stall Elessar or if he was just curious. Either way, Elessar smiled at the question, giving them a few more valuable seconds.

"Ah yes, her legacy. Queen Elizabeth's desperate attempt to leave something that could overthrow my king. A pity for you it lies in the hands of two people too cowardly to use it."

Charlie was so engrossed in the revelation that he appeared completely oblivious to his peril. "Is that why you are after Ben's parents? Because they have this 'legacy' thing?"

"They won't have it much longer, once I have found them. And Ben is going to help me do just that."

"I don't know where they are," Ben said, hiding his dismay with a display of defiance.

"Oh, I know that. But I have a feeling your parents know where *you* are. You will be the bait that brings them to us."

"They won't fall for that."

"I think they will. Especially if they know their poor son is to be executed forty-eight hours from now at dusk."

Ben felt a rush of fear run down his spine, but he kept his cool. His mind was working quickly. He had to get out of here. The taxi station was just ahead, but it would take a miracle to get past Elessar, two dark elves and twenty ratlings. Their only chance of escape was back the way they had come, but the patrol behind them would arrive any moment now.

He needed a distraction – a big distraction.

Ben reached for his pouch, but even as he did so Elessar turned to the well-built elf next to him.

"Take them to the Floating Prison."

The dark elf extended both hands, palms outward. They started to pulse with a purple glow.

"Run!" Ben shouted.

Charlie reacted first, Natalie a fraction later. Neither were quick enough. Three purple beams lanced out. Ben flung his arms in front of Charlie and Natalie in desperation.

A crescent shield materialised, encasing all three of them. The purple beams ricocheted off it and split into dozens of small streaks of light, which rebounded back at the enemy.

The ratlings squealed, many of them falling to the ground. The dark elves, who were at the front, took the brunt of the impact. One went down, but the other two, including Elessar, shielded themselves with a flick of the hand.

In that brief moment of chaos, Ben saw the shock and surprise on Elessar's face. He was distracted. The remaining ratlings were looking around in a stupor. Without the dark elves to command them they looked lost. Ben heard the patrol arrive behind them, but they too were stunned by the scene.

Ben drew the last remaining pellet from his pouch and threw it on the ground in front of him. Blue fog burst from the pellet and within moments he was coughing and choking, barely able to see his hand in front of his face.

"Come on!" Ben said.

Without waiting to see if Charlie and Natalie had heard him, Ben leapt forward blindly, skipping over and treading on fallen ratlings. A claw tried to grab his jacket, but he yanked free. In a flash he was through the fog and the barricade and running full throttle to the taxi station.

With his heart pumping, legs pounding and adrenaline flowing, Ben wasn't able to appreciate the station. There was a line of small carriages, each pulled by a variety of winged animals. Many of the taxi drivers were standing by the road, watching their escape in astonishment. Ben could have sworn one or two of them were even urging them on. He risked a glance over his shoulder. Natalie and Charlie were close behind, but hard on their heels were at least a dozen ratlings, snarling and sniffing in pursuit.

The taxi at the front was a two-wheeled cart pulled by a winged horse on which the driver sat. Ben threw himself into the cart, quickly followed by two bumps as Charlie and Natalie followed suit.

"National Forest, please, south entrance," Natalie said, somehow sounding calm despite her exhaustion and panic.

"Right you are, ma'am," the driver said in an accent that sounded strangely familiar.

He tugged on the reins and kicked his heels. The horse responded by lurching forward and extending its wings, but the ratlings were in full flow and closing the gap at an alarming rate.

Spears hurtled towards them and Ben ducked as they whizzed by. One ratling gave an almighty leap and managed to cling onto the cart. Ben rammed his elbow hard into its claw and the ratling let go with a cry of pain. Even as he fell, two more took his place. Ben, Charlie and Natalie started hammering at the claws frantically, but there were too many. On Ben's left a ratling had gained purchase and was crawling its way up. The smell from its snarling mouth almost knocked Ben out.

"We need to take off!" Ben shouted.

The driver urged the horse on and its wings started flapping.

A claw grabbed Ben's chest and he fell forward. Charlie grabbed him, but the ratling was strong and Charlie was slowly losing the tug of war.

A flash of blue hit the ratling and it fell off the cart with a howl.

Natalie had managed to stand up and was firing her Spellshooter like someone possessed. Her hair was flung back and there was a wild, frenzied look in her green eyes.

The ratlings fell back. The carriage angled up and with a jerk it left the ground.

A ball of purple fire came at them from nowhere. Ben heard the flame ripping through the air moments before it cannoned into the back of the cart.

The cart rocked and Ben and Charlie held on for dear life. Natalie cried in alarm, arms flailing as she sought to keep her balance. Everything seemed to happen in slow motion. Ben reached forward but missed Natalie's outstretched hand by inches. She fell backwards and, with a look of pure horror, disappeared off the side.

She hit the ground a short distance below and the ratlings swarmed over her.

"Turn around!" Ben shouted, spinning to the driver.

"Can't do that, mate," was the gruff response.

Ben watched in anguish as Elessar swept the ratlings aside and hauled Natalie to her feet. She was struggling madly, but at least she was alive. The cart was gaining altitude quickly and the scene below became smaller with every second.

Ben collapsed back on the seat, breathing raggedly.

"They're coming after us," Charlie said, peering over the edge of the cart.

The ratlings had commandeered a couple of taxis and taken to the skies in pursuit. Ben only saw one dark elf on board; Elessar and the other elf remained behind with Natalie. Ben watched them desperately until they were just specks below.

His concern for Natalie was put on hold the moment he saw the chasing taxis. The ratlings were closing in.

"Excuse me," he called to the driver. "Can we go faster?"

"Don't worry, mate," the driver said, peering behind at the chasing taxis. "Those stinkin' ratlings won't catch us. More than my job's worth if they do."

Ben stared at the driver in astonishment. He wasn't a half-elf at all – he was a Londoner. He wore jeans and a puffy jacket adorned with the England football team crest.

Their cart accelerated away from the taxis.

Ben relaxed a little. The wind buffeted his face, but his jacket countered the cold so well he almost felt toasty. The buildings below looked like models and the people nothing more than Lego men. It wasn't long before the town gave way to a rolling carpet of green hills.

Charlie took out his handkerchief and wiped his brow. He was breathing raggedly and his face was flushed.

"Oh god, this is a disaster," he said. "I don't know who's in greater trouble – Natalie in the hands of Elessar or us, heading towards some god-forsaken forest without the faintest clue what we're doing."

"I would say her," Ben said.

"What do we do now?" Charlie continued, appearing not to have heard Ben. "We can't leave Natalie, but we have no idea how to rescue her. We still need to find the wood elves, but without her what chance do we have?"

"You're blabbering, Charlie."

"With good reason! If this cart disappeared and we started plummeting to our deaths, we'd be in less trouble than we are now."

"I think you're over-stating things a bit."

Charlie wiped his brow again and took a deep breath. "I'm sorry. Do you have a plan? I'd take anything right now."

"First, you need to calm down," Ben said. It had been a while since Charlie had been this upset. "Let's talk about Natalie first. Elessar has already told us where she's going – the Floating Prison."

"But where's that?"

"No idea, but I'm hoping the wood elves will know."

Charlie nodded and finally composed himself. "Elessar wanted to use you as bait for your parents. Attempting to rescue Natalie will play right into his hands."

"I know, but we don't have much of a choice," Ben said.

Charlie didn't argue and there was a grim determination on his chubby face. They had only known Natalie for a couple of days but suddenly it seemed a lot longer.

"At least we know why Elessar is after your parents. Elizabeth's legacy is something your parents have. Apparently it has the power to stop Suktar, which is why the dark elves want it."

"So it turns out the dark elves aren't after my parents at all. They're after something they have."

"Exactly," Charlie said, slapping his thigh.

Ben found it hard to share Charlie's elation; he was thinking about the rest of Elessar's revelation.

"Whatever this thing is, Elessar said my parents were too cowardly to use it. Does that mean they have the power to stop King Suktar, but won't use it?"

"No," Charlie said. "What is odd is how your parents came to have such an item."

"Maybe they stole it."

The words were spoken softly. The thought gave Ben the chills, but it was starting to make sense. What if his parents had a criminal record because they stole this thing from the Institute?

"No." Charlie was shaking his head, his voice firm. "We can't jump to conclusions."

But Ben couldn't stop thinking about his parents. All this time he had never doubted their reason for disappearing, but now he felt a glimmer of uncertainty. He took a deep breath and managed to put aside his doubts; thankfully, there were plenty of other things to occupy his thoughts.

"Something still doesn't fit," Ben said. "Why did that dark elf kid mention Elizabeth's legacy when I deflected his spell?"

"Good point," Charlie said. He tapped his chin thoughtfully, but had no suitable reply.

The great forest slowly began to dominate their view; even from a distance the trees were an impressive and intimidating sight, tall and proud. They spanned the horizon as far as the eye could see.

With the revelation of Elizabeth's legacy, Ben had almost forgotten about their pursuers, but it all came rushing back the moment he heard the whooshing sound from behind. A purple flare sailed towards them, falling short of their cart. Ben saw three taxis in pursuit, each filled with a handful of ratlings and the single dark elf firing the spells.

"They are measuring the distance," Charlie said, with a mixture of anxiety and fascination. He stared into the space where the flare had fallen. "That one was twenty yards short."

"Can we go any faster?" Ben asked.

"We're flat out, mate," the driver said. "Unfortunately, we only have one pegasus pulling, your pursuers have two."

The flares continued to fire at the cart every few minutes, with Charlie shouting out distances.

"Fifteen yards."

It was like being in a 3D movie. The purple bolt started off as a speck in the distance and slowly grew larger as it approached, before falling away.

"Ten yards."

Ben was beginning to feel the heat from the flares.

"Five yards." Charlie's voice had gone up an octave. Ben could almost reach out and touch the purple sparks.

The driver cracked his whip. "We're almost at the forest."

A bolt zipped by the left wheel.

A sickening thought hit Ben. "Even if we make it to the forest unscathed, we will soon have lots of those annoying ratlings plus a few dark elves on our tail. Are you ready for more running?"

"No," Charlie said immediately. "Not even if my life depended on it."

"Which it does."

"Still no."

To Ben's surprise, the driver spoke up. "You won't need to worry about them once you hit the forest."

"What do you mean?" Charlie asked.

They reached the forest as he spoke. What Ben could see between the branches looked dark and uninviting.

"Watch," the driver said.

The pursuers fired again, but they had clearly slowed down and the bolt got nowhere near them. Suddenly they turned and veered away.

"They are afraid of the forest," the driver said, flashing a toothy grin at them.

Charlie raised an eyebrow. "If they are scared, shouldn't we be scared too?"

"Frankly – yes."

They started descending and, just as it seemed they would land on the tree tops, they entered a large circular clearing. It looked like an abandoned picnic site. The grass was overgrown and there were several upended wooden tables and benches scattered haphazardly. Ben spotted a large sign and a semblance of a path leading into the forest.

The driver landed with a bump near the centre of the clearing. They stepped out and Ben groaned with pleasure at the chance to stretch his legs.

"How much do we owe you?" Charlie asked.

"It's normally fifty pounds, but I'll give you a discount for giving me the chance to tick off those dark elves. Let's call it forty."

Charlie gave him the money. He thanked him and handed Charlie a small spell pellet.

"Just fire that, and I'll come and pick you up; only from here, mind. I won't go into the forest."

Ben watched him fly away, until it was just the two of them alone in the clearing, surrounded by the forest.

— CHAPTER TWENTY-FIVE —
Follow the Light

"Not the most welcoming of signs, is it?" Charlie said.

They were at the point the path started into the forest.

"South Trail # 1

"Danger: Do not proceed beyond this point."

It was clear nobody had been here in a while. The forest had almost consumed the path with grass and shrubbery.

"Where did the library book say the elves had been spotted?" Ben asked.

"Most of the sightings occurred four miles down this trail."

"Well, we'd better get going then," Ben said, rubbing his hands together.

The forest was like no other he'd been in. The trees were mostly pine and their branches started at some height, creating a great canopy. The green light filtering through gave the place an enchanted feel and Ben half expected a unicorn to come bounding through. He could feel life radiating from the trees and it created an energy that made his skin tingle. There were all sorts of noises coming from the tree tops and other sounds deeper within the forest.

"What's the plan?" Charlie asked.

"Simple really. We find the elves, ask them a few questions about my parents and the Floating Prison, then leave."

"That's not really a plan," Charlie said, swatting a stray branch aside. "It's just a bunch of things you want to do. What happens if we can't find the elves? Or if we find them but they're not friendly?"

"I'll think of something," Ben said, throwing Charlie a lopsided smile.

"One of these days that's not going to work," Charlie sighed.

Ben set a steady pace and they kept a sharp eye out for anything unusual, trying to quell any unease fuelled by Natalie's stories. They saw a lynx, several deer and even a brown bear, which ambled across the path, but nothing more.

The path started to deteriorate as they progressed deeper into the forest and, after less than an hour, there was nothing left of it.

"Where did it go?" Charlie asked, staring at the forest floor.

Ben brushed a few branches aside. "It must have worn away over time. We've been heading roughly straight the whole time so if we continue we should stay on track."

The sun was starting to set when Ben decided to stop briefly for food. The forest had changed little during their four-mile hike, but then they had only made the smallest of inroads into this vast land of trees. Even at this relative edge of the forest, Ben knew if they lost their bearings they would be completely lost.

They took out their sandwiches and settled down by the base of a giant pine tree.

"I never thought I'd say this," said Charlie, licking his fingers as he finished off his baguette, "but I'm starting to hope we encounter these wood elves sooner rather than later. It's getting dark and I don't fancy sleeping here."

They resumed their hike, a steady march through the mighty pines, but neither of them saw the slightest sign of an elf. With the rapidly fading light, spotting them was becoming less and less likely.

A sudden thump came from behind and Ben turned. Charlie had tripped over a branch and was getting to his feet, rubbing his backside.

"I can't see where I'm going anymore," Charlie said, as he picked himself up.

Ben rubbed his eyes. He wanted to continue, reluctant to admit defeat, but even his legs were starting to feel the long hike.

"There's no point going on. We won't see any wood elves like this unless we bump into one."

They picked a spot to rest in between two large trees, with enough canopy above to protect them from rain. They talked to fend off their unease while darkness descended. Without the sunlight the forest became an ominous, daunting place. Soon Ben had to squint to see his hand in front of his face.

"Take your pouch out," Charlie said.

As soon as the pouch left his pocket it cast a warm glow on their little camp, fighting back the darkness. Ben and Charlie placed their pouches in the middle creating a pseudo camp fire.

"How did you know they did that?"

"Natalie told me." Charlie stared at the small glow. "I hope she still has hers. I bet it's really dark in prison."

Eventually tiredness crept in. They agreed to rotate a shift so that someone was always on guard throughout the night. Charlie volunteered to go first, insisting sleep was impossible here. Ben had no such problems; with his back against the trunk, he closed his eyes and almost immediately started drifting off.

A whooshing noise cut through the air. Ben opened his eyes just as an arrow thudded into the tree an inch above his head. At the same time another arrow thunked into Charlie's tree.

There was a moment's shock as they looked at the arrows. They scrambled to their feet.

"Stay put," Ben hissed. He could see the fear in Charlie's jittery movements. Ben searched for the intruder, but the light from the pouches didn't extend far.

A hollow voice floated into the clearing. "You are trespassing. The arrows are the only warning you will get. Leave now."

Ben saw no one. The voice was impossible to trace; it seemed to come from everywhere.

"We should go," Charlie said, fighting for calm.

"No." Ben cupped his hands to his mouth to create a little megaphone. "My name is Ben Greenwood," he shouted. "You might know my parents."

A pause. Silence.

"You are trespassing," the voice repeated. "The arrows are the only warning you will get. Leave now."

Charlie rubbed his forehead. "I don't think that helped, Ben."

But Ben shook his head, a glint in his eye. "They didn't deny it."

"You are trespassing. The arrows are the only warning you will get. Leave now."

"No," Charlie admitted, "but it sounds like a stuck record player."

"Please," Ben said, speaking to the forest. "I'm trying to find my parents. Just tell me if they were here."

Further silence. Ben's heart sounded like a beating drum counting the seconds.

A small figure stepped into the clearing. He was an elf child. There was a glow surrounding him that gave the elf an angelic look.

"You were given a warning, but you chose to ignore it."

"Shall we run?" Charlie whispered. The fear had gone from his voice. It was hard to be truly scared when faced with a child elf no taller than your waist.

"No." Ben turned to the elf. "Listen, we just—"

You will join your Institute friends. The child's voice resonated inside his head. *They too ignored our warning. You will work for us, rebuilding the forest your people damaged.*

The voice was soft, reasonable, but compelling. Ben wanted to ignore it and repeat his call for help, but instead he found himself listening.

Your name is no longer important. Whatever purpose you had is no longer important. When we feel you have paid your due, we will release you.

Ben was vaguely aware that Charlie was listening in rapt attention. His eyes were starting to glaze.

Follow the green light. It will direct you to your new home.

The light came from behind them. It was as if someone was aiming a powerful filtered torch into the clearing.

Follow the light.

The child elf stared at them with a pleasant smile. Ben shook himself, trying to get the voice out of his head, but it kept repeating – patient, calm, but impossibly insistent.

You will forget your name. You will forget your purpose. Follow the light.

The urge to listen was overwhelming. His mind felt sluggish. He took a step towards the green light.

Charlie had disappeared from the clearing. Ben could just make out his shadowy figure in the distance, following the green light. Ben wanted to call out, but his vocal chords weren't working. He was losing control of his body. His mind started to blank. Summoning the very last remnants of determinism, he suppressed the voice inside his head enough to think.

His name was Ben Greenwood. He was here to find his parents.

His parents. Their smiling faces floated into his mind. Ben locked every ounce of his focus on to them, softening the power of the voice.

He turned away from the green light and toward the child elf, who was still smiling pleasantly.

Ben took a step forward. Some unknown force grabbed the back of his jacket and one step forward became two steps back. Ben grit his teeth and lifted a leg. It hovered in the air and swung as if he were going to step back again.

There was no force pulling him back. It was all in his head. Ben screamed in defiance and managed a tiny shuffle forward. His head exploded with pain. Ben took another step forward. The pain intensified, but the elf was now almost within reach.

Colours exploded in front of Ben's face and the world seemed to sway. He managed to stay on his feet, but he could no longer see properly. In his mind's eye he visualised the elf's position. One more step and he reached out, his hands grasping the soft fabric of the elf's shirt. He yanked it towards him, lifting the elf off his feet, so those big, green eyes were inches from his own.

"Stop whatever you are doing," Ben said, in a husky whisper, "or I'll break your little neck."

There was no fear in the elf's eyes, just serenity, and perhaps a hint of amusement.

"Very good, human," the elf said, in his child voice.

Ben sensed movement behind a second before he felt the pain. Something hit him on his head and he blacked out.

— CHAPTER TWENTY-SIX —
Wood Elves

Ben woke to the smell of fresh grass with absolutely no recollection of where he was. His enchanted jacket was still dry, but his trousers were damp from dew. He moved his hand slowly to the back of his head and he felt a little bump, which hurt to touch.

Pain brought the memories flooding back.

The wood elves. The green light.

Ben's eyes shot open. Daylight was flooding through the tall trees. The birds were chirping and the forest seemed normal.

He got to his feet, feeling a little sore. His stomach rumbled. He was so hungry; it felt like he hadn't eaten for a week. Distracted by his empty belly, it took him a second to realise he wasn't alone. Far from it.

He was surrounded by wood elves. They were standing in a perfect circle around the trees Ben and Charlie had set camp in. His initial reaction was panic, remembering the mental war with the child elf the previous night, but reason stopped him from fleeing. The elves had clearly been here some time. If they wanted to get rid of him, they could have done so while he was sleeping.

They all had faint auras like the child last night, though some of the elves seemed to glow more than others. The combined effect was a halo that enclosed him and the trees. The elves wore green and brown clothes, blending in with the forest, but the elf right in front of him stood out with gold trim on his shirt and breeches.

"Good morning, Ben Greenwood," the elf said. There was a warmth in his face that Ben found reassuring. His voice was soft and had a peculiar echo to it.

"Who are you?" Ben asked.

"Why don't we do introductions after your friend has woken?" the elf said.

Ben had been so glued to the elves he hadn't noticed Charlie sleeping nearby. Last night he had been hypnotised by the green light and disappeared into the forest. Had the elves brought him back or had he recovered?

"Charlie," Ben whispered, giving him a nudge.

Charlie was slow to wake until he saw the wood elves, at which point he scrambled to his feet.

"My name is Lantis," the elf said. "I am, in your language, the 'lord' of this forest. After your commendable show of strength, Ben Greenwood, my advice was sought. As soon as they mentioned your name, I came directly."

The way Lantis spoke, the manner in which he responded to Ben's name and the warmth in his voice were all good signs. But Ben still felt nervous when he asked his next question – there was so much riding on it.

"Do you know my parents?"

Lantis smiled. "I know them well, your father especially. They were here last week."

"Last week?" Ben turned, sharing his excitement with Charlie. "Do you know where they went?"

"I don't. But they never tell me where they are heading."

Ben felt deflated, but only a little. His parents had been here! Last week. He looked around with a funny smile, as if they were still hidden somewhere in the trees.

"What were they doing here?" Charlie asked, seeing that Ben was busy revelling in the news.

"They were resting. Suktar keeps them on their toes and this is one of the few places he cannot easily reach."

The news sobered Ben. "Why do they keep running and hiding? Why don't they go to the Institute for protection?"

He didn't ask the questions he really wanted answered. Why did they leave him in the first place? Why don't they come back home?

Lantis sensed Ben's doubts and placed a hand on his shoulder. "They aren't hiding, Ben, I promise you that."

"What are they doing then?"

"I swore an oath to your parents not to say. I am sorry."

Ben's mind went back to the hidden memory so recently revealed at the Institute and he spoke softly.

"My dad said he was going to search for someone."

A flicker of surprise crossed Lantis' face and Ben knew he had something. Charlie saw it too; his eyes widened and he pointed a finger at Lantis.

"That's it, isn't it? That's the key to all this. Who are Ben's parents searching for?"

Lantis stared intently at each of them.

"Yes, they are searching. But more than that I will not say."

"Why though? They have Elizabeth's legacy. Isn't that what Suktar wants?" Ben asked.

Lantis did not answer.

"Can you at least tell us what Elizabeth's legacy is?" Charlie pleaded.

"That I can tell you. Have you heard of Elizabeth's Armour?"

Ben shook his head, but to his surprise saw Charlie nodding.

"Natalie told me about it. Queen Elizabeth wore a silver suit of armour during her great conquests of the Unseen Kingdoms. It was said to bring her luck because she never lost. The armour was buried with her when she died," Charlie said.

"Very good. That is exactly the story everyone is told."

"But not the true story?"

"No. Your Institute had conquered or allied with many of the kingdoms with little resistance, until they landed on the shores of Erellia."

"King Suktar's realm," Charlie said, giving Ben a glance.

"That's right. Suktar was planning a mighty invasion and it was on those shores the Institute suffered their first defeat. Over the next decade Erellia conquered many kingdoms with shocking brutality and the Institute was forced to retreat. Elizabeth realised the danger Erellia posed not only to the kingdoms but also to the British Empire. So she took her case to the High Council."

"The High Council?"

"A society consisting of twenty-four of the most powerful wizards. I do not know how Elizabeth found their headquarters or how she convinced them, but she returned with a suit of armour powerful enough to combat the threat of Suktar's army. To this day, it remains the only thing Suktar truly fears. The armour is Elizabeth's legacy."

The revelation caused a momentary silence. Ben was vaguely aware that his mouth was hanging open.

"What about the spell on me?" he asked eventually.

"Your parents came straight here after the dark elves raided their house. They convinced us to cast a spell that harnesses the power from Elizabeth's Armour in order to protect you."

Ben exchanged a meaningful glance with Charlie. So that was why the dark elf mentioned Elizabeth's legacy when his spell was deflected.

"What does it do other than deflect spells?" Ben asked.

"The spell relies on the qualities of the Armour, which are largely unknown. I can tell you it is only effective against dark elves."

Ben felt the mystery finally becoming clear, but Charlie's intense stare indicated he still wasn't done.

"How did Ben's parents get Elizabeth's Armour in the first place?"

"On this I am also sworn to secrecy," Lantis said. "Indeed, you already know far more than the Institute."

"Did they steal it?"

Ben directed the question at Lantis with such intent he thought for a moment he was going to get an answer. But Lantis remained silent.

"I don't think the way they got it is important right now," Charlie said.

"It's important to me," Ben said with a hint of anger. He sighed and ruffled his hair. "I need to know."

"Do you trust your parents?" Lantis asked.

"Of course."

"As do I. They are two of the best humans I know. Do not worry about how they obtained the Armour."

Ben wiped his forehead with the back of his hand.

"You're right. I shouldn't doubt their motives. I just wish I understood them more."

"You will in time," Lantis said softly.

The moment was broken by an almighty rumble coming from Charlie's stomach.

"Sorry," he said with a cringe. "I'm not usually this hungry in the morning."

Ben felt the same way. He delved into his bag and took out the last of their sandwiches.

"Your hunger is to be expected," Lantis said, as he watched them munch down their food.

"Why? Does that trance spell you cast on us last night drain the body?"

"It wasn't last night," Lantis said. "It was two nights ago."

Ben almost choked. "What?"

"You've been out for thirty-six hours. I'm sorry, it took me some time to get here and my colleagues saw no sense in waking you."

Charlie had turned pale. "It's tonight."

"What's tonight?" Lantis asked, sensing their sudden alarm.

Ben grabbed his bag and strapped it over his shoulder.

"The dark elves spread a rumour that I'm going to be executed, in an attempt to capture my parents."

"But you're not."

"No, but my parents don't know that." The more Ben talked, the more he realised how desperate the situation was. "Nobody except the dark elves know where we are."

"Where is this execution supposedly taking place?"

"The Floating Prison."

Lantis gave his first sign of worry, a subtle creasing of his smooth forehead. "Let us hope your parents are not fooled."

"Do you know where the Floating Prison is?" Charlie asked.

"It is a small island that floats somewhere in the sky, though nobody knows where. It's Suktar's personal jail. As you can imagine, escaping is impossible."

"It can't be impossible," Ben said. "There must be a way in, so there is obviously a way out."

"The entrance is through a gateway, but its location is unknown and it changes each day. As for the exit, there is a different gateway that also changes daily."

Ben ran a hand through his dishevelled hair. "Do you know where the entrance gateway is today?"

"No, and I would strongly advise you against finding out. Going to the Floating Prison serves no purpose. If your parents do find a way in, it will be a lot easier escaping without worrying about you."

"The dark elves captured a friend of ours," Ben said. "She is going to be executed as well. So we don't really have a choice."

"I'm sorry to hear that," Lantis said.

"Who would know where the entrance gateway is?"

"The only people who might possibly know are the Institute. They have a mighty network of people across the Unseen Kingdoms."

"We're not on great terms with the Institute right now," Ben said. "Is there anyone else who might know?"

Lantis shook his head and Ben cursed. The Institute was the last place he wanted to return to, but if it was the only way to the Floating Prison, what choice did he have?

— CHAPTER TWENTY-SEVEN —

Unwanted Rescue

They left the wood elves and set a good pace back to the forest clearing. The sun was poking through the tall trees and Ben guessed it to be approaching midday. That meant they had about eight hours before dusk. Eight hours to save Natalie and find his parents.

"I don't want to be a pessimist—"

"Then stop talking," Ben said.

"...but I've been thinking about our to-do list. First, we have to fire that spell the taxi driver gave us and hope he arrives. Then we have to sneak onto the Dragonway avoiding the dark elves, get back to the Institute, find the location of the Floating Prison, rescue Natalie and make an escape. Have I missed anything?"

"My parents," Ben said. "Once we're at the Floating Prison, I want to find them."

"Your parents – of course. Also, while we're there I wouldn't mind catching up with Elessar over a cup of tea."

Ben couldn't help but smile. "Let's just concentrate on getting back to the Institute and worry about the other stuff later."

"I'd prefer to worry about it now," Charlie said. He swatted aside a stray branch. "Are we doing the right thing? I don't want to sound like a coward and I certainly don't want to abandon Natalie, but wouldn't it make more sense to report her kidnapping to the Institute? They have a far better chance of rescuing her than we do."

"My parents don't trust the Institute and neither do I."

"What about Wren?"

Ben considered the question. "I trust her, but we have no idea if she'll be there when we return."

The trek back seemed shorter than the original journey and it wasn't long before Ben could make out the clearing through the trees. Charlie handed Ben the spell pellet and he tucked it into his pouch. This was one spell he could not mess up or else they would have no way back to the Dragonway.

"What's that?"

Charlie was pointing at a hint of colour beyond the trees, in the clearing.

A ripple of movement. Voices.

Ben and Charlie stopped less than twenty yards from the forest edge and darted behind one of the huge pines.

"What can you see?" Ben whispered.

Charlie had his back pinned against the tree. Slowly he turned his head and peered round. "I see a couple of those creatures that look like a cross between a lion and an eagle."

"A griffin?"

"That's the one," Charlie said. "They have riders."

"Are they dark elves?" Ben asked. His own view was obscured by branches.

Charlie squinted. "I don't think so." His eyes widened. "They have stars floating above their shoulders."

"The Institute," Ben said.

"How did they find us?"

Ben barely heard the question. He was thinking furiously, re-adjusting his hastily made plans. Yes, this was better – riskier but better. They needed to take risks; they only had eight hours.

"Follow me and try not to talk," Ben said.

Charlie gave an unrestrained gasp as Ben unpeeled himself from the tree.

"Ben, are you mad?" Charlie whispered furiously. "Ben!"

He ignored Charlie's frantic pleading and walked through the last of the trees and into the large circular clearing.

There were three of them. Two sat on griffins, but it was the man in the middle, sitting atop a gleaming black pegasus, who caught Ben's attention. He was big, with serious eyes and four red diamonds floating above his right shoulder.

"Ben Greenwood," the man said in a calm, even voice. "My name is Matthew. It is good to see you. We have been waiting some time."

Ben watched the man closely. The four red diamonds meant he was probably one of Draven's right-hand Wardens, but his composure was the polar opposite to that of his senior.

"How did you find us?"

"We have many contacts in Borgen. I have come to take you home."

Ben hesitated. "Home? I thought the Institute wanted me confined in Taecia."

"There have been developments," Matthew said. "Draven has instructed me to return you back to your home in Croydon and post a Warden to make sure you are safe."

Ben thought fast. A couple of days ago going home would have been wonderful, but now it was a disaster. He needed to get back to the Institute. Matthew didn't look like a man whose mind was easily swayed. Ben took a gamble.

"One of your apprentices, Natalie, has been captured by the dark elves. She is going to be executed at sunset at the Floating Prison."

Ben expected some sort of response, but Matthew barely flinched.

"I will inform Draven as soon as I've seen you safely home. Now, we'd better get going."

The two Wardens on griffins jumped down and beckoned them forward. Ben threw a desperate look at Charlie, but he was no help at all.

"This doesn't need to be forceful," Matthew said, seeing their lack of movement.

The two griffin riders started towards them, Spellshooters by their side.

"My parents!" Ben said in a rush and the two men paused. "The dark elves have spread a rumour that I'm also going to be executed in order to lure my parents to the Floating Prison."

This produced even less reaction than the news of Natalie. "We know. Why do you think we are taking you home? To get you as far away from the dark elves as possible."

Ben cursed silently. He wanted to tell them he needed to get to the Floating Prison, but what was the point? They would never understand his desire to find his parents.

The men resumed their advance. Ben glanced back. They could flee into the forest, but Charlie would never be able to keep up with him.

"You should run," Charlie said. There was steel behind his pale face. "I can buy you a few seconds. You can make it back to the wood elves."

"Good idea," Ben said, as he readied himself for the oncoming Warden. Ben had no intention of leaving Charlie.

A screeching noise pierced the air. Ben looked skywards, searching for the source, hands covering his ears. Charlie tripped and landed on his backside.

In the distance, flying swiftly beneath the clouds, was a huge dragon-like animal. Someone was riding its back. Ben could just make out the rider's flapping cloak as the beast approached.

"God damn," Matthew said, his voice hard. He barked a command to his two men. "Back on your griffins. We've got company."

The dragon circled above them. It was a wyvern, Ben realised, remembering the huge animals on the roof of the Institute. It had a long, narrow neck and a crocodile-like mouth. Ben took a step back as the wyvern came in to land and the ground shook on impact. When Ben's eyes finally went from the wyvern to the rider, his heart leapt.

It was Alex.

His blue, hooded cloak looked strangely impressive and contrasted with the trendy, tight-fitting jeans and black, pointed shoes. Eyes sparkling, he reminded Ben of a five year old up to no good.

"Good afternoon," Alex said, giving them a little salute. He towered over everyone on his wyvern. "Apologies for being late. You're a sly fox, Matthew; you nearly threw me off the trail. Have you considered switching departments? I could use someone like you."

Matthew had a face of stone. "This mission is not your concern, Alex. I have orders from Draven to take these two boys home."

"How lovely for you," Alex said, making a show of inspecting his nails. "However, I have a wyvern that can eat you whole, so your orders don't mean squat."

Matthew glanced warily at the wyvern, but his determination never wavered. "I have orders."

"I had a feeling you might say that."

Alex pulled the wyvern's rein and it reared its huge neck, towering over Matthew with a mighty roar that gave Ben goosebumps.

The wyvern snapped its neck forward like a snake striking, but Matthew's black pegasus was already moving and with a mighty leap it took to the sky. One of the griffin riders went with him. They started circling the wyvern like a couple of annoying wasps.

"Ben!"

The remaining Warden had dismounted and was running right at them, Spellshooter in hand.

Ben squared up to the Warden, eyes focused on his Spellshooter. The tip started to glow and the Warden took aim. A flash of white exploded. Ben dived to his right and felt the spell whiz by. He rolled and sprung to his feet just in time to see the Warden jump on him. With a burst of energy Ben squirmed free and threw himself at the Warden's legs. Both of them went down. They rolled around in the grass, Ben barely hearing the screeches and blasts from the other battle. He had a hold of the Warden's wrist and was trying to point the Spellshooter away. But the Warden was too strong and slowly the Spellshooter turned towards Ben's chest.

Thump. A huge branch smashed the Warden on the head. He dropped his Spellshooter and looked up in a daze. Another blow caught him full on the face and he slumped to the floor, motionless.

Charlie stood over them, branch raised, as if another blow might be needed.

"He's out," Ben said, picking himself up.

They turned to the other battle scene and gasped.

The griffins, the pegasus and their riders lay on the ground, unconscious. Alex sat sideways on the wyvern, legs crossed as if he were enjoying the midday air.

"Are we ready?" Alex asked. He saw Ben and Charlie staring at the fallen Wardens. "They're fine. Abbey's breath is quite toxic, but they'll recover. I don't envy the headache they'll have."

"Abbey?"

"My wyvern," Alex said, giving her a little pat. She lowered her neck until her long crocodile head touched the ground. "On you get."

"You want us to get on that thing?"

"Yes, and make it quick. She's not that thrilled at having to take all three of us."

"Where are we going?" Ben asked.

"The Floating Prison obviously. The entrance is back in Taecia, so we've got a bit of flying to do."

Ben took a deep breath and approached the beast. His unease grew as he examined the wyvern's scaly neck. How were they supposed to stay on that? But as he climbed up, the beast's scales stuck to him like Velcro. With a bit of coaxing, Charlie eventually joined them.

The wyvern lifted its neck and suddenly they were ten feet high. With a great flap of its wings, the wyvern took to the air. It soared up with such acceleration Ben's neck was nearly thrown out of place. He took in great gulps of air as the forest quickly receded into a blanket of green.

"The Institute has been working day and night to find you since you gave Draven's Wardens the slip. The dark elves weren't happy and our treaty with them looks like it's about to go up in smoke. The Executive Council finally realised kissing up to the dark elves wasn't working, which is why they're trying to get you home and as far away from the dark elves as possible."

"But you're not?" Ben asked.

"I know your parents. They will attempt a rescue if they think there is the slightest chance you've been captured. But not even they can escape the Floating Prison without help."

"But why take us?"

Alex turned and gave Ben a rare flash of sincerity. "I heard about that spell your parents laid on you and how it seems to repel dark elf magic. We're going to need that if we have any chance of success."

So Alex didn't need them at all, just Ben's spell. He wasn't surprised, but he still felt a little disappointed.

"Do you know about Natalie?"

"Yes. My guess is the dark elves will disguise her as you. They will execute her at the island's highest point to get the best chance of spotting Greg and Jane. There is a huge rock formation on top of the tallest hill that gives a panoramic view of the whole island. By the time Greg and Jane get close enough to recognise the disguise, they will be trapped."

"So, just to be clear," Charlie said, "we have to rescue Natalie and potentially Ben's parents by approaching the most exposed place on the island?"

"You got it."

"How well guarded will the Floating Prison be?"

"Very. Even the gateway entrance will be watched, hence the wyvern."

"That's not as comforting as it sounds."

Alex shook his head. "Don't worry about it; I have a plan."

"I hate that line," Charlie muttered under his breath.

Ben hoped Alex's plans weren't as ad hoc as his. Charlie did have a point – the rescue mission seemed hopeless, even by his standards; but he trusted Alex for one very good reason.

"Do you know my parents well?" Ben asked.

"Very well," Alex said, the flippancy in his voice disappearing momentarily. "I count them as my closest friends."

It was just the answer Ben had been hoping for. His next question made his stomach churn with nerves, but he forced it out; he had to know the answer.

"Do you know what crime my parents were accused of?"

There was a pause. "Yes, I do." Another, longer pause. "At least, I know part of it. Only your parents know the whole story, despite my efforts to learn the truth."

Ben didn't like the silence that followed, but he knew what Alex was doing. He was trying to figure out the best words to use. The anticipation had Ben squirming on his seat.

"It happened over twenty years ago when they lived in a cottage in Sussex," Alex said. Ben had seen pictures of the cottage with its acres of open gardens. "An intruder, a dark elf in disguise, entered their house. There was a fracas. The dark elf was killed and your parents were done for murder."

The word "murder" echoed in his head and made his heart falter. But he resisted the tide of emotions threatening to swamp him.

Charlie asked the question Ben had been about to voice. "So they got done even though someone broke into their house? Surely they acted in self-defence?"

"Not quite," Alex replied. "Yes, the dark elf broke into their house and yes, they acted in self-defence. But the dark elf had escaped. He had made it halfway down the cottage path before Greg shot him down."

Ben frowned. "Why would he shoot a fleeing dark elf?"

Alex turned around, his grey eyes filled with intensity. "That, Ben, is a very good question."

"Had the dark elf stolen something?" Charlie asked.

"No. The dark elf came and left with nothing, hence the mystery."

Their peaceful flight was a stark contrast to Ben's spinning mind, disturbed only by the wyvern's flapping wings and occasional snort. So his parents hadn't gone to jail for stealing the Armour from the Institute. His dad had been convicted for shooting a fleeing dark elf and his mother was probably an accomplice to the crime.

Alex was clearly confused by the dark elf's presence at the cottage, but Ben wasn't. What if the dark elf had been searching for Elizabeth's Armour? He must have learnt his parents might have it, so he tracked them to their house. He didn't escape with the Armour, but clearly he learnt something so significant his dad felt he had to stop the elf escaping.

Was Elizabeth's Armour really that important? Important enough to kill for? Lantis said it was the only thing that could defeat Suktar. Did that justify his dad's crime?

The questions waged a war in his head. He wanted to talk to Charlie, but it was clear Alex didn't know about the Armour.

There must be a good reason for someone as senior and close to his parents to be kept in ignorance, so Ben kept quiet.

They left the forest and were soon flying over endless sea. Occasionally Ben made out a ship below or a plane above. He kept a close eye on the sun; it seemed to be getting lower at an alarming rate. Hours had passed, and Ben felt sore and stiff from holding onto the wyvern, when they finally sighted land again. Taecia's coastline materialised below and they soared inland, above hills and small lakes.

The constant sound of wind and flapping wings was broken by Alex.

"The gateway lies in the next valley, right by a lake. Our best chance is surprise, so I'm going to hit them hard and fast. Lean forward and flatten yourselves as much as you can to minimise yourself as a target. Any questions?"

The anticipation sent Ben's heart racing. He could only imagine what Charlie was thinking.

Sure enough, it was Charlie who spoke.

"I don't want to sound like a pessimist, but could you give us a figure, a percent, of our chance of success? Are we looking at fifty–fifty, or is that too optimistic? Because I thought these dark elves were dangerous."

"They are dangerous," Alex replied, shooting them a quick smile. "But so is a wyvern and so am I."

"You didn't answer my question," Charlie said to himself.

Feeling the wyvern beneath him and with Alex at the helm, Ben realised for the first time they were going into this conflict with powerful allies.

Just how powerful he was about to find out.

They sailed over a hill and the wyvern dived into the valley like a hawk spotting its prey. The acceleration was intense. Charlie screamed, but it was muted by the whistling wind. Leaning to the side, Ben could make out the lake in the distance and a handful of figures by the bank. They seemed small and insignificant compared to the might of the wyvern. But they weren't small for long; the wyvern was closing quickly. Ben saw something ignite by the lake and a moment later, a huge purple fireball was coming right at them.

"Flatten yourselves!" Alex cried.

Ben just had time to lean into Alex, feeling Charlie cling to him from behind, when the wyvern pitched left. The fireball missed them by inches, the heat warming the air.

More fireballs followed. One seemed destined to hit them until the wyvern fired his own to counter it. Ben couldn't help peering out from his covered position and gasped when he saw how quickly the valley was rising up to greet them. He could see the purple uniforms of the dark elves and their extended arms, hands glowing. Alex had his Spellshooter out and was firing peculiar, red and white, twirling missiles, which reminded Ben of candy. They were effective, honing in on their targets and knocking the dark elves for six. Several of them were already fleeing.

"Get ready to land!" Alex said, his voice wild with exhilaration.

The wyvern's small legs came out, it steadied its wings and with a small thump they landed in the valley.

Many dark elves lay motionless on the ground, but a few were still fighting. Ben leapt off the wyvern and used it as a shield, putting the huge animal between him and the elves. He saw several flashes and the wyvern roared in pain. It stood up on its hind legs, extending to its full height so for a second they were no longer shielded by its body.

There were few dark elves left, but they were fighting gamely, duelling with Alex who was firing, ducking and rolling with a speed Ben hadn't thought possible.

The last one went down and Ben ran round to join Alex. His smile was grim, triumphant, but his eyes were focused on a couple of dark elves scampering through the valley.

"I need to finish them off before they can call for back-up. I will meet you on the other side. Don't wait here, it's too dangerous."

Alex leapt back onto the wyvern, looking every inch a Western cowboy.

With incredible speed, he fired something at Ben and Charlie in rapid succession. Ben felt something hit his chest and saw a thin film envelope him.

"That should help keep you out of trouble," Alex said, giving them a crooked grin and a wink. He slapped the wyvern and took off, chasing the fleeing dark elves and leaving the two of them alone in the valley.

— CHAPTER TWENTY-EIGHT —
The Floating Prison

Ben watched Alex fly away, his heartbeat slowly working its way back to normal. Everything had happened so quickly; the raid had only lasted minutes, but Ben remembered every second so clearly it seemed longer. He felt breathless despite contributing very little to the action.

He shook himself into action. "Let's get going. Where is the gateway entrance?"

The question snapped Charlie out of his stupor. He searched the valley floor but saw nothing unusual. He looked again, more thoroughly this time. Still nothing.

"I know hindsight is a wonderful thing," Charlie said, "but do you think we should have asked Alex what we're looking for? Because I can't see a thing."

"There!" Ben said. He was pointing to a spot of grass less than fifty yards away, next to the bank of the lake. There was a peculiar ripple in the air about the size of a doorway. They approached it cautiously.

Ben lifted a leg. He was going to step through the gateway when Charlie grabbed him. "Hold on a second!"

"What for?" Ben was so eager to go through, it took considerable willpower to stop himself.

"Once we go through, we can't come back."

"I know that. So?"

Charlie's eyes provided the answer. This was the point of no return. "From everything we've heard about the Floating Prison, it seems like it would make more sense to wait here."

"It won't be safe for long." Ben replied. "If just one of the dark elves crests that hill and spots us, we're done for. They will follow us through the gateway. We should go now, while nobody knows we're here."

Ben felt Charlie's unease and he put an arm around his shoulder.

"As soon as we're through the gateway, we'll find somewhere to hide and wait until Alex shows up. I'm sure that spell he cast on us will help somehow."

Charlie finally nodded. "I don't like the way he just ran off like that."

"He had to stop the dark elves getting help," Ben said.

"I know. I just wish he could have warned us that this might happen."

Ben felt some of Charlie's concern, but brushed it aside in his desire to get going. He walked up to the gateway until his nose almost touched the ripples. Tentatively, he poked a finger through. It felt cool – the temperature was clearly colder on the other side. He retracted his finger and inspected it. Everything looked normal.

"Here we go," he said.

He held his breath and stepped through.

It felt like the first step off an aeroplane when you leave the pressurised cabin and feel the atmosphere of your new destination. There was a cold wind and his enchanted jacket automatically adjusted to compensate. He turned around and saw immediately why there was no turning back. The gateway from this side didn't exist; it was as if he had arrived by stepping through nothing.

Ben took in his new surroundings quickly and relaxed a fraction when he discovered he was alone. He was on a winding dirt path bordered on the left by sparse brambles. Beyond the brambles was a steep hill and on top of that Ben could make out the prison. He gasped in wonder. It looked like a giant hexagonal jewel made into a building. It was black and looked every bit as majestic as the brightest gem. There were no windows or doors, as if the designer knew such thing would detract from the prison's flawless beauty. He couldn't even begin to imagine how you would get in.

Ben eventually turned his attention to the other side of the dirt path and gave a start. Thick bog land stretched downhill for a short distance before ending abruptly. Beyond the edge there was nothing. Thousands of feet below Ben saw water. He was right on the island's edge. Ben felt dizzy and looked away, concentrating on solid ground.

Charlie soon appeared out of thin air as he too passed through the gateway. "Is it safe?"

"Yes, we're alone."

The predictable gasps from Charlie came as he saw the prison and the island's edge. He tore his eyes away and started looking nervously up and down the path. It curved out of sight limiting their view.

"I don't like it here. We should find a place to hide," Charlie said.

They found a ditch nestled within the brambles close by where they could still see the gateway. It was deep enough so only their heads were visible above ground, concealed by the brambles.

Ben gazed at the sun on the horizon and cursed. Wherever the gateway had taken them, it was later in the day than Taecia. He estimated it no more than an hour before sunset.

Despite the confined space in the ditch, Ben kept bouncing up and down on his haunches, wanting to be ready the moment Alex arrived. He wasn't concerned when Alex didn't turn up after five minutes of waiting; after all, several dark elves had escaped and chasing each one would take a bit of time, especially if they put up a fight. But when ten minutes had elapsed without any sign of Alex, Ben got his first twinge of concern.

"Something isn't right," Charlie said.

"He'll be here soon."

Fifteen minutes passed and Ben cursed. He was now looking at the sun every thirty seconds, watching its unrelenting approach to the horizon. With every passing minute, Ben became more restless. Where was he? Alex knew the time crunch. Could he have been caught? Having seen him in action with the monstrous wyvern, he doubted it. He must still be tracking down the dark elves. Ben waited as long as he could bear, but eventually he was forced into a decision.

"We have to get going," Ben said.

"Are you mad? We might as well jump off that cliff."

Their argument was cut short by voices. They flattened themselves against the ditch and peered towards the gateway. Three figures appeared from nowhere, stepping through the gateway and stopping on the path.

Ben's heart sank.

Alex was flanked by two dark elves. He had been caught.

"Why are we stopping?" Alex asked. His voice was clear, for they were less than twenty paces away. He didn't sound scared, but then Alex didn't strike Ben as someone who was easily afraid.

"The children are here."

Ben's stomach did a somersault. Elessar's soft, compelling voice was unmistakable. He turned, his purple eyes scanning the brambles. They were well concealed, but Ben ducked anyway.

Alex didn't turn round. "Are you sure?"

"I can see the orange beacons from your spell. I told you they would wait."

Charlie gasped, giving away their position completely. Ben's mind felt sluggish; he was confused. Alex was one of their only allies. He was a close friend of his parents; he couldn't be a traitor.

"Pick them up," Alex said. He sounded almost bored. "I will meet you on the hill. Make sure you bring your side of the bargain with you."

"You will get it after the execution, not before. I will not sacrifice the pouch before I am certain we have the Greenwoods."

"Really?" Alex finally turned around. His face was contorted with such anger, he was unrecognisable. "I can stop Ben's heartbeat with the spell I have on him, so don't mess me around."

"You do that and you won't leave here alive."

"Maybe not, but neither will you," Alex said, his face twisting into a nasty smile.

Elessar narrowed his eyes. "I thought we had an agreement. It was you who came to us, remember?"

"Wrong. I never had an allegiance. I worked at the Institute because the pay was good. But when your armies started consuming the Unseen Kingdoms, I needed dark elf cooperation to maintain my lucrative trade routes. That's all this is – *business*. Now, are you in or out?"

There was a moment's silence as the two faced each other in a stand-off.

"I will give you the pouch when we reach the hill," Elessar said finally.

Alex nodded and, without further ado, marched up the winding path, away from them and out of sight.

Elessar watched him go and then turned back towards them. Ben was barely peeking out of his hiding place, but Elessar's eyes somehow found him and he smiled.

"I see you," Elessar mouthed.

"Oh crap," Charlie whispered.

For an instant Ben was paralysed with shock. Elessar and the other dark elf were walking towards them in a slow, unconcerned fashion that implied they had all the time in the world.

"Move!" Ben shouted, pushing Charlie who was doing a creditable impression of a rock.

Charlie jumped and then thrust himself through the brambles and out of the ditch. Ben followed, but as he clambered out he knew they were too slow. The dark elves were almost on top of them. Charlie turned to run, but Elessar raised a hand and sent a spell in the shape of a swirling boomerang that tripped him up and roped his hands and legs. Charlie fell face first onto the dirt path, having run no more than a few paces. Ben anticipated the same spell and tensed himself, but it never came. Elessar drew a sword and with inhuman speed thrust it at Ben's neck. Before Ben could blink, the sword was at his throat.

"Good evening, Ben Greenwood. Let us get the pleasantries out the way. Your friend has no purpose here. If you put so much as a foot out of place, he dies and we get to see if your protective spell can stop me beheading you. Do I make myself clear?"

Ben nodded, or tried to, as it was difficult with the sword pricking the skin of his Adam's apple.

"Excellent. Well, we should get going. You wouldn't want to miss your own execution, would you?"

Charlie and Ben were marched along in front of the dark elves. Charlie was still bound and was reduced to shuffling forward; Ben could feel the dark elf's sword in his back every time he slowed.

He felt so confused his head was spinning; only the pain from the sword kept him steady. It didn't make sense. It wasn't possible, but the change in Alex was unmistakable.

"Why?"

It was Charlie who asked the question. Ben couldn't offer any explanation and so they continued in silence. With great effort, Ben attempted to take his mind off the betrayal. They had left the prison behind and were now walking inland, up a gentle slope. The landscape was wild, the long grass wet and muddy. Huge boulders were sprawled across the hillside, some of them as big as houses and carved into shape by the relentless wind.

They entered a clump of trees, and the moment they came out the other side, Ben saw their destination. It was a much larger hill, dwarfing everything around it. The top was a plateau and on it were several huge boulders. One lay on top of two others, creating the impression of two walls and a roof. There were people on the plateau: dark elves, though just how many was difficult to tell at this distance. Underneath the "roof" was another figure, who stood out because of her small size and wavy hair.

Natalie.

"I see her too," Charlie said, seeing Ben tense.

They began their ascent up the large hill. The sun was fast approaching the horizon and every time he looked at it his stomach churned. Were his parents here on the island? If they weren't, he was in deep trouble.

"Any plan?" Charlie whispered, managing a small, nervous smile. "I'd take anything right now."

"My parents," Ben said, putting as much certainty into his voice as possible, but the tremor made it rather unconvincing. "They are here, I know it. They will rescue us."

"I hope you're right."

The last few steps before they crested the giant hill were surreal. Ben was walking to his execution, yet deep down there was a well of hope that staved off despair. In moments he could be seeing his parents again. But right now it wasn't his parents he was thinking of; it was Natalie. She stood underneath the giant, horizontal stone, her hands and legs magically bound. She had a cut on her forehead and looked exhausted.

She looked at Ben and then Charlie as they reached the hilltop, her green eyes full of anguish.

"Oh why did you come? It's a trap."

"We hadn't noticed," Ben said, glancing at Charlie. But Charlie wasn't listening. He was staring at a lady slumped to the side, her back resting against one of the vertical stones.

It was Wren.

She looked beaten, her dress was torn and her normally pinned up hair was a mess. Her eyes were closed and her breathing faint. Ben stared at her in despair. Deep down he had hoped Wren might somehow learn of Alex's deception and come to their aid. Maybe she had, but she had failed.

The sword at Ben's back poked him and he and Charlie were directed under the large stone next to Natalie.

"Alex, tie him," Elessar ordered.

Ben looked up just as Alex fired a spell into his chest. Ropes magically appeared, binding his hands and feet. So Elessar knew Ben's spell only worked against dark elf magic.

"We are ready, Your Highness," Elessar said with a bow, his eyes fixed firmly on the grass by his feet.

"Now we wait."

The new voice almost knocked Ben over. It was soft like Elessar's but spoken with ten times the power, making Ben's hair stand on end. He turned to the speaker, but his eyes started to burn the moment he looked at him. He was taller and broader than any other dark elf he'd seen. He wore a small crown and draped over his shoulders was a magnificent purple cloak adorned with gold hieroglyphs. If the crown hadn't given away the elf's authority, there were four huge bodyguards with swords that could slice a tree in two.

Ben had always pictured King Suktar older – after all, he was alive during Elizabeth I's reign. But if anything, his face had a hint of youth in it.

There were at least a dozen other dark elves around the edge of the plateau, searching the surrounding hills for his parents. He spotted Alex standing a little distance away, next to Elessar.

Ben had restrained himself until now, but seeing Alex with Elessar talking amongst themselves was too much.

"Oi!" he shouted. "You treacherous lowlife, I trusted you. You're going to pay. My parents will bring you down!"

Alex didn't have the guts to look his way and Ben spat at him, though it fell well short. He got a thump on the back of his head for his trouble.

"Are you okay, Ben?" Natalie asked.

"Yeah, I'm fine." His head was spinning, but he shook it off.

"If I were you, I'd stop chatting and start praying," Elessar said, his eyes staring at the sun. "Your parents have less than ten minutes to show their faces."

It was now noticeably darker and Ben was having to squint to see the hill below, though the dark elves seemed untroubled by the lack of light. Ben could have sworn the sun started to accelerate as if suddenly drawn to the horizon.

"This is it," Charlie said, speaking softly so that only Ben and Natalie could hear. "If they don't come now, we're done for."

"They'll come."

Charlie's pale face looked on the verge of panic. "What if they don't? I'm only fourteen. I don't want to die. God, I've wasted my life. I haven't done anything with myself."

Ben wasn't listening. His eyes were glued to the surroundings. Where were his parents?

"Your fate is starting to look rather bleak," Elessar said, interrupting his thoughts. Ben stared at the disappearing sun with growing frustration.

Time was almost up, he realised. He continued to search for any sign of his mum or dad. Other than the occasional sprawling tree and the mighty boulders, the landscape was bare and unsuited to hiding or launching a surprise attack. The grass was thick, but would they really crawl all the way up the hill to avoid being seen?

Everyone now had their attention on the hillside, even the king. As the sun dipped below the horizon, Ben began to believe for the first time that his parents might not turn up. The thought made his legs unsteady and he almost lost his footing. They would never let him die without putting up a fight, so that meant his parents weren't on the island. Had they been unable to find it? Maybe they didn't get the dark elves' message about the execution. It didn't matter now. What mattered was they weren't here.

The sun dipped out of view without the faintest sight of his parents. Elessar kept searching with a look of desperation, unable to accept defeat. Finally, he turned towards his king.

"You failed, Elessar," the king said. Ben risked the burning sensation in his eyes. A subtle lowering of Suktar's eyebrows was the only sign of his disapproval.

"I am sorry, Your Highness." Ben had never heard Elessar flustered before, but his discomfort was scant consolation now. "I assumed they cared for their son's life."

"You assumed wrong. The king will not be pleased. Get rid of them all except the Greenwood boy and meet me back at the palace where we will decide a punishment suitable to your failure."

So this elf wasn't the king. Who then? The answer came to him immediately: King Suktar's son. The prince his parents were accused of killing. If only Colin or Draven had been around! Not that it mattered anymore.

Elessar kept his eyes focused on the grass. "Yes, Your Highness."

"Are you certain you have Wren Walker under control or should I stay to make sure there are no further foul-ups?"

"I cast the spell on her myself, Your Highness. Not even Wren can break free on her own."

"I hope not, for your sake."

A small whirlwind appeared around the prince and his four guards. It intensified until they were lost in the vortex, the wind nearly sweeping Ben from his feet. As quickly as it had come, it disappeared, and the prince and his guards had gone.

"I really thought I understood humans, but your parents proved me wrong," Elessar said, clicking his tongue. "Not everyone seems to care about their offspring. A pity for me and a pity for you, as your life is now at an end."

Shock hit Ben like a blow to the face and real fear flowed through him for the first time. He tried to keep it from showing, but as Elessar drew his sword, testing its edge, Ben started shaking.

"I am eager to get home, so let's not draw this out. Who's first?"

Elessar spoke so casually it felt like a dream. Was this really happening? Ben wanted to pinch himself, but his hand was shaking too much.

"I am," Ben said. Was that really his voice? He shuffled forward and knelt down, unsure who was controlling his body.

"How noble," Elessar said, almost bored. "Unfortunately, I need you alive."

He grabbed Natalie and made her kneel. She struggled until Elessar's purple gaze rendered her motionless.

Ben's blood was pumping painfully in his ears. He leapt forward, but a steely hand from behind yanked him back. He screamed, but Elessar could have been deaf for all the response he showed.

Time seemed to slow. The sword swung forward, swiping towards Natalie's neck.

A small silver sledgehammer cannoned into Elessar's face, sending him flying ten feet into the air. There was a stunned silence and it took Ben a second to realise the hammer had been a spell. Ben turned, expecting to find his parents.

But it was Alex, his Spellshooter still pointing at Elessar's fallen body.

— CHAPTER TWENTY-NINE —
The Greenwoods

Ben was just as stunned as the surrounding dark elves. Conflicting emotions threatened to overload him. For a second he could have heard a pin drop.

The dark elves' astonishment turned to fury and they turned as one to Alex. The cries came from every corner of the plateau and they charged. Alex was suddenly facing a dozen dark elves coming at him from all sides, swords drawn, hands pulsing with magic.

Alex fired another spell. This one arced over the oncoming elves and hit Wren, casting her in a halo of light.

"Get up, Wren!" Alex shouted, his voice containing only a fraction of the panic it should have.

Wren raised her head. The dazed look in her eyes vanished as she took in the scene and quickly got to her feet. She raised her hand and half a dozen tiny missiles launched from her fingers, whizzing their way to the dark elves. Ben saw a couple go down and a few more re-direct their charge towards Wren.

In the brief respite, Alex raised his Spellshooter and fired a spell into the evening sky. It exploded in a mighty shower of sparks like a firework.

To Ben's amazement, a dozen missiles went off in the distance. They were heading rapidly towards the hill. Ben, Charlie and Natalie barely had time to shuffle under the stone roof when the spells hit the ground like an air strike. The noise was deafening. Dark elves and huge lumps of earth went flying into the air.

Coming up the hill, screaming as they charged, were a dozen Spellswords. The dark elves ran down to face the new adversary and suddenly the fight was even.

The hill was now a battlefield, with spells flying everywhere amongst cries of anger and pain. Ben feared for the Spellswords at close quarters against the elves' swords, but they fired spell into their palms and blades materialised. Ben saw Alex fending off two elves with a sabre whilst engaging another in a shooting battle.

Ben wanted to help, but he was still bound. Even if he were free, what good could he do? He was completely useless here. It was maddening.

A tap on his shoulder diverted his attention from the battle and a moment later his bonds disappeared.

"Time to get out of here," Wren said, her calmness in contrast with her appearance. Within moments she had also dispelled the bonds from Charlie and Natalie.

Wren led them down the hill, but they had barely left the plateau when a sparkling purple bolt streaked towards Wren's head. She raised her hand and the spell hit an invisible shield, but Wren staggered as if remnants of the spell had penetrated.

"Going somewhere, Wren?" Elessar asked. He walked through the battlefield, heedless of the carnage around him, with two dark elves following in his wake. One side of his face was covered in blood. His normal arrogance and composure were gone, and his mouth was curled in a snarl.

"Take Ben, kill the others," Elessar ordered. "I will deal with Wren."

Wren turned to Ben, her grey eyes betraying only a flicker of urgency. "Get out of here."

Ben nodded as Elessar fired another bolt at Wren. She blocked it and stepped forward to meet him. The two other dark elves attempted to circle around Wren, but she fired two jets of gold at them without even looking. One dark elf went down, but the other dodged the spell.

"Oh dear," Charlie said, staring at the remaining dark elf bearing down on them. The elf had his sword drawn and was walking carefully, his face grim. Ben, Natalie and Charlie were back-peddling down the hill, watching the dark elf get ever closer.

"Should we turn and run?" Natalie asked.

"No good," Ben replied. "He will catch us."

"What else can we do?"

Ben kept his eyes firmly on the dark elf. "Spread out. Give him three different targets to go for."

They spanned out, still walking backwards. The dark elf gave each of them an appraising look, before altering his path to Ben.

"Now what?" Charlie asked.

"I'm working on it."

The dark elf was no more than a dozen paces away and closing fast. Ben searched the hill for help, but all the nearby Spellswords were locked in battle.

Surely the elf wasn't going to use that sword? Elessar wanted him alive. Ben's only chance was surprise. He grit his teeth and tensed himself. As he was about to launch forward, his foot stumbled on something soft. He lost his balance and fell to the ground.

He had stepped on a fallen Spellsword. Ben's horrified gaze went to the bloody, lifeless face. His Spellshooter lay next to him in the thick grass.

The Spellshooter.

Ben picked it up, aimed it at the dark elf and rested his hand on the trigger.

The dark elf's eyes widened.

The spells inside the barrel instantly filled Ben's mind. He could feel the power pulsing from the coloured pellets. They made the spells in Natalie's Spellshooter look insignificant. While still back-peddling, Ben focused and pressed the trigger.

Nothing happened.

He tried again. Still nothing. The dark elf was now so close, his sword was almost within striking distance. Quelling his rising panic, Ben took a deep breath and cleared his mind. He summoned every ounce of willpower. Sweat pouring down his forehead, he willed the pellet to explode forth.

The barrel illuminated bright blue, but the spell still resisted. Ben screamed with effort and for a moment the pellet started floating down the orb. But before it could make it into the barrel, it ran out of steam.

Ben stared at the Spellshooter in desperation.

The dark elf lunged, aiming the butt of his sword at Ben's head. Ben side-stepped and threw the Spellshooter at the elf with all the willpower and determination he had used moments earlier. The Spellshooter hit the elf full in the face and exploded. Ben was thrown one way, the dark elf the other. Ben scrambled to his feet, but the dark elf remained on the grass in a lifeless heap.

"Are you okay?" Natalie asked anxiously.

Ben nodded, his eyes searching the battlefield for another Spellshooter. There! He ran over and picked it up.

"We can use these to help," he said.

"Are you mad?" Charlie asked. "You want us to run up to a dark elf, shove a Spellshooter in their face and then hope the resulting explosion doesn't kill us?"

Natalie nodded, her green eyes anxious. "It's too dangerous, Ben. Throwing a Spellshooter can make the spells inside explode. It's a miracle you're okay."

Ben felt torn. He desperately wanted to help. There was fighting everywhere, with several bodies lying on the hill, as well as spells flying all over the place like a fireworks display gone wrong.

A stray fireball sailed over their heads.

"We've got to go!" Natalie said, grabbing Ben by the arm.

Ben was about to argue when he saw a flash of red in the distance. It came from a nearby hill. Ben squinted, focusing on a clump of rocks near the top. There it was again! It looked like a powerful torch being aimed at him.

Was someone up there?

"Ben!" Charlie's voice was frantic. "What are you doing? Let's go!"

Ben didn't take his eyes off the hill. "Something is up there."

They immediately stopped trying to drag Ben away and looked.

"My parents," Ben said, his voice a whisper. As he spoke, he saw two unmistakable silhouettes on top of the hill.

Charlie suddenly forgot all about the battle. "Are you sure?"

Ben looked them both in the eye. "I'm positive. Follow me."

Ben knew running would attract attention, so he resisted his natural instinct and maintained a steady pace down the hill. Several times Ben saw a dark elf spot them, but a Spellsword always cut them off. Gradually the sound of battle receded and they found themselves alone at the base of the hill.

"We made it," Natalie said, her face lighting up.

Charlie was looking back up the hill. "I still feel like we're going to be hit by a stray spell."

The battle was still raging, but it was difficult to make out who was on top. Ben couldn't see Alex or Wren; he hoped they were okay.

"Now what?" Natalie asked.

"Now we find my parents."

Ben led them to the smaller hill and into a cluster of trees at its base. The branches hid what was left of twilight and they got their spell pouches out to help illuminate their way. Ben kept looking up, searching for the clearing at the top of the hill. His heart was thumping and sweat ran down his forehead. Were his mum and dad still up there? His stomach gave a lurch when he spotted the clearing and he raced the final stretch, bursting through the tree line at a sprint.

He stopped, breathing hard, eyes searching eagerly. There were a few scattered boulders much like the last hill, but everything was smaller.

There was no sign of his parents.

Ben scrambled up to the boulders and peered behind each of them.

"Where are they?" Charlie asked. He and Natalie had entered the clearing and were looking at him in confusion.

"They were here," Ben said with a note of desperation, still looking, unable to accept defeat. Charlie and Natalie joined him, but there was little to search except the boulders. After re-checking each one twice, they went to the largest one and sat down disconsolately.

"They were here," Ben said softly.

"We believe you," Natalie said, and Charlie nodded.

"I can't understand why they keep running."

Neither Charlie nor Natalie had a suitable reply.

Ben's eyes drifted to a nearby boulder. His parents could have been sitting there less than twenty minutes ago. There was a small stone on top of it that caught his attention. Ben could have sworn the stone had been black a moment ago, but now it seemed to have a dull green hue. He squinted. The more he stared at the stone, the brighter it became.

"What's that?" Charlie asked. The stone was now giving off a green glow.

Hope surging, Ben sprung up and ran over. It was a spell pouch. They stared at it in amazement. Ben picked it up and held it close. He opened the drawstring. A small green pellet stared back at him.

Ben exchanged excited looks with Charlie, but Natalie wore a frown.

"Don't touch the pellet," she said.

Ben and Charlie looked at her in surprise. "Why not?"

"It could be booby-trapped. Some pellets activate on touch."

Ben's free hand hovered over the open pouch. "What are the odds of someone planting a trap for us here? The dark elves were busy last I checked."

The more Ben stared at the pellet, the more he felt like taking it out. His hand started trembling and, before he knew what he was doing, he had delved into the pouch to pick it up.

There was a flash of blinding light and the world disappeared into blackness. Ben was floating, aware but without a body. His panic subsided as an image materialised before him.

Another memory.

The colour and details were as rich and perfect as before. He was in a sumptuously decorated hallway with thick, red carpet, gold enamelling on the intricately carved wooden panels and magnificent portraits lining both walls.

Ben knew right away this memory wasn't his. He was watching a scene unfold through someone else's eyes. Before he could work out whose it was, the memory sucked him in and the world took over.

"Would you take a seat, Mr. Greenwood?" Lord Samuel asked with thinly masked impatience. "Your pacing is most off-putting."

337

"My apologies," Michael said, but he made no motion to sit down. "It is an old habit; I am used to being on my feet."

Samuel made no attempt to hide his disgust, but the others didn't seem to care; Charlotte even smiled, momentarily wiping away her troubled frown.

Charlotte's anxiety was evident among all the directors, bar Michael. They sat on elegant chairs spaced generously against the wall, constantly glancing towards Queen Elizabeth's royal suite. Any moment now her door was going to open.

Michael could guess his fellow directors' thoughts because he shared most of them. Why had the Queen summoned them? Her visits to the Institute were increasingly infrequent; she was no longer young and the unrest back home kept her busy. Michael noticed Lord Samuel licking his lips. No doubt he was wondering what all were – was Queen Elizabeth going to resign her position as commander of the Institute? If so, who would replace her?

For Michael, the mystery of the meeting brought back fond memories of the day he had discovered the Institute. Was that really ten years ago? How times had changed. He had five green diamonds floating above his shoulder, making him senior to those lords and barons who had made his early Institute life so difficult. Now only a few, such as Lord Samuel, didn't treat him as an equal.

Michael's reminiscing was broken by the opening of the royal suite door. He felt his fellow directors stiffen.

A guard appeared. "Lord Samuel. Would you please come through?"

The chair creaked under Lord Samuel's bulk as he stood up. He was clearly pleased that he had been called first and gave the others a pompous nod before disappearing through the door.

The minutes seemed to drag out and even Michael started to feel tense. Finally, the door opened and Lord Samuel re-emerged, his face redder than usual. He looked straight at Michael with a scowl of open hostility, before stalking off. What was that about? The other directors appeared equally baffled.

"Lady Charlotte Rowe," the guard said.

Charlotte rose, her anxiety washed away by fierce determination. Michael gave her an encouraging nod as she walked into the royal suite.

Time passed just as slowly before Charlotte came out again. Unlike Samuel, there was no anger, just a thoughtful expression as she left.

The remaining directors came and went until Michael was left alone in the hallway. He was surprised to find he felt slightly disappointed at being last.

"Michael James Greenwood," the guard said.

Michael approached the doorway and entered the royal suite, his heart beating a little faster.

Queen Elizabeth sat on a gilded chair at the centre of a spacious, exquisitely furnished room. To her left was a display of her famous armour in all its glory, the golden sword floating inches from the ground. Michael smiled, remembering the first time he'd seen the sword, at his entrance examination for the Institute. That had been an interesting day.

Michael bowed and the Queen beckoned him forward. There was nowhere to sit, but he was more comfortable standing anyway.

The Queen looked tired. She tried to conceal it, but Michael knew her too well. Her auburn hair and pale face were as flawless as ever, but there was a weariness in her eyes and her back wasn't quite as straight as usual.

"Michael Greenwood." Elizabeth let his name hang in the air. There was a hint of a smile on her face. "After all these years I never thanked you for repaying my faith." Michael looked at her with surprise and Elizabeth continued. "My advisers, Lord Samuel among them, tried to dissuade me from promoting you, the baker's apprentice, and Charlotte to the Institute's highest echelon."

"Then it seems as though I should be thanking you," Michael said with a bow. "However, if I may correct you on one point – I was no longer a baker's apprentice; I became fully qualified several years ago."

Elizabeth's smile wiped the weariness from her face. "That is why I like you, Michael. You speak your mind, even to me."

Michael waited patiently for her to continue. This idle talk was clearly a prelude, but he knew better than to press her.

Elizabeth turned to her armour and her humour faded. "My armour is not safe here."

The announcement caught Michael by surprise. "How can that be? Surely there is no safer place than the Institute?"

"Safe from the outside perhaps, but not from within."

Michael felt his stomach lurch. "You suspect treachery?"

"The lure of power is an irresistible force."

Michael instinctively thought of Lord Samuel. Suddenly, the man's troubled face made more sense. What had the Queen said to him?

"My armour must be kept safe for Suktar's eventual return."

"Suktar's return?" Michael said, a little too loudly. Then in a softer voice. "I hoped he hadn't survived after we defeated him in Taecia."

"We may have routed his army, but Suktar got away. The High Council warned me the Armour's magic could not be fully harnessed by a single individual. In my arrogance and greed I ignored them. There were repercussions, especially to myself."

The Queen paused, closed her eyes and took a deep breath. Her hands gripped the armrests, fighting a sudden tremble. When the Queen's eyes reopened, Michael noticed a subtle gold tint to them.

"He will return," the Queen continued, calm once more. "It may not be for decades or even centuries, but we must be ready when he does."

"What is your plan, Your Majesty?" Michael asked, for she clearly had one. That's what this was all about.

"My Armour shall never again be owned by one man or woman. It shall be split amongst you and the four other directors."

Michael stared at Elizabeth's Armour, allowing the magnitude of her order to sink in. The story behind the forging of the Armour was one of Queen Elizabeth's most guarded secrets. Much was speculated, but little was known about its power.

"The Institute is not to know of my Armour's fate. It must be kept safe, handed down to your descendants, until Suktar returns."

"I am honoured," Michael said, with a bow.

"Do not be. I have burdened you with a great responsibility."

"Will your son not wonder why he isn't to inherit it?"

"I will deal with my son," Elizabeth said firmly. Yes, there was a definite hint of gold in those brown eyes. "Henry of all people must not know my Armour's fate. If he has even the slightest inkling of its whereabouts, he will go mad searching for it. Should Henry don the Armour, the consequences would be dire."

Michael very much wanted to know the reason behind such ominous portents, but knew better than to ask. He turned his attention to the magnificent suit of armour. Each piece had a specific purpose.

"What am I to be entrusted with?"

"You shall take the sword. It was crafted for the sole purpose of ending Suktar's life. That objective will fall on your bloodline."

"May I know which pieces the others will take?"

Elizabeth thought for a moment. "I will tell you only this – Lord Samuel has the shield. He must be at your side, protecting you against Suktar's mightiest blows. You two have the greatest burdens." Elizabeth sensed Michael's unease. "I know your opinion of him, but Lord Samuel's courage cannot be doubted. It is a trait I hope his family carries with them."

Michael bowed. That left the helmet, the boots and the breastplate. Each served a particular purpose. He wondered who was taking what.

Michael assumed the meeting was over, but Elizabeth was looking at him again, gauging him.

"As guardian of the most powerful element of my Armour, the task of re-assembling it when the time comes will fall on the Greenwoods."

Michael met her stare with a note of pride. Queen Elizabeth had seen him last not because he was least important; quite the opposite.

"It shall be done, Your Majesty," Michael said.

There was a flash of white light and the memory faded. Ben felt himself being sucked back into his body.

"Ben!"

Charlie was shaking him. He and Natalie were bent over, staring with anxious faces. Ben was lying on the ground, his back wet with mud.

"Are you okay?" Natalie asked as Ben got to his feet.

Ben was too stunned to speak. Bits of the memory kept replaying in his head. Michael Greenwood. Queen Elizabeth I. Her Armour. Her son. Suddenly everything made sense. His parents were searching for the rest of Elizabeth's Armour. The realisation made him want to scream with joy and sigh with relief all at once.

"What happened?" Charlie asked urgently, holding Ben's shoulders.

It took Ben a moment to find his voice. In that brief interlude, something caught his eye behind Charlie and Natalie.

Movement in the trees, footsteps, voices.

Charlie and Natalie began to turn round, but Ben grabbed them.

"Behind the boulder!" he said, and they scrambled to safety. Ben risked a peek, his heart hammering.

Wren and Alex appeared through the trees. Alex looked a mess. His face was bloody, his hooded cloak torn and his jeans scorched and ripped. Yet he somehow retained a relaxed stance.

Wren, by contrast, seemed no worse than when she had faced off with Elessar. If anything it looked like she had managed to tidy herself up. Her hair was now in a long ponytail and what Ben could see of her dress in the remaining light looked cleaner than before. The only sign of battle was a gash on the side of her face.

Ben, Charlie and Natalie rose in relief.

"There you are! We need to get off this island," Wren said. "Reinforcements will arrive soon. Are you all okay?"

Charlie and Natalie nodded.

"My parents were up here. I saw them," Ben said.

Ben thought they might not believe him, but he couldn't have been more wrong. The weariness in Alex and Wren vanished. Alex hobbled around the small hilltop like a man possessed, touching boulders, sniffing the grass. Wren didn't move, but Ben got the impression she was somehow searching just as thoroughly.

"Here!" Alex said. He was leaning down by the smallest boulder. "Tracks. Thirty minutes old."

Wren came over swiftly. "They'll be gone by now," she said with disappointment.

Alex and Wren stared for some time in the direction of the tracks.

"Did they leave anything here?" Alex asked, turning towards Ben.

Ben suddenly felt strangely reluctant, but he showed them the spell pouch. Alex took it eagerly and peered inside. "It's empty."

"There was a pellet inside, but it activated as soon as I touched it."

Both Alex and Wren were looking at him very closely. "Did anything happen?"

Ben felt all eyes on him now, including Charlie's and Natalie's. He thought quickly, knowing any hesitation would be treated with suspicion. "It threw me backwards and I blacked out."

"Is that all?" Wren asked. God, she had a penetrating stare! Ben wondered if those grey eyes could magically detect a lie.

"Yes, that's all," Ben said, forcing a look of innocence and meeting Wren's eyes without a flinch.

Alex cursed, scrunching the spell pouch into his pocket. Wren continued to stare at Ben a moment longer. When she finally looked away, Ben had to resist the urge to sag his shoulders with relief.

"We should get going," Wren said.

Ben could feel Charlie and Natalie looking at him as they set off down the hill through the trees. He desperately wanted to tell them about Michael Greenwood's memory, but it would have to wait.

— Chapter Thirty —

Apprenticeship

"We owe you an explanation," Wren said.

Ben wondered when they were going to get around to that. He had so many questions he barely knew where to start.

"Everything that has happened here revolves around your parents. We were trying to find them."

"It's a long story," Alex continued, "but we think Greg and Jane might be the only people able to stop Suktar."

Ben felt both their eyes on him again. It took some effort to remain cool. Did they know about Elizabeth's Armour? Did they suspect he knew?

Wren continued. "You may remember I went to Riardor to help repel a dragon raid, which is why we didn't see each other the morning after your stay at Hotel Jigona. Normally the dragons get discouraged after a day, but this particular raid was unusually persistent. It was only when Alex sought me out and told me about Colin and Draven's deal with Elessar that I realised what was happening. The dragon raid was being created by the dark elves in an attempt to keep me away from the Institute. I returned at once, but you had already left."

"To Borgen to find the wood elves," Ben said.

Alex took over. "Shortly after, Wren and I received an unusual summons to the Commander's office."

"The Commander?"

Ben must have raised his voice because everyone turned to him in surprise.

"What did he want?" Ben asked, with forced composure.

Alex gave him an odd look before continuing. "The Commander was in one of those rare moods when he acts like a leader. He told us about your execution and ordered Wren and I to drop whatever we were doing to rescue you. Somehow he had detailed maps of the Floating Prison and knew exactly how to get in and out."

Ben was careful to mask his confusion. How much did the Commander know about Elizabeth's Armour? Alex continued and Ben reluctantly pushed thoughts of the Commander aside.

"Wren and I thought we could save you and make contact with your parents at the same time. All our attempts to find your parents had failed – they were sure to surface to rescue you."

"But they didn't," Ben said.

Wren and Alex exchanged uncomfortable looks.

"We made an error of judgement," Wren said.

"What she means is – we messed up. They must have seen Wren and myself on the hill and assumed we were there to rescue you. Our plan was to trick your parents like we tricked you. We wanted to make it look like I had changed sides and betrayed Wren. Unfortunately, they didn't buy it."

Ben rubbed his forehead. "If you wanted my parents to show up, why not just wait out of sight? That way my parents would have had to rescue us."

"Now that's a good idea," Alex said with a smile, staring pointedly at Wren.

Wren shook her head. "That was Alex's original plan, but I felt that it was too risky, especially when we learned Ictid would be present."

"Ictid?"

"King Suktar's son, the Prince of Erellia. He is a dark elf of incredible power. Even Greg and Jane would have had trouble pulling off a rescue attempt with him there. I wanted to be on hand if anything went wrong. Unfortunately, your parents thought we were there to rescue you."

"I waited until the very last moment," Alex said. "I was sure if we didn't do anything, your parents would intervene."

Ben felt his stomach sink a little. "But they didn't."

"I have no doubt if I hadn't stopped Elessar, your dad would have."

"Then why did you intervene?"

Alex turned to Wren who answered. "I wouldn't take the risk. I told Alex to act if there was no sign of your parents."

Ben recalled the moment Elessar had tried to execute Natalie. Could his parents really have intervened if Alex hadn't? It seemed impossible. He recalled Elessar's sword inches from Natalie's neck. How could they have possibly stopped that?

"Why didn't you tell us what you had planned?" Ben asked, frowning at Alex. "My heart stopped when I saw you with Elessar."

"I'm sorry about that," Alex replied, having the good grace to appear momentarily sombre. "Your reactions were necessary to fool both Elessar and your parents."

It was starting to make some sort of sense, but Charlie clearly wasn't finished."When did they capture Wren? From what you told us, she returned to the Institute just after we left for Borgen."

"Ah, finally we come to the part of my brilliant plan Wren didn't object to," Alex said, struggling to raise a triumphant bloody hand. "I met with Elessar and convinced him I was done with the Institute and willing to trade Wren and Ben for valuables." Alex took out a small bulging pouch and wiggled it. It glowed purple and radiated an energy that made Ben wonder at its contents.

"Elessar fell for that? Because he doesn't strike me as the type easily duped."

"Elessar and I were already well acquainted; I have been working for him these past six months. The dark elves are always trying to infiltrate and destroy the Institute from within. In the hope I might learn more about their search for Greg and Jane, I convinced them I was ready to switch sides. I had to cough up a few costly Institute plans, but it earned me Elessar's trust."

"Alex already had a reputation for being a bit of a loose cannon, so it didn't take a great leap of faith for Elessar to make an alliance," Wren said.

"What she means to say is I don't confine myself to the needless red tape imposed by the Institute. So I struck a deal with Elessar and we set a trap for Wren."

"Which I allowed myself to walk into," Wren continued. "It was the only way I could get close to the action."

"But how did you know they wouldn't kill you after capturing you?" Ben asked.

"She didn't," Alex said, "but I managed to persuade Elessar it would be better to add Wren to the bait and dispose of her after."

"So the whole thing was to get Ben's parents," Charlie said softly.

Alex nodded. "Indeed. Unfortunately, they called our bluff. We must think of another way to get hold of them."

Ben kept a calm face, but inside his heart was racing. Charlie, lacking Ben's knowledge of his new memory, was still frowning.

"If you think Ben's parents are so important to stopping Suktar, why don't they come back?"

"That's a very good question, Charlie," Wren said. "Initially we thought it was due to the Institute's ridiculous declaration of treason, but I have a feeling they will not return even if it's removed."

Ben felt Wren's stare but said nothing. He wondered again if she knew anything about Elizabeth's Armour.

He became vaguely aware they weren't heading back the way they had come. Of course, the location of the exit gateway was always different to the entrance. At the base of the hill they were joined by the Spellswords who had survived the battle. Together they formed a loose circle, with Ben, Charlie and Natalie in the middle. Wren and Alex moved a little distance apart to talk quietly between themselves.

Ben paid little attention to the darkness and unwelcome landscape as they walked. He kept replaying his ancestor's memory, still trying to take everything in. Michael James Greenwood was his ancestor. Was that the same Michael James marble statue at the Institute? It must be. For some reason his surname had been omitted from history. Ben felt a shiver up his spine knowing he was related to the original Director of Spellswords, a legend within the Institute and one of Queen

Elizabeth's right-hand men. What an unbelievable secret for his parents to conceal. What other secrets did they have? One thing was perfectly clear: going back home was not going to help find his parents. He needed access to the Unseen Kingdoms. To get that, he needed to join the Institute, but that was a problem. The Institute was strictly invitation only. Neither Wren nor Alex had made any such offer. What was going to happen when they got back to Taecia? Were they going to send him home for good? The thought caused him endless worry and he worked frantically on a solution, knowing with each passing minute he was running out of time.

He was so deep in thought he barely noticed when they stepped through the exit gateway. It was only when he heard the roar of dragons that he realised they were back at the Dragonway in Taecia.

"I'll see you back at the Institute, Wren," Alex said. He turned to Ben, Natalie and Charlie and gave them a little salute. "Let's do lunch sometime."

He hobbled away and with him went Ben's hope that Alex might offer him an invitation to the Institute.

The remaining Spellswords drifted off to their own trains. With their Spellshooters holstered, they looked more like commuters than warriors.

That left Ben, Natalie and Charlie alone with Wren. At some point on the journey back she had somehow managed to tidy herself up. Her hair was piled on her head in a neat bun and the gash on her head was clean. Was she wearing another dress? It shouldn't have been possible, but Ben could have sworn it was different to the one she had worn in battle.

Ben was aware he had seconds before Wren said goodbye, possibly forever. If she didn't ask him now, she never would.

"Would you mind if I had a word with you in private, Ben?" Wren asked.

"Sure," Ben replied, hoping his surprise masked his relief.

Wren led Ben a little way down the station platform until they were alone.

"Normally the discovery of the Unseen Kingdoms and the Royal Institute is a wondrous and defining moment in a young boy's life. I am sorry you and Charlie have had such an intense few days."

Ben couldn't help smiling. "It's not been that bad."

The truth was these last few days had made the rest of his life look mundane.

Wren was looking at him thoughtfully. "Your parents are wonderful Spellswords and two of my closest friends, but I always felt they were hiding something – something important. I have only known you for a few days, but already I sense the same thing. What is it about you Greenwoods?"

Ben looked into Wren's grey eyes. He trusted her; there was no doubt about that. He wanted to confide in her, but Queen Elizabeth's orders to Michael Greenwood were clear. The

Institute was not to know. His parents had gone to great lengths to ensure just that.

"I think you should trust us," Ben said. It sounded lame, but he couldn't think of anything else to say.

Wren nodded in agreement. "I do, Ben. As soon as Alex and I return to the Institute, we will get that ridiculous declaration of treason on your parents removed."

"Thank you," said Ben. "What's going to happen with the dark elves? Is the treaty with them now up in smoke?"

"I fear it might be, but we'll see. I don't think they are ready to declare war on us just yet," Wren said. She glanced down the platform and for a horrible minute Ben thought she was about to leave. Thankfully she turned back to him. "I am sure you must be wondering about your future with the Institute."

Ben felt his stomach lurch. "I hadn't really thought about it."

Wren's half smile left him in little doubt that she didn't believe him. "Even without the courage and competence you have displayed, your family line entitles you to the apprenticeship, should you wish to enrol. Charlie has also earned the right to apply, as we are always searching for suitable members beyond the existing ancestry."

Wren motioned towards Charlie and Natalie, and they started a slow walk back down the platform. Ben made a show of thinking about the offer, which lasted all of five seconds. He had a strange urge to start dancing.

"You know, I'd like to give it a go. I'm sure I can bully Charlie into joining with me."

"I'm glad. You can begin the enrolment process at our Croydon office."

They re-joined Charlie and Natalie, who were looking curiously at them.

"Natalie, I don't want to see you in the Institute for at least forty-eight hours. I'm sorry I can't give you more time to recover, but you are too valuable to me." Natalie beamed at the compliment and Wren turned to Charlie. "I hope to see you again soon, Charlie. And when Ben relays my offer, don't for a minute doubt yourself. You will do wonderfully. Now, I must be going. The Executive Council will be waiting for me."

The three of them watched Wren go. When she had passed out of sight, Charlie and Natalie turned to Ben.

"What was that about?" Charlie asked. "What offer?"

Their dragon pulled into the station, smoke pouring from its nostrils. The carriages opened and a few late-night stragglers emerged.

Ben grinned. "I'll explain on the way home."

THE END

FROM THE AUTHOR

Thank you for reading *Royal Institute of Magic* - I hope you enjoyed it. If you are interested in following Ben's journey as he starts his apprenticeship at the Institute, you can buy the next book in the series:
Royal Institute of Magic: The Shadowseeker

If you would like to stay in touch, please visit my website at **www.royalinstituteofmagic.com** where you can also sign up to the newsletter in order to receive information on upcoming releases, exclusive content, and free giveaways!

If you feel so inclined, I would also greatly appreciate it if you could write a little review on **Amazon.** It only takes a few minutes and gives other potential readers a better idea of what the book is like.

Writing can be a pretty lonely business, so it's always nice to hear from readers. Please feel free to get in touch at **victor@royalinstituteofmagic.com** and I'll reply within 24 hours - promise!

I look forward to hearing from you.

Regards,
- Victor

ABOUT THE AUTHOR

Victor Kloss was born in 1980 and lived his first five years in London, before moving to a small town in West Sussex. By day he builds websites, by night he writes (or tries to).

His love for Children's Fantasy stems from Enid Blyton, Tolkien, and recently, JK Rowling. His hobbies include football, golf, reading and taking walks with his wife and daughter.

Visit Victor's website at www.royalinstituteofmagic.com or contact him at victor@royalinstituteofmagic.com.

ALSO BY

Elizabeth's Legacy (Royal Institute of Magic, Book 1)

The Shadowseeker (Royal Institute of Magic, Book 2)

CPSIA information can be obtained
at www.ICGtesting.com
Printed in the USA
BVOW04s1807261116
468969BV00003B/179/P